Crime Files Series

General Editor: **Clive Bloom**

Since its invention in the nineteenth century, detective fiction has never been more popular. In novels, short stories, films, radio, television and now in computer games, private detectives and psychopaths, prim poisoners and overworked cops, tommy gun gangsters and cocaine criminals are the very stuff of modern imagination, and their creators one mainstay of popular consciousness. Crime Files is a ground-breaking series offering scholars, students and discerning readers a comprehensive set of guides to the world of crime and detective fiction. Every aspect of crime writing, detective fiction, gangster movie, true-crime exposé, police procedural and post-colonial investigation is explored through clear and informative texts offering comprehensive coverage and theoretical sophistication.

Published titles include:

Maurizio Ascari
A COUNTER-HISTORY OF CRIME FICTION
Supernatural, Gothic, Sensational

Hans Bertens and Theo D'haen
CONTEMPORARY AMERICAN CRIME FICTION

Anita Biressi
CRIME, FEAR AND THE LAW IN TRUE CRIME STORIES

Ed Christian (*editor*)
THE POST-COLONIAL DETECTIVE

Paul Cobley
THE AMERICAN THRILLER
Generic Innovation and Social Change in the 1970s

Michael Cook
NARRATIVES OF ENCLOSURE IN DETECTIVE FICTION
The Locked Room Mystery

Emelyne Godfrey
MASCULINITY, CRIME AND SELF-DEFENCE IN VICTORIAN LITERATURE

Christiana Gregoriou
DEVIANCE IN CONTEMPORARY CRIME FICTION

Lee Horsley
THE NOIR THRILLER

Merja Makinen
AGATHA CHRISTIE
Investigating Femininity

Fran Mason
AMERICAN GANGSTER CINEMA
From *Little Caesar* to *Pulp Fiction*

Fran Mason
HOLLYWOOD'S DETECTIVES
Crime Series in the 1930s and 1940s from the Whodunnit to Hard-boiled Noir

Linden Peach
MASQUERADE, CRIME AND FICTION
Criminal Deceptions

Alistair Rolls and Deborah Walker
FRENCH AND AMERICAN NOIR
Dark Crossings

Susan Rowland
FROM AGATHA CHRISTIE TO RUTH RENDELL
British Women Writers in Detective and Crime Fiction

Adrian Schober
POSSESSED CHILD NARRATIVES IN LITERATURE AND FILM
Contrary States

Lucy Sussex
WOMEN WRITERS AND DETECTIVES IN NINETEENTH-CENTURY CRIME FICTION
The Mothers of the Mystery Genre

Heather Worthington
THE RISE OF THE DETECTIVE IN EARLY NINETEENTH-CENTURY POPULAR FICTION

R.A. York
AGATHA CHRISTIE
Power and Illusion

Crime Files
Series Standing Order ISBN 978–0–333–71471–3 (hardback)
Series Standing Order ISBN 978–0–333–93064–9 (paperback)
(outside North America only)

You can receive future titles in this series as they are published by placing a standing order. Please contact your bookseller or, in case of difficulty, write to us at the address below with your name and address, the title of the series and one of the ISBNs quoted above.

Customer Services Department, Macmillan Distribution Ltd., Houndmills, Basingstoke, Hampshire RG21 6XS, England

Hollywood's Detectives

Crime Series in the 1930s and 1940s from the Whodunnit to Hard-boiled Noir

Fran Mason
Senior Lecturer in Film Studies and American Studies,
University of Winchester, UK

palgrave
macmillan

First published 2012 by
PALGRAVE MACMILLAN

Palgrave Macmillan in the UK is an imprint of Macmillan Publishers Limited, registered in England, company number 785998, of Houndmills, Basingstoke, Hampshire RG21 6XS.

Palgrave Macmillan in the US is a division of St Martin's Press LLC, 175 Fifth Avenue, New York, NY 10010.

Palgrave Macmillan is the global academic imprint of the above companies and has companies and representatives throughout the world.

Palgrave® and Macmillan® are registered trademarks in the United States, the United Kingdom, Europe and other countries.

ISBN: 978–0–230–57835–7

This book is printed on paper suitable for recycling and made from fully managed and sustained forest sources. Logging, pulping and manufacturing processes are expected to conform to the environmental regulations of the country of origin.

A catalogue record for this book is available from the British Library.

A catalog record for this book is available from the Library of Congress.

10 9 8 7 6 5 4 3 2 1
21 20 19 18 17 16 15 14 13 12

Printed and bound in Great Britain by
CPI Antony Rowe, Chippenham and Eastbourne

Contents

Series Preface

Since its invention in the nineteenth century, detective fiction has never been more popular. In novels, short stories, films, radio, television and now in computer games, private detectives and psychopaths, prim poisoners and overworked cops, Tommy-gun gangsters and cocaine criminals are the very stuff of modern imagination, and their creators a mainstay of popular consciousness. *Crime Files* is a ground-breaking series offering scholars, students and discerning readers a comprehensive set of guides to the world of crime and detective fiction. Every aspect of crime writing, detective fiction, gangster movie, true-crime exposé, police procedural and post-colonial investigation is explored through clear and informative texts offering comprehensive coverage and theoretical sophistication.

Preface

Although the hard-boiled literary detective style had developed in the 1920s and became a significant sub-genre of detective fiction in the 1930s in the works of Hammett and Chandler, the Hollywood studios were slow to transfer hard-boiled texts to the screen. Apart from MGM's adaptation of Hammett's *The Thin Man* in 1934 and early versions of *The Maltese Falcon* (in 1931, aka *Dangerous Female*, and as *Satan Met a Lady* in 1936), there was very little production in this area until John Huston's version of the latter text in 1941. This is because detective films of the 1930s and 1940s were mainly based either on the classic style of detective narrative found in the whodunnits associated with the 'Golden Age of Mystery' or on an action-based thriller format, usually as 'B' features that were cheap to make and which could be developed into a series of sequels. Even when hard-boiled fiction appeared in Hollywood in the 1940s it was often adapted to service the detective mystery series, as is the case with the softening of Chandler's *Farewell, My Lovely* when it was used as the basis for the narrative of *The Falcon Takes Over* (1942). The detective film in this period is usually not, therefore, the hard-boiled style most often associated with Hollywood detectives, but the amateur sleuth or master detective format that was developed in B-Movie mystery series such as 'The Falcon', 'Sherlock Holmes', 'Charlie Chan' and 'Mr Moto'. In creating these series, Hollywood primarily drew on American sources when adapting literary texts, such as Hammett's *The Thin Man*, S. S. Van Dine's 'Philo Vance' novels, Earl Derr Biggers' 'Charlie Chan' series or John P. Marquand's 'Mr Moto' stories. It also, however, recycled its own earlier adaptations (the 'Boston Blackie' and 'Lone Wolf' series), developed its own detectives ('The Crime Doctor'), or transferred the English style to an American context by using Conan Doyle's Sherlock Holmes, Leslie Charteris' The Saint and Michael Arlen's Falcon. Until the first adaptations of hard-boiled or *noir* works by Hammett, Chandler and Cain appeared in the early to mid-1940s, the dominant style therefore was the whodunnit detective mystery rather than the suspense thriller.

This study seeks to examine the dominant tendencies in the detective crime series of the 1930s and 1940s which have often been overlooked in favour of studies of hard-boiled or *noir* detectives even though the output from the crime series far outweighs that of the latter forms. In part, the crime series have been overlooked because they are considered to be contrived, inauthentic or formulaic as 'generic' B-Movie product, whereas hard-boiled films either express a perceived authenticity that makes them meaningful explorations of American society or else they are deemed to transcend genre to become more complex (often by being considered in their interfusions with *film noir*), so that they deal with difficult things such as desire, ideology, social relations, the operations of money in capitalism, and the various corruptions, perversions, deviancies and transgressions arising from the representation of these to produce ambiguity and confusion where the crime series films produce simplicity and certainty. Some of the series are formulaic, certainly, most notably the Columbia series 'The Lone Wolf' (after an interesting incarnation of the role by Melvyn Douglas in *The Lone Wolf Returns*) and 'Boston Blackie', but this does not mean that the crime series don't have any interest. This is not to claim that the films overtly deal with social concerns. It must be remembered that the vast majority of the crime series were B-Movies and that they were therefore produced to provide an entertaining diversion to accompany the main feature. They do not therefore often overtly engage with political, cultural or social concerns, except during the wartime spy films, and care needs to be taken to avoid reading too much into light diversions.

The films do, however, articulate at various points matters relating to ideological formations within the United States, even though it is difficult to see in the crime series films an open response to the New Deal ethos of Roosevelt's presidency. Indeed, the films themselves are quite often uncertain or fractured in their mapping of ideology and this has much to do with their B status and their flexible definition of the mystery format which produces a profuse number of codes from one film to another in the series and even within films, so that there are often competing or conflicting meaning systems in operation. For example, conflicting codes of masculinity are produced in the representation of the Falcon because his active sexual desire is sometimes presented as charming, confident and attractive, but on other occasions it is shown to make him bungling because his constant interest in sex gets him into trouble. He can therefore be hyper-masculine and competent or incompetent and inefficient at different times, sometimes even in the same film (*A Date with the Falcon* [1941]). It is not a conscious ploy to seemingly confirm a sexualised masculinity before debunking it because often it is the generic codes in operation that determine the representation. Thus, in *A Date with the Falcon*, when the film requires comedy, the Falcon can be made to look foolish by making a hasty retreat on to a window ledge, but if the superiority associated with the amateur detective is required he can then light a cigarette and calmly smoke it while a crowd down below urges him to jump.

This is only one example and there are many others, including the conflicting codes surrounding Charlie Chan and Mr Moto because of the complex and contradictory representations of their ethnicity, the representations of law and crime that develop in the criminal detective series ('The Saint' and the 'Falcon') which offer interesting discourses concerning the disorder the detective creates in pursuing an investigation whose purpose is to return society to order, and the representation of Sherlock Holmes within an American ideological system that still wants to value aspects of his Englishness. All these will be considered in this book, as well as the development of the comedy thriller format in 'The Thin Man' films, which were given class-A or prestige status as headlining films, and the rise of hard-boiled and other types of crime film in the 1940s which helped to bring the detective crime series to an end in 1949 when the last of the 'Charlie Chan' films, *The Sky Dragon*, was released by Monogram. A particular concern throughout will be on the production of the crime series as B-Movies designed to support a headlining feature on the double-bill that became the standard model of cinema exhibition in the 1930s. This mode of production is significant because it influences and diffuses the codes of the detective genre through the operation of a form of cinematic vaudeville that articulates a range of generic codes to provide entertainment over and above the mystery narrative, so that even though the use of comedy, romance, music and other forms might appear to be intrusive, it is argued here that they are a key aspect of the fun that the crime series provide.

1

Exploring Detective Films in the 1930s and 1940s: Genre, Society and Hollywood

Hollywood's version of the whodunnit in the 1930s and 1940s was not always of the classical style associated with the progenitors of the literary detective genre (Poe and Conan Doyle) or the writers of Golden Age clue-puzzle mysteries (such as Christie and Chesterton). The whodunnit does, nevertheless, provide the template for most of Hollywood's crime series, even if sometimes it is only to furnish a mystery sub-plot in films that emphasise action or suspense. The 'Charlie Chan' films, for example, which formed the longest running of Hollywood's crime series, privilege the mystery form of the whodunnit, including the conventional unmasking of the murderer in the denouement. There were also numerous 'Philo Vance' films throughout the period, the best known of which, *The Kennel Murder Case* (1933), is paradigmatic of the clue-puzzle style in its rendering of a locked-room mystery involving more than one person trying to kill the same man at about the same time on the same evening. Even in series that were more variable in style, such as the 'Sherlock Holmes' films, where the emphasis was often on suspense, there was still always some form of mystery or riddle to occupy Holmes while he contended with criminals whose identity he had already revealed, such as The Dancing Men Code in the espionage film *Sherlock Holmes and the Secret Weapon* (1942) or the mystery of how the victims are killed in a thriller such as *The Spider Woman* (1944). There are a number of reasons why Hollywood preferred to use a version of the whodunnit style during the 1930s and 1940s. The whodunnit aligned with the economic restrictions of 'B'-Movie production, which required a cheap and rapid turnaround of films, because stories could be recycled relatively easily, often merely by changing the setting and the names of characters, and because action could be confined to a few sets. There were also narrative imperatives for the use of the whodunnit because its emphasis on the concealment of the criminal allowed interest to be maintained until the denouement. In addition there were moral concerns connected to the Motion Picture Production Code because, while the whodunnit formula focused on criminality, the types of crime represented were usually unrelated to the gangster violence that the Hays/Breen Office was concerned about (Black, 1994: 108) and this made its representation of crime morally 'safe'.

The Hollywood whodunnit

The whodunnit style that predominates in the Hollywood crime series is, however, a more multifarious form than its literary equivalent. Despite the recycling of established motifs such as the enigma, the interpretation of clues, and the denouement, Hollywood's preference for action-based narratives and the need to visualise detection within these confines means that it is often interfused with the thriller mode to allow suspense and action to come to the fore.[1] Hollywood's version of the whodunnit (and the styles that displaced it in the late 1940s) can still, however, be understood by reference to critical accounts of the literary detective form. These accounts have focused, for example, on the role of the detective and the nature of detection (Knight, 2004: 30–63; Rzepka, 2005: 90–113), the importance of ratiocination and the scientific method (Knight, 2003: 77–94; Scaggs, 2005: 33–54), the puzzle of the mystery as a form of game for the reader or audience to play (Cawelti, 1976: 105), the differences between the whodunnit and American hard-boiled forms (Soitos, 1996: 24; Messent, 1997: 7; Pepper, 2000: 10–34), the relationship between crime and morality (Palmer, 1991: 133–5; Pyrhönen, 1999), and the development of sub-genres such as the policier, crime thriller and the police procedural (Scaggs, 2005: 85–104).[2] Many of these features or motifs were significant within Hollywood crime texts in the period before the rise of the hard-boiled film, although they were very often modified because they had to attend to the imperatives of either visual representation or institutional arrangements. The problem of representing the intellectual process of detection as a central feature of the mystery narrative, for example, was a particular concern because it needed to be visualised for the audience. Concerns with morality and crime were also reframed because of the impact of the Motion Picture Production Code which was articulated in 1930 and fully in force from 1934. Criminal-detectives such as

The Saint, Falcon or Lone Wolf, for example, were turned into servants of law and society, a transformation that also affected their activities because their criminal inclinations were either recast as harmless pranks or channelled into detection, so that burglary became a means to discover clues rather than theft for personal gain.

The features of the classic detective formula that recur in the Hollywood crime series discussed here align quite closely with John Cawelti's taxonomy of literary detective fiction. Cawelti argues that there are four aspects that define the detective formula: situation, pattern of action, characters and relationships, and setting. Situation refers to the dominant narrative of the mystery provided by an unsolved crime and its elucidation, while pattern of action refers to the narrative arc that follows on from this premise and comprises '(a) introduction of the detective; (b) crime and clues; (c) investigation; (d) announcement of the solution; (e) explanation of the solution; (f) denouement' (1976: 82). The situation and the narrative as defined are particularly relevant to the films of the Hollywood crime series, especially when Cawelti notes that the denouement (the apprehension of the criminal) and the solution (the explanation of the crime) can be combined (Ibid.: 90). In the classical Hollywood narrative paradigm, these aspects are generally elided or follow in quick succession to integrate narrative threads in the resolution so that, although it is very often implied that the Hollywood detective has deduced the solution before the final scenes, he or she usually only provides the explanation in a denouement that also includes the capture of the criminal. On occasions, however, it is only in this final scene that the detective discovers the identity of the culprit (*The Falcon and the Co-eds* [1943]) or springs a trap either to capture the criminal (*The Scarlet Claw* [1944]) or to goad them into a confession (*The Saint in Palm Springs* [1941]), although 'The Thin Man' series presents the final denouement as a way for Nick Charles to work through possibilities until he reaches the right conclusion. Further aspects of the narrative are provided by Cawelti's category of characters and relationships which not only includes the detective, but also the criminal, the victim and 'false suspects' (Cawelti, 1976: 96), all of whom provide the material (in the form of clues or testimony) to drive the detective's investigation. Finally, there is the setting, which most obviously refers to the locations favoured by the classical detective story, but which also refers to the space that delimits the action so as to separate the detective's textual world from the 'complexity and confusion of the larger social world' (Ibid.: 97). Cawelti, however, also comments that the setting can often be used to represent stability in a world disrupted by crime (Ibid.: 98) and this introduces another significant motif in detective fiction, discussed by several critics: the detective's role in returning society to order (Schatz, 1981: 124; Copjec, 1993: 171; Messent, 1997: 8; Leitch, 2002: 173; Knight, 2003: 88 and 90; Scaggs, 2005: 46–9). Depending upon perspective, this might simply involve ensuring that crime is only a minor disruption rather than a sign of chaotic social relations (Field, 2009: 19), or might provide the detective with an ideological function so that the return to the status quo associated with the solution of a crime is an overt legitimation of bourgeois ideology (Mandel, 1984: 47).

This suggests that the detective is a figure of authority who is more than someone who merely solves crime or carries the burden of the narrative. Nevertheless, the detective's primary narrative role is the investigation of a mystery and his or her social role is often secondary to the cerebral problem that he or she has been set. Mandel, for example, notes that '[T]he real subject of the early detective stories is thus not crime or murder but enigma' (1984: 18) and this means that the detective must also be an interpreter and seeker after knowledge who gathers the world as information in visual cues and props before 'using her or his reasoning powers to penetrate below the surface of things' (Messent, 1997: 5). While clues and information are necessary in detective stories, their presentation has always been problematic within the cinematic form. A clue can be introduced by a passing reference in a novel without drawing attention to its importance, whereas to hold an object in shot in cinema seemingly 'overstresses' its significance (Knight, 2004: 111). Detective films can use a misleading shot as a form of red herring to direct attention towards objects that are actually insignificant, but the B-Movie crime series tend to have a much more mechanical approach to such matters and very often use visual clues to provide narrative information in an instrumental manner. This pattern is also a product of classical Hollywood's overall penchant for dynamic narratives (based on tension, conflict and suspense, or action and incident), but the particular demands for clarity and pace found in B-Movies, which generally have a running time of between sixty and seventy minutes, mean that screen time cannot be used up on static representation of props.[3] There are exceptions, but where this is the case, the use of visual clues is usually integrated into the onscreen action. In *Sherlock Holmes in Washington* (1943), for example, Holmes searches a room for clues to find out how a British agent transported secret plans to the United States. A collection of cameras, a negative containing the small image of a matchbook, a microscope, a slide projector and several matchbooks of the kind appearing in the negative are all put on the screen not only for Holmes to find, but also to visually display his thought processes as he moves quickly around the screen space from one object to another. As importantly, information is conveyed at the same pace as Holmes' movement, so that the objects are located in a set of clear causal relationships to embed them in the larger story of the mystery when Holmes concludes that the clues indicate that the agent put the secret plans on microfilm which he then concealed in a matchbook.

Despite such exceptions, evidence in detective films tends to be revealed not in the form of props but through dialogue in interviews or conversations. This mode of collecting and revealing evidence also generates movement from scene to scene as the detective uses the information learnt from one character to guide him either to another character or to a location where new evidence can be gathered. The detective's trajectory through the narrative, therefore, is to move from one source of information to another, most usually in the form of reported testimony, suggesting a consonance between the cinematic narrative of the crime series and literary hard-boiled fiction, which shares a similar emphasis on testimony from suspects or witnesses, as both Mandel (1984: 36) and Scaggs (2005: 59) note, as opposed to the whodunnit's focus on objects to be interpreted. The tendency to rely on reported evidence is not, however, a product of the hard-boiled style's influence on cinema, but a result of the need for dynamic narratives and causal relationships between episodes or scenes within the classical Hollywood paradigm. Despite the relegation of the clue-as-object to a subsidiary role, crime series nevertheless still offer the same ideological imperative that underpinned the scientific method in the classical literary detective form which, in its fetishisation of the clue-as-object, sought to prove the objectivity of reality. The world is objective and open to interpretation for the film detective and the screened reality that he or she inhabits is ultimately where truth resides in spite of deceptions on the part of criminals and suspects. The film detective makes the world knowable by solving mysteries because, like Sherlock Holmes according to Moretti, he or she possesses the 'stable code' (1988: 145) that helps align signifier with signified. It can be argued, indeed, that the textual reality inhabited by the detective is solely a world of objects in spite of the general absence of physical clues because the characters the detective encounters become objectified as evidence to be observed so that they can be placed within a taxonomy of knowledge which allows them to be understood as units of meaning once their motives, relationships and actions have been learnt or accurately interpreted. To the detective, the world is a place of 'things' in which other characters are functional, their only purpose to advance the investigation. The Falcon, for example, controls and re-directs sexual interest on the part of the female characters he encounters towards his investigation, thereby transforming desire into the affectless collection of information.

The instrumental treatment of narrative content also has relevance for matters of morality within the detective film through the transformation of crime from a social and moral matter to a mystery that is ostensibly empty of meaning because it is articulated simply for the purpose of entertainment, a feature that is also derived from literary detective works. As products of the classical Hollywood studio system, detective films in the 1930s and 1940s were necessarily governed by the Motion Picture Production Code and had to accord with its imperative not to present crime in a positive way. It is axiomatic, therefore, that Hollywood presumes crime is wrong, but the imperative to provide entertainment means that criminal acts are not necessarily treated in moral terms because they function primarily to generate mystery, tension or action in the detective's pursuit of an investigation. The criminal is therefore less a moral problem than a necessary opponent who sets in motion the suspense, thrills and incident that form the entertainment. The punishment or detention of the criminal in the denouement is often less a matter of morality or legality than an opportunity to provide excitement or gratifying release from tension in the case of action-oriented resolutions, or pleasurable satisfaction in the revelation scene in enigma-based films. While it is certainly the case, for example, that Moriarty is represented at the beginning of *The Adventures of Sherlock Holmes* (1939) as morally repugnant because he values the orchids he tends more than the life of a man he has murdered, his presence in the film is not to articulate disapproval of criminality, but to provide the mysteries that will generate events and incidents. Moriarty's bringing to book is similarly empty of moral concern because it is primarily the means to afford action (in the race across London to prevent him bringing his plan to fulfilment), excitement and tension (in his struggle with Holmes atop the Tower of London), and spectacle (when he falls to his death). Many other examples which privilege entertainment over morality in the denouement can be offered from the crime series, such as Nora Charles' rescue of her husband Nick in *Shadow of the Thin Man* (1941), the gunfights at the end of *The Falcon Out West* (1944) and *The Falcon in Hollywood* (1944) or the perverse pleasure of characters being hoist by their own petard, such as Valdin in *Bulldog Drummond's Bride* (1939) who is killed by a bomb meant for others. The importance of the ending is therefore to emphasise narrative closure and, while conclusions have ideological or moral implications, these are institutionally subordinated to the satisfactory closing of the entertainment provided by the narrative.

One of the problems for the Hollywood studios in adapting the whodunnit to screen is that the observation, interpretation and deduction associated with it are not the stuff of visual entertainment. The 'Torchy Blane' adventure *Smart Blonde* (1937) illustrates the difficulties of transferring the whodunnit style to cinema. The film is a succession of conversations, primarily conducted by Torchy, a newspaper reporter, and her police officer fiancé, Steve McBride, as they move from one source of information to another, paralleling each other in a pattern that is made overt in a mirroring sequence during which Torchy and McBride, in separate scenes, interview two women involved in the life of the main suspect. The effect of this mirroring is to establish relations of equivalence between the two scenes so that no particular value is attached to the evidence uncovered in either, but this also reflects on the narrative as a whole because there seems to be very little meaning in the story of the investigation as it moves from one interview to another. Because there is little incident, the investigation is very flat and the pleasure of the text is primarily provided by the vibrancy of Glenda Farrell's performance as Torchy and her bantering relationship with McBride.

The 'Torchy Blane' films sought to address the flatness of the whodunnit narrative of *Smart Blonde* by privileging incident and action over mystery in *Fly-Away Baby*, aka *Crime in the Clouds* (1937). The film involves the pursuit of a suspect around the world, with the identity of the criminal apparently known early on so that there seems to be very little mystery until the narrative reveals at the end that someone else is responsible for the crimes. This occurs on a zeppelin flight from Germany to New York and the conclusion, in which the criminal plunges to his death as he seeks to escape by parachute, wraps up the mystery, which has only actually been introduced in the last reel, in a perfunctory manner. The prior material, except for an early scene in which the murderer is interviewed, is revealed to have been a wild goose chase, most particularly the round-the-world flight that has filled most of the film. A similar situation is also present in a hoax murder that takes up half the running time of *The Adventurous Blonde* (1937) and both cases suggest that the Hollywood detective film, particularly in its B-Movie form, is as based on incidental padding, digression and misdirection as it is on a linear movement towards conclusion. This means that the B-Movie narrative partakes of the contradiction implicit in most mainstream cinematic narratives in being driven by both the need for a linear plot that leads to resolution and by the need to suspend the ending until sufficient material (narrative information or entertaining situations) has been delivered.

The films of the detective crime series, therefore, have twin imperatives towards delay and resolution, with the former being provided by what Bordwell calls 'retardatory material', which he describes as comprising 'comedy (e.g., byplay with incompetent police), romance (a young couple falls under suspicion, or the detective is prey to romantic inclinations), and the commission of more crimes' (1985: 64). This view mirrors Porter's analysis of the 'deflection or rebound from progress toward resolution' in literary detective fiction, which involves processes such as 'rival investigations or love motifs that intermittently suspend the principal investigation, and false trials and false solutions' (1981: 32) or, in Coward and Semple's analysis, the use of 'bumbling and inefficient' police (1989: 51).[4] While Bordwell refers specifically to hard-boiled Hollywood film, his analysis is relevant to most detective texts of the classical Hollywood period. The comedy of manners and verbal interplay in 'The Thin Man' series, for example, acts as incidental entertainment by providing textual material that does not contribute to the causal narrative, although it does help to delay the movement towards resolution by removing Nick and Nora from 'linear plot-telling' (Young, 1994: 265). Bordwell notes that the further commission of crimes in detective movies is one of the more significant ways in which 'retardatory material' is used, but such events, in accumulating incidents, have a secondary effect. While the continuation of criminal activity can often help to clarify the narrative information, by eliminating suspects (sometimes through their murder) or by providing clues that lead towards resolution, these incidents can also muddy the investigation by casting doubt on already existing solutions or theories, thereby acting as textual obfuscation or mystification that both impede the narrative of investigation and obscure the truth of the crime. It can be argued that such events are of more importance to the detective text than the arrival at truth in the resolution, because without them the narrative would consist only of a crime, clues indicating the identity of the criminal, a deduction of these clues and the arrest of the perpetrator.

These incidents fill the text and allow the detective to remain narratively active, suggesting that detective films are more padding than anything else, but these mystifications also provide the 'misleading motivation' that Tomashevsky, writing about fiction, says is designed to 'distract the reader's attention from the real situation' (1965: 80).

In addition to being part of the game in the literary text, they form an important part of the cinematic detective text by providing sub-narratives to the criminal narrative being investigated. However, because they are misleading, they help to mystify the main narrative with the result that the audience can often not distinguish what is the main narrative and what is a sub-narrative. For example, in *Charlie Chan in City of Darkness* (1939), there are three mystery narratives, one involving blackmail, another concerning burglary, while a third (the source of the murder mystery) deals with a spy ring. Even though they are mystification, the first two narratives are given most screen time, to imply that the answer to the murder mystery can be found in one of them, but they also have the effect of displacing the espionage narrative that forms the primary mystery until the final reel. A further effect of retardatory material is to problematise the generic lines of the whodunnit because many of the delays in the crime series involve the introduction of comedy, romance, action or suspense. It is difficult to describe the mystery story developed in the Hollywood detective series in terms of the formal detective story of literature with its characteristic whodunnit or clue-puzzle (Knight, 2004: 85–9; Leitch, 2002: 172). Even though films in the 'Charlie Chan', 'Falcon', 'Mr Moto' and 'Thin Man' series, for example, almost invariably have a whodunnit form in which the identity of the main criminal is only revealed in the concluding scenes (although interestingly the 'Sherlock Holmes' films do not always have this formula), the Hollywood detective film tends towards the thriller form, whether of the mystery, suspense or action varieties. They very often, therefore, involve cross-generic coding in which multiple formats within the mystery style are deployed, such as hard-boiled, whodunnit, action and suspense in *The Falcon Takes Over*, or draw in tropes from other genres, whether these are the comedy elements that are typical of the B-crime series generally or more specific interconnections such as the Gothic or horror codes that are articulated in some of the 'Sherlock Holmes' films (*Sherlock Holmes Faces Death* [1943], *The Scarlet Claw* and *The House of Fear* [1945]), the gangster form in *The Saint in New York* (1938), espionage in the war-time films of the series, or *noir* tendencies in some of the late 'Sherlock Holmes' and 'Falcon' films.

Mystery, suspense and thrillers

This cross-coding is only an exaggeration of existing tendencies within the format of the detective story as it had been created and developed in fiction. Many critical accounts of literary detective fiction draw on

Todorov's 'The Typology of Detective Fiction' in distinguishing between the classical form and the thriller or *série noire*, the former associated with the whodunnit and its focus on deduction and analytic reason, and the latter, more problematically, with the hard-boiled style (Leitch, 2002: 65; Gates, 2006: 13–4; Field, 2009: 26–8). Todorov argues that the whodunnit is characterised by having two stories, 'the story of the crime and the story of the investigation' (1977: 44), the first of which (the pre-narrative *récit*) is over before the second begins and has no narrative within the text except through its reconstruction or recollection in the story of investigation because it is 'an absence' (Ibid.: 46). This latter story, however, involves no action, only the gathering of information through the inquiries of the detective, who is a detached observer of events immune from danger. In the thriller form, on the other hand, 'the narrative coincides with the action' (Ibid.: 47) and the detective is fully involved in 'danger, pursuit [and] combat' (Ibid.: 48) which threatens his or her safety because the thriller protagonist is immersed in the world of criminality. Another important difference between the two forms is that the whodunnit is defined by the mystery plot, whereas the thriller is focused more on 'curiosity' (the explanation of causes for visible effects by the provision of back-stories or simple questions of what will happen next) and 'suspense' (the expectation of certain events that follow from the initial cause of the narrative and how their specifics will be worked out). This distinction between whodunnit and thriller has generally been adopted by critical accounts of detective fiction so that Soitos (1996: 23–4), for example, uses it as the basis for a binary set of paradigms defining the whodunnit in opposition to hard-boiled fiction.

There are difficulties with such an opposition because Todorov adds a further category to whodunnit and thriller forms, that of the 'suspense novel', which most critics have ignored or conflated with the latter category.[5] Todorov argues that the suspense novel exists between the whodunnit and the thriller, commenting that it combines the mystery and two stories (crime and investigation) from the former with the primacy of the narrative of action that characterises the thriller. He adds that the suspense style 'served as a transition between the whodunit [*sic*] and the thriller' even though 'it existed at the same time as the latter' (Todorov, 1977: 50) and includes the work of early hard-boiled writers such as Hammett and Chandler within its domain. The thriller becomes clearer in its reference in such a formulation and bears little resemblance to the hard-boiled style with which it is most often associated because this form still shares with the whodunnit an enigma to be solved rather than the 'curiosity' of the thriller format. It is the action thrillers of the 'Bulldog Drummond' movies and 'Dick Tracy' serials and films that Hollywood produced in the 1930s and 1940s that most closely resemble Todorov's thriller format. The films in Paramount's low-budget 'Bulldog Drummond' series, for example, are ostensibly detective fictions, but have very little in the way of mystery. The first of the series, *Bulldog Drummond Escapes* (1937), deals with the imprisonment of Phyllis Clavering (who reappears throughout the series as Drummond's fiancée) by Norman Merridew, but reveals both its villain and his crimes early on. The only mystery in the film derives from curiosity over the reason for Phyllis' captivity and most of the narrative entails rescuing Phyllis while trying to prove Merridew's guilt to the recurring character of Colonel Nielson, the police commissioner. Other entries in the series share the same lack of mystery and further emphasise the action elements within the thriller plots. *Bulldog Drummond Comes Back* (1937), the first to star John Howard, involves another abduction of Phyllis by a criminal who identifies himself in order to set Drummond a set of riddles to solve (the film's 'curiosity') in the hope of saving her, while *Bulldog Drummond's Peril* (1938) alternates between showing two groups of criminals enacting their plans in the quest to gain control of a formula for artificial diamonds and Drummond's pursuit of them. These films are dominated not by mystery but by suspense in a 'cops-and-robbers' mode, to which Phyllis draws attention in *Bulldog Drummond's Peril* and *Bulldog Drummond's Bride*.

The cinematic version of the cops-and-robbers format is important in the films of the detective crime series and its presence suggests that they are as much thrillers as they are whodunnits. Most of the 'Lone Wolf' films tend towards the cops-and-robbers format until the end of the Warren William period when films such as *Secrets of the Lone Wolf* (1941) and *One Dangerous Night* (1943) provide whodunnit narratives, while the later films of the 'Torchy Blane' series also offer this form, as in *Torchy Gets Her Man* (1938) in which Torchy and McBride go up against a counterfeiting gang. The 'Dick Tracy' series of films made at RKO in the 1940s, which were preceded by four serials made at Republic between 1937 and 1941,[6] are the most obvious example of the cops-and-robbers format with the titles of the films announcing the duel between Tracy and a criminal in two cases: *Dick Tracy vs. Cueball* (1946) and *Dick Tracy Meets Gruesome* (1947). The villains that Tracy confronts are usually henchmen rather than the criminal geniuses that characterise the thriller form adopted by the detective crime series, which are more ingenious in their deployment of a variety of thriller styles. These include the detective versus the criminal mastermind, the detective versus a gang, the 'MacGuffin' format, or the caper, chase or pursuit narrative as types of specific plot; or the articulation of different modes such as suspense, thrills, action, or mysteries in the form of puzzles or games. Most often, the series thrillers combine narratives by drawing on different generic sign-systems to offer up several modes at one time. Such overlaps and borrowings are not unusual with regard to genres or sub-genres, as Steve Neale has demonstrated (1990: 57), and indicate that any genre is flexible in its use of signifying patterns. The detective crime series of the classical Hollywood period share the same flexibility and derive narratives not only from the whodunnit format, but from a range of different genres and sub-genres, each with their own representation of particular types of crime and criminal. *The Falcon Strikes Back* (1943), for example, draws on the criminal mastermind narrative (Geraldine Lipton, a notorious fraudster), a caper involving her gang (a bond fraud), the criminal monster (in the form of the insane murderer Dugan), and the whodunnit (the Falcon's pursuit of clues through two sets of crimes), as well as marshalling motifs from espionage (albeit as misdirection), Gothic (the final encounter between Dugan and Mrs Lipton), and *noir*-style betrayal (the double-crosses within the gang), even as it also manoeuvres its generic references within the kind of light-hearted romp that is associated with the comedy thriller. The multivalent generic references of *The Falcon Strikes Back* are not untypical of the detective crime series produced by Hollywood in the 1930s and 1940s, even if the mystery style of the whodunnit (and its associated tropes of enigma and deduction) commonly acts as a focus for the assembly of other crime-related textual forms.

Detectives, personas and individuality

The kind of crime text that is on show in the crime series is often determined by the persona of the detective because the style of film very usually depends upon the kind of situation that is most appropriate for the protagonist. Matters of generic verisimilitude would, for example, prevent Dick Tracy from pursuing a case to an isolated Gothic-inspired mansion such as that which Sherlock Holmes investigates in *The House of Fear.* Similarly, Holmes might be considered out of place in the cartoonish criminal underworld represented in *Dick Tracy vs. Cueball*, even if, after defeating the Hoxton Creeper in *The Pearl of Death* (1944), he might be able to convincingly face Splitface (*Dick Tracy* [1945]) or Gruesome. His 'type' as a detective, however, makes him appropriate for the textual worlds of whodunnit, Gothic mystery, espionage, and *noir*, all of which he appeared, albeit less successfully in some than others, so that *Pursuit to Algiers* (1945), an international thriller, is often considered one of the weakest of the Holmes films (Thompson, 1988: 50) because of a misalignment between persona and text. There are therefore certain discourses attached to particular detectives that make them fit the worlds within which they are placed. Sherlock Holmes can be framed within a text with Gothic resonances, for example, because the discourses of ratiocination and deduction that characterise his method not only make him an appropriate champion of reason against the supernatural, but also provide motivation for a narrative that resolves with the revelation that apparent supernatural causes are actually the product of human criminal agency.

The persona of the actor performing the role of the detective also plays a significant part in determining the form and style of the detective's textual world. It is not the discourses surrounding Sherlock Holmes that allow him to enter Gothic worlds, even if he does so in Conan Doyle's fiction in *The Hound of the Baskervilles* (1939), but the discourses surrounding Basil Rathbone's incarnation of Holmes as a result of his performance in the film version of *The Hound of the Baskervilles* that allow Holmes to enter further Gothic mysteries. Gates discusses Parish and Pitts' view that the B-crime series catered to star personas and summarises their argument that 'Basil Rathbone *was* Sherlock Holmes; Tom Conway *was* the Falcon; Warner Baxter *was* the Crime Doctor; and Warren William *was* The Lone Wolf' (Gates, 2006: 72, citing Parish and Pitts, 1990: xi). It should be noted, however, that Tom Conway onscreen is a construction of the persona of 'Tom Conway' through the performance of the roles he played, including the roles he undertook at the same time in the horror films of the Lewton unit which confirmed, shaded or developed the persona created by the Falcon. It would be more accurate to say, therefore, that there are discourses that attach to the Conway screen persona that produce meanings which allow him to fit the charming but morally ambiguous Falcon as well as the stern and suffering figure of Paul Holland in *I Walked with a Zombie* (1943). In particular, it is the very ambiguity of his persona that creates the doubtful motives that allow his character of Holland in *I Walked with a Zombie* to appear as the cause of misery for his wife and younger brother before it is revealed that it was their affair that caused his suffering.

The same use of prior or parallel textual discourses in creating persona is the case for other stars playing detectives. William Powell and George Sanders were able to perform roles as Nick Charles in the case of the former and The Saint and the Falcon in the case of the latter, not because their signs of 'Britishness' created associations of villainy, as Gates argues (2006: 72–3), but because their personas accumulated discourses associated with being aristocratic or patrician (within the context of Hollywood's understanding and deployment of such figurations) that could be articulated in a variety of ways. In both cases, the personas were dashing, charming and witty with an air of superiority, but these could be deployed flexibly depending upon what the situation required to make them caddish or roguish in one cluster of meanings (the latter most often being called upon in their detective personas); dangerous or cruel in a more overtly 'villainous' way; loyal, noble or self-sacrificing; or bored, languid or world-weary. Sanders' portrayal of The Saint, for example, draws on many of these meanings, but softens the cruelty, while retaining an air of danger, to make the persona roguish rather than caddish or devious. The performance of the star persona in the same role over several films does, however, reiterate the same patterns of meaning, as Mary Beth Haralovich notes in her discussion of Sherlock Holmes on film (Haralovich, 1979: 54), even if on occasions, as with The Saint, these can be modified. It is less the case, in these circumstances, that the star is the role than that the performance of the star persona is the film. Clearly, other factors are important, such as setting or supporting characters, so that the Falcon, for example, is not quite the same figure without Goldy Lock accompanying him because certain possibilities (physical humour) are no longer available, while the creation of Holmes' persona by Basil Rathbone is also affected by playing opposite Nigel Bruce as Dr. Watson. However, the persona tends to determine the possibilities available, whether this is with regard to setting, type of narrative, specific incidents or situations that are allowable, or style and mode, although there are occasional exceptions such as the 'Michael Shayne' series in which Lloyd Nolan as Shayne has a variable persona depending upon the style of the film. In *Michael Shayne, Private Detective* (1940) he is downbeat and rather bungling because the film is in the comedy thriller mode, in *Dressed to Kill* (1941) he is observant and wise because it is a whodunnit, and in *Blue, White and Perfect* (1942) he is an action hero because the film is a Nazi-busting movie.

One feature in the representation of the detectives that significantly influences their meanings is their status with regard to law and crime because this determines their relations to society. Of particular import is the detective's ability to stand above society, resist its temptations, deal with its problems and finally mete out justice. The detective in the classical detective story has always been a singular figure 'alone capable of dissipating the threat to the social order that is posed by an act of criminal violence' (Palmer, 1991: 124) and, as several scholars have noted, his or her amateur status is significant in setting the detective apart from the forces of law and the criminality that the police deal with on a daily basis (Moretti, 1988: 143). This means that the detective is not entangled within the bureaucracy of crime and the everyday 'legwork' that policing entails, often using a sidekick (Goldy or Lefty in some of the 'Falcon' films or, until he is replaced by a younger brother, Number One Son in the 'Charlie Chan' series) or the police (Lieutenant Abrams in 'The Thin Man' series or Inspector Lestrade in the 'Sherlock Holmes' films) for these purposes. More importantly, although the detective is reliant on the police for aspects of the investigation, even as he outdoes them in intuition and deduction, he or she is able to stand outside the disorganised excess of information accruing in the bureaucratic and procedural areas of the law as a social institution which itself acts as a metonymy for the muddled and baffling (and baffled) landscape of society as a whole, with its confused motivations, mystifications, false leads and appearances, and general lack of structure. The detective of the crime series is often configured as a transcendental subject who is someone able to stand above his or her own subjectivity from which position the transcendental subject can perceive his or her own conscious being and observe its relations to wider formations (such as society or other consciousnesses). Such a figure could also be described as a 'subject-outside-history', unaffected by the social, cultural, economic, ideological and political relations, apparatuses or institutions that comprise historical forces, albeit only as an impossible fantasy of a subjectivity freed from their movement. The classical detective has been a particular focus for the fantasy of transcendental subjectivity from Dupin and Sherlock Holmes through to the rise of the hard-boiled detective, although the latter is a problematic figure in this regard. Two key aspects of the transcendental subject are to be outside structures of labour and monetary exchange (to be independent, in other words, of the means of capitalist production, whether as producer or product) and to be free from state apparatuses (institutions, bureaucracy, ideology) in order to make the classical detective a model or fantasy figure outside of or above the social relations within which most people exist.[7]

The amateur detective, particularly in the mode of the gentleman detective, fulfils these criteria by being outside money, labour and institutional attachment to the forces of the law and the State. It is not necessarily that such figures are independently wealthy, but that they are never shown as having any relation to money, as if somehow they are divested of any need for it, even when they must hire hotel rooms (*Charlie Chan at Monte Carlo* [1938]), take trains across the American continent (*The Falcon Out West*) or fly from London to France (*Bulldog Drummond's Bride*) or from London to Washington (*Sherlock Holmes in Washington*). It is unsurprising, therefore within, generic paradigms that most of the amateur detectives in the classical Hollywood crime series are gentlemen, adventurers or individualists. Of the amateur detectives, only Torchy Blane and Boston Blackie are remotely working class and neither is overtly coded as such despite the former having a fast-talking, brassy persona derived from the urban dramas made by Warner, the studio that produced the 'Torchy Blane' series, which frame her in these terms. Indeed, Boston Blackie, as an ace safe-cracker who has reached the height of his profession before moving into official society, is represented as one of the aristocrats of criminal and working class society, having a figure who is effectively his butler in the form of The Runt. There are similar ambiguities in the case of Nick Charles, in 'The Thin Man' series, because of his past life among criminals as a professional detective before he enters high society. The remainder of the amateur detectives are predominantly from the upper echelons of society, such as Philo Vance and Michael Lanyard (Lone Wolf), while Gay and Tom Lawrence (the two incarnations of the Falcon), Simon Templar (The Saint), Bulldog Drummond, and Sherlock Holmes are all either aristocratic or from the professional and intellectual class, and, as significantly, all English. This outsider status is important in establishing the detective as an individualist, free from social relations even if some of the detectives have to strive to maintain their self-sufficiency. The struggle to maintain autonomy is often a significant concern for criminal-detectives such as Boston Blackie, the Lone Wolf, The Saint and the Falcon, who often have to prove their innocence of a crime by finding the real culprit. This is not merely a narrative trope to make them active as detectives, thereby setting the story of the investigation in motion, but also a way of conveying the quest for individuality as a struggle in representing the ways in which they are beset by attempts to curtail their freedom through imprisonment as a metonymy for the bonds created by society.

Most significant in this concern with autonomy is the detective's freedom of movement across society and his or her ability to enter restricted or controlled spaces. Detectives in the crime series are given licence to enter any space because they are police officers or associated with the police or because they take upon themselves the right to do so, often through breaking and entering (Nick Charles, The Lone Wolf, the

Falcon), the use of disguise (Sherlock Holmes) or trickery (The Saint). The series detective is therefore generally characterised by mobility, both spatially and socially, able to overcome barriers or restrictions (implicit or defined) by slipping into areas others are unable or unwilling to enter, whether these are bank vaults, hideouts, salons, criminal dens, or private homes, in order to move through high society, middle-class and working-class worlds, and the criminal underworld, even if they require a mediator in the form of an assistant to do so on occasions. They very often take on the iconography of the thief or the police officer in the process, to become temporarily their 'other', even if only in facsimile or dissimulated form, but above all such freedom suggests their status as transcendental subjects because they cross cultural, social and economic boundaries as if they did not exist. The same is also the case with the hard-boiled detective, as Ralph Willett observes of Dashiell Hammett's Continental Op (Willett, 1996: 43–4), but the sense of the investigation as a form of entanglement and the private eye's specific location within a particular city, suggests that he has a more delimited or restricted space through which he can move, while the fact that the private eye has to defend his own spaces (office or home) from being penetrated by police or intruders also indicates not only that he has a more precarious control of space generally, but also, as a result of identification of self with private space, that he is under threat from the city he inhabits.

B-Movie production

The Hollywood detective crime series of the 1930s and 1940s are not only defined by their relationship to the generic codes of the format they adopt within the series as a whole or across the different films within each series. Their production as B-Movies also has an impact on the films' style, narrative and content. Indeed, the B-Movie production of most of the series often helps to either confirm generic codes or to vary them to produce a pastiche or cross-generic style. Although there had been cheaply produced films within the Majors before the rise of the B-Movies, the main period of the development of B-Movies occurred from the middle of the 1930s onwards as a response to economic difficulties experienced by the Hollywood studios between 1930 and 1933 which saw them showing net losses in 1932 before three of eight majors (Paramount, Fox and RKO) went into bankruptcy or receivership in the following year (Schatz, 1996: 159). Between 1930 and 1933, average weekly attendance dropped from 110 to 60 million

(Miller, 1973: 2) and cinema owners, which included the vertically integrated Big Five (MGM, Warners, Paramount, Fox and RKO), sought new ways to draw in audiences. Balio recounts how versions of lotteries such as 'Bank Night and kindred contests, such as Prosperity Night, Movie Sweepstakes, and Treasury Night' (1993: 28) were used to sell tickets, but it was the development of the double feature that was the most important response to the economic travails because it changed exhibition practices across the United States in both first-run and independent cinemas until the Majors cancelled their B productions when divorcement killed off the double-bill in the late 1940s (Kerr, 1986: 234) and a number of the crime series discussed here went into Poverty Row production ('Charlie Chan', 'Michael Shayne', and a version of the 'Falcon' series). The double-bill allowed cinemas to change their programmes twice or more a week and thereby provided a variety of offering for audiences, albeit very often only with a change of supporting feature or the replacement of two programmers with two more of the same status. Initially, it was the affiliated theatres who were the main users of double bills, but their success led to first-run theatres following suit because the latter found they couldn't charge the same price for a ticket for a single film that other theatres were charging for two.

According to Miller (1973: 30) the double-bill, with a headlining or 'A'-feature and a supporting film with B-grade production (most often also including cartoons and a newsreel) quickly became pervasive in the United States, with 85 per cent of movie houses adopting the practice by 1936, by which point all of the majors had developed their own B units to service the demand for second feature fare (McClelland, 1978: 14; Taves, 1993: 316).[8] Not all B-Movies came from these units, however, not only because there were many Poverty Row independents producing cheap films to act as filler in the double-bill (Maltby, 1995: 66), such as Republic, World-Wide, Grand National and Monogram (which produced the 'Mr Wong' crime series), but some films made by the Majors with an 'A' budget failed to receive the success, critical or popular, that was expected of them and were subsequently relegated to supporting status. In addition, there were what Taves (1993: 317) refers to as 'lower-level A's', also referred to as '"shaky A's," "gilt-edged B's," "in-betweeners," or "intermediates"' which straddled the boundary between A and B picture and which could be shown at either end of the bill depending upon where they were exhibited. Such films, also termed 'programmers' by Miller (1973), might be a bottom or top of the bill film depending upon 'distribution and exhibition arrangements' (Spicer, 2002: 32). The films in MGM's 'Andy Hardy' series were somewhat in this category, as also were the 'Charlie Chan' films, which began production with reasonably high budgets before the development of the double-bill (Miller, 1973: 8), but which could appear in either position on a bill once the double feature had become a staple of exhibition practices. Because of its necessity within the double feature, the B-Movie also became a key part of the block-booking system through which the Majors guaranteed a steady income by including them in a package along with a headline production (Maltby, 1995: 66). This ensured that the studios received income not only from the headliners, but also the low-budget films, which became a staple of the industry as an economic rather than an aesthetic product until divorcement and the decline of the B-Movie in the late 1940s, even though the profit made on a B-Movie was low, \$10,000 on a picture made for \$70,000–80,000 according to Cross (1981: 7) as opposed to the higher profits based on percentages that accrued on class-A pictures. However, as Taves notes, the flat fees that were charged for B features meant that 'the expected gross to the studio from a B could be more reliably determined in advance because of the flat fee' (Taves. 1993: 314) and this meant that B-Movies invariably showed a profit that couldn't always be guaranteed by a prestige film.

B-Movies therefore serviced a purely economic need and there was hardly any attempt to generate aesthetic value within the format, even if occasional B-Movies could be unexpected successes. It is for this reason that B-Movies have received little critical attention, even though they amounted to about half of the Majors' product in the 1930s, not only because of their perceived lack of artistic merit, but also because they emphasise the industrial nature of Hollywood studio production in the 1930s and 1940s, their very existence revealing that A or prestige pictures were also conceived by the studios as 'product' to fill seats. There are, however, clearly differences between the two types of picture, most importantly with regard to budget which affected all other areas, particularly the length of shoot which averaged only about three weeks, but could be scheduled for as little as a week (Taves, 1993: 318). Although B units shared the same process of production as used for A-films, the personnel involved were distinct, so that directors, screenwriters, and players usually only worked on either As or Bs, even if some moved on from Bs to As (Rita Hayworth, for example, appeared in both the 'Blondie' and 'Charlie Chan' series while Glenn Ford appeared in the former and Robert Young in the latter), dropped from As to Bs (John Barrymore, who appeared in three 'Bulldog Drummond' movies), or occasionally provided supporting roles in As (e.g., Nigel Bruce and Warner Oland).[9] B-Movies did not, therefore, have access to star personnel and had to make do with existing sets or lots (often re-using sets from more expensive productions), because there was no budget to do anything other than dress what was already available, or use library footage to create backgrounds (Cross, 1981: 20). On occasions, films would try to convince audiences that cheapness of production was actually narratively motivated. In *Bulldog Drummond Comes Back*, for example, Drummond openly mentions as he is shuttled around places he has already visited that he is being given the 'run-around' by the villains, but this only draws attention to the limited number of sets being used. Similarly, in *The Falcon in Mexico* (1944), a narrative is created for the Mexican guide, Manuel, that has him constantly swapping cars to cover up the fact that the long-shots of the Falcon's arrival at various locations are drawn from stock footage in which different cars appear.

The development of B units also had advantages because they allowed the studios to remain active throughout the year and to balance overheads because stock, sets and personnel were in constant use. In the case of Columbia, which had fewer economic resources than most of the other majors, B-Movies to service the cinemas owned by the Big Five were the life-blood that kept the studio in production, with an occasional prestige movie being made by a director such as Frank Capra (Kuhn, 1999: 22–3). Series films were extremely important in this regard, with most of these being in the B category, although some ('The Thin Man' and 'Gold Diggers' films) had prestige production. The creation of the double-bill as standard exhibition practice in the United States by the mid-1930s and the creation of B units to fulfil the demand for film product created conditions suitable for the development of 'series' films generally and crime series in particular, with Fox putting most of its resources for B production into series (Miller, 1973: 46). A variety of series developed across different genres, such as the western ('Cisco Kid' and 'Durango Kid'), comedy (the 'Ritz Brothers', 'Blondie', and 'Mexican Spitfire'), romance ('Maisie'), action adventure ('Tarzan'), and horror (the 'Wolfman' and 'Mummy' series as well as compendium monster films involving the 'Wolfman', 'Frankenstein' and 'Dracula' once the latter films had moved from prestige to B production), but crime was a particular focus for the production of series films. The general demand for regular product that the series provided and the quick turnover of scripts that was needed made the crime format attractive because of the availability of ready-made scenarios that could be recycled from other films or crime series or from the wealth of literary and radio whodunnits on the market. By the time of the rise of the B unit in the mid-1930s, Charlie Chan was already a recurring character in fiction and film and there had been several 'Philo Vance' and 'Sherlock Holmes' films, while The Saint and other detectives were also developing back catalogues in fiction that could provide scripts once the rights had been acquired. The pulp ethos that created the 'simple, standardized, and repetitive' product that Taves notes as an important feature of B-Movies (1993: 333) also helped to make crime films ubiquitous in B production and the most numerous of the series (Cross, 1981: 60).

The cinematic vaudeville of the B-Movie

To define B-Movies only by the cheapness of their production would do them an injustice, not only because such a view ignores the differences among studios (with regard to favoured genres or differences in production values), but also because it overlooks the ways in which film makers sought to produce an entertaining package within the limited running time available (usually just over an hour). The shortness of the films was a particular difficulty for the producers, screenwriters and directors of B-Movies because the narrative space it offered wasn't sufficient to develop the different plot lines that afforded complexity in A-features. Narrative material, therefore, had to be thinned out to avoid the abundance provided by sub-plots with a concomitant loss of variety. For example, when Chandler's *Farewell, My Lovely* was adapted as *The Falcon Takes Over* (1942) a number of excisions or modifications were made to streamline the plot, including the removal of several characters who provide a good deal of incidental story material: a phoney doctor who holds Marlowe the detective in his sanatorium in a drugged state when he gets too close to discovering the truth of the jewel heist gang, the two corrupt police officers who help to put him there, and an honest police officer who helps Marlowe reach the gangster Laird Brunette. In addition, some characters are given more prominent roles, most notably Velma and Brunette (who become members of the heist gang they have nothing to do with in the novel), or substituted for others, such as the police officers Randall and Nulty who, in the novel, occupy separate sub-plots that add to the narrative complexity but who in the Falcon adaptation are replaced by the simplified double-act of O'Hara and Bates. These modifications winnow out much narrative incident that might threaten to push *The Falcon Takes Over* beyond the running time allowed for supporting features, but also leave gaps that must be replaced so that the film doesn't come in below the usual duration for a B-Movie of about 60–70 minutes.

Such reductions in narrative material are partly the result of costs (because more characters means more money spent on acting personnel),[10] but they are also the result of the need to avoid the narrative inflation created by having a large supporting cast whose characters need to be introduced and then developed sufficiently to make their presence credible within the logic of the narrative. B-Movies generally therefore have a direct, but truncated storyline focusing on a small number of characters, but this can be problematic if it thins the narrative too much, particularly in the whodunnit variety of detective film which requires sufficient complexity (usually provided by a sufficient number of subsidiary cast members to provide suspects) in order to conceal the truth of the solution. On occasions, the necessary mystification is provided by an instrumental approach to the use of subsidiary characters in which they are introduced for a few scenes before being discarded. Such is the case in the 'Sherlock Holmes' film *Terror by Night* (1946), in which a middle-aged couple, Mr and Mrs Shallcross, are used briefly as suspects when Watson believes they have confessed to the murder being investigated, only for them to be jettisoned from the story when it is discovered that they only confessed to the theft of a teapot from a hotel. This seems a very simple and mechanical use of the characters, but the situation is more complex and it is this complexity which demonstrates that B-Movies are not simply formulaic, but can be very ingenious in their narrative construction. The Shallcrosses serve more than one purpose in the narrative because in addition to providing textual mystification, albeit briefly, they also provide a comic interlude as part of the film's package of entertainment, not only in the comedy of bathos with regard to the teapot, but also in the byplay created by the comedy of errors involving Watson. In addition, the scene in which they are involved comes just after Sherlock Holmes has decided to search a coffin in the baggage car, the search of which, less than a third of the way through the film, would uncover the secret that would solve the case and bring the narrative to an end. The introduction of the Shallcrosses is a necessary delay in the narrative of investigation, but their scene also has a final function because, as Kristin Thompson points out (1988: 64), it helps to re-direct the investigation away from the search of the coffin, thereby creating new narrative spaces.

It isn't always the case that B-Movies have this innovative and economical approach to the construction of narratives and oftentimes they are just economical. Films of the detective crime series are full of narrative short-cuts, such as secret doors, to allow an easy escape in order to keep a criminal (and occasionally a detective) narratively active, or secret compartments where clues can be found easily so that the detective doesn't have to spend a lot of screen time searching a room thoroughly. Although these narrative abbreviations are contrivances, they are also important elements of the detective film's regime of generic verisimilitude (consistency with the law of genre) which Steve Neale argues are 'least compatible with regimes of cultural verisimilitude' (credibility according to discourses of 'reality'), but which also often create the greatest pleasure for the audience of a genre text (Neale, 1990: 48). The B-Movie also uses an instrumental approach to the transmission of information which, due to the exigencies of narrative time, needs to be delivered quickly and clearly. Thus, in the 'Torchy Blane' film *Blondes at Work* (1938), confusion over a telephone that doesn't ring is quickly cleared up when McBride discovers the murder weapon obstructing the sounding of the bell. Similarly, relationships, friendships and bonds of trust are established very quickly in B-Movies if they don't exist already. For example, in *The Saint in New York*, The Saint befriends Sebastian Lipke, the taxi driver, during a cab ride and wins the trust of Inspector Fernack within minutes of meeting him. In the economy of the B-Movie, very little is left to implication, so that bottles of poison are clearly marked 'Poison' (*The Adventurous Blonde*) and cans of gunpowder 'Explosives' (*Mr Moto Takes a Chance* [1938]), but narrative abbreviations or contractions are more pervasive than minor details such as this, becoming part of a wider instrumental approach to narrative. Many B-Movies embody Boris Tomashevsky's discussion of narrative functionality in relation to the 'compositional motivation' created by 'motifs' in which he refers to Chekhov's view that 'if one speaks about a nail beaten into the wall at the beginning of a narrative, then at the end the hero must hang himself on that nail' (Tomashevsky, 1965: 79). B-Movie narratives offer quite clear causal relationships between motifs in this way, but very often they don't wait until the end of the film to resolve them in the way that Tomashevsky describes, but do so almost immediately after they have first been deployed. Such an approach is on show in *After Midnight with Boston Blackie* (1943), for example, when Manleder, an associate of Blackie, brings along a camera at one point, ostensibly to capture photographs of crimes being committed, although the narrative purpose of the camera is actually to provide flash bulbs for Blackie to throw so that he can distract the gangsters following him into a cellar and then overpower them as they look in the direction of the small explosions the bulbs create.

Despite this tendency to reduction with regard to narrative material, there is also a paradoxical inflation within B-Movies in order to offset the possibility that the film might under run. In *The Falcon Takes Over*, discussed previously, so much has been winnowed out from Chandler's *Farewell, My Lovely* that the film has to compensate by adding comedy sequences that fill out the narrative (involving the Falcon playing drunk or the slapstick that results when his sidekick Goldy is found at the scenes of murders on no less than three occasions). Similar forms of 'padding' can be found in other B-Movie films, whether it is the long journey that Larry Talbot takes to find Frankenstein's castle in *Frankenstein Meets the Wolfman* (1942), the farce-based courthouse sequence at the end of the 'Torchy Blane' adventure *Blondes at Work*, which has no bearing on the narrative of investigation but which delays the announcement of a confession that would otherwise have ended the film much earlier, or the helter-skelter action sequence at the end of *Bulldog Drummond's Bride* which lasts nearly a quarter of the film's running time. Such textual inflation is not simply about filling the narrative, however, but also derives from the B-Movie's fundamental purpose, which is to provide entertainment as a supporting feature to the headlining film. Such 'padding' is not in these circumstances necessarily extraneous, nor are the pared down and instrumental narratives of B-Movies simply to do with bringing in a film within its allowable running time. The 'padding' can be part of the entertainment of the film and the narrative contractions treated as devices that reduce narrative time in order to allow the deployment of more non-plot based forms of entertainment. Richard Maltby's argument that 'Narrative functions as part of the provision of pleasure in cinema entertainment, not as the point of it' and his further comment that 'We may enjoy chase scenes in an action movie, the songs in a musical, or the performance of a favorite [*sic*] star, while remaining disengaged from the overly familiar or repetitive plot-line' (Maltby, 1995: 324) are particularly resonant for the B-Movie in this regard.

The B-Movie as a whole can perhaps best be understood as a set of attractions, considered as a form of 'cinematic vaudeville', and the B-Movie crime series, because of its need for material that retards the progress of the narrative toward closure (which includes its mystifications) in order to keep the detective active in the narrative, is particularly prone to this form of textual organisation. As has already been noted, the B-Movie crime film becomes indistinct with regard to its generic conventions, incorporating multiple forms of crime codes in addition to the mystery format of the whodunnit. In addition, crime films in all of the series discussed here incorporate cross-generic elements, such as slapstick, banter and farcical misunderstanding, romantic involvements, or the thrills and spills associated with the action or adventure format. Gates notes the tendency to mix comedy and detection in the crime series of the 1930s and 1940s as part of its comforting vision of a 'stable and happy society' (2006: 76), but the cinematic vaudeville provided by comedy goes beyond this. It pertains more clearly to Kerr's description of the hybrid B-Movies that developed in Poverty Row studios which mixed 'melodrama and mystery, gangster and private eye, screwball comedy and thriller' (1986: 232) in order to provide fare that would differentiate the supporting feature from the main A-feature. Kerr also notes that exhibition practices developed in the 1930s and 1940s that offered contrasting styles in the double-bill so that '*The Saint in New York*, for example, was billed with *Gold Diggers in Paris*, *Blind Alibi* with *Holiday*' (Ibid.). This suggests that cinemas presented their products in much the same way as a vaudeville theatre, offering different forms of entertainment on a bill that also included, for example, cartoons, comedy shorts and newsreels.

The B-Movie develops an internal pattern that provides a textual form of vaudeville within a narrative frame, although this narrative is itself only one part of the entertainment on the bill and often, indeed, becomes merely the thread that connects the other kinds of entertainment on offer. In *The Falcon in Mexico*, for example, there are several scenes involving musical entertainments which, although integrated into the narrative because certain incidents occur during or after their performance, are not in themselves necessary to the plot. These are supplemented later by carnival sequences, which provide incidents that are more embedded into the plot (a murder and the Falcon taking on the disguise of a dead man to draw out the murderer), but their presence is also in many ways supernumerary to the narrative. While it could be said that these sequences are simply a way of cutting costs by using stock footage inter-cut with material shot specifically for the film, this would ignore the visual pleasures provided by the both the exotic setting and the performances offered within the carnival scenes. Such textual material is not merely an interlude in the narrative, even if it seems to be an interruption in the goal-oriented organisation of events that leads to closure, because it is deployed as an attraction that complements (and perhaps even displaces) the entertainment provided by the mystery narrative. While such material might appear to be an intrusion or a supplement, it is nevertheless a very important part of the pleasure provided by the B-Movie which needed to provide something for everyone as part of the overall package of entertainment on the cinema bill.

The cinematic vaudeville that the B-Movie offers can be considered, therefore, as a set of routines organised in the manner of a bill of entertainment in itself, providing some action, thrills, romance, mystery, suspense and comedy, as well as musical entertainment on occasions. Different films emphasise a particular aspect according to genre (thrills in horror, mystery or action in crime films), but they also provide other attractions so that, for example, *Congo Maisie* (1940), from MGM's 'Maisie' series, includes exotic adventure, song and dance routines, magic tricks and comedy to supplement its primary romance narrative. Such is the importance of cinematic vaudeville in B-Movies that in detective films the mystery that motivates the narrative becomes merely one of the routines. Indeed, the denouement usually creates a routine of its own, sometimes in the form of action, although most often it seems closer to a magic act, rather than a deductive explanation of events, with the detective performing a magician's 'reveal' when he names the criminal.[11] Thus, for example, Basil Rathbone's performance of the detection as Sherlock Holmes is just one part of the B-Movie bill, no different in many ways to the comedy act provided by Nigel Bruce's Dr Watson, who can even be considered to be more important within the B-Movie aesthetic because of the entertainment he provides. The organisation of material as cinematic vaudeville means that the B-Movie offers genre confusion similar to the form of pastiche that Dyer refers to as 'pasticcio'. In this style, combination, interruption and abundance are most significant: 'However much a pasticcio may have a dominant or underpinning formal tone or structure, or may make sense by virtue of implicit meaning, still much of the flavour resides in the sense of profusion' (Dyer, 2007: 19). The characteristics of diversity and distraction that accrue as a result of the accumulation of different textual components, which Dyer also sees as features of the 'circus, vaudeville, revue and early cinema programmes' (Ibid.: 16), applies significantly to the B-Movie. This is not to claim that this is the only place where combination or genre hybridity occurs because, as Bordwell, Staiger and Thompson have argued, genre hybridity can be found in most Hollywood films of the studio era in the use of the romance plot across all genres (1985: 16–17).

The films of the crime series seem particularly prone to profusion and combination and not only in their incorporation of suspense, thriller and espionage forms within a whodunnit mystery narrative. The need to delay the denouement means that the narratives are constantly distracted from their goal by the mystification that is characteristic of the genre but also by the incorporation of cross-generic material.

Each crime series usually incorporates comedy through the use of an assistant (The Runt in the 'Boston Blackie' films, Watson in the 'Sherlock Holmes' series, Lee, Jimmy or Tommy Chan in 'Charlie Chan'), as well as in the use of inefficient police officers, both of which create comedy routines that have a burlesque or vaudevillian flavour, such as the routine Dr Watson performs with the Shallcrosses in *Terror by Night*, as well as farce or comedy of errors. In addition, the crime series provide action sequences and thrills in a melodramatic mode (very often in the form of nick-of-time rescues or fights in precarious situations such as on rooftops), romances, musical performances, and any other distractions or divagations appropriate to the situation in order to divert the film away from the movement towards closure. *The Falcon Out West*, for example, has as its narrative motor the investigation of the murder of a ranch-owner in New York, but it moves to the West in order to add western tropes to those of mystery, romance and slapstick humour. The same film also exemplifies the tendency of the crime series to shift away from their usual setting not only to vary the format by presenting an already used plot in a new location, but also to place the detective within new generic parameters. This is most obviously the case with the espionage films that most detectives found themselves within after the United States' entry into World War II, such as the Lone Wolf adventure *Passport to Suez* (1943), but can also be seen in the Gothic style of, for example, *The Scarlet Claw* (in which Sherlock Holmes finds himself in a village in Canada) and in the use of the milieu of the criminal underworld to evoke gangster figurations in *The Saint's Double Trouble* (1940) or the *noir*-mode in *The Falcon in San Francisco* (1946). In combination with the retardatory material that delays the denouement, this cinematic vaudeville suggests that the detective crime series of the period can be best understood in terms of a concept of narrative 'bafflement', both in the mystifications that provide confusions, but also in the way that these and the cinematic vaudeville delay, side-track or 'baffle' the linear plot with non-essential scenes or routines.

2

'Such Lovely Friends': Class and Crime in 'The Thin Man' Series

Metro-Goldwyn-Mayer Inc.'s (MGM) 'The Thin Man' films are unusual among the detective crime series of the 1930s and 1940s because they maintained their A-Movie status as main features throughout their run. Other crime series topped the bill at times, usually because they were mid-level product ('shaky As' or 'programmers') that could be exhibited as support or main features ('Charlie Chan'), but also because some series ('Bulldog Drummond' and 'The Lone Wolf') were accorded an A-Movie budget in their early stages before subsequently dropping to B-Movie status. 'The Thin Man' films have something of a problematic position in this regard because although they cannot be considered B-Movies, nor are they obviously A-Movies, not least because the series was set off by a quickie that became a hit. *The Thin Man* (W.S. Van Dyke II, 1934) was filmed in 12 days for $231,000 and, although it went on to make $1,400,000, its budget was closer to that of a programmer in MGM terms.[1] That the film was based on a piece of pulp fiction, albeit a 'soft-boiled' confection of whodunnit and hard-boiled forms, makes its categorisation ambiguous, as does the mix of generic styles typical of the B-Movie, and it is mainly the gloss of screwball comedy that, as Hardy notes, moves it 'away from hard-boiled whodunit [sic] towards the sophisticated run of cocktail-fuelled marital comedies that were to proliferate in the mid-1930s' (Hardy, 1997: 79). It is the problematic generic status of *The Thin Man* and the other films in the series, however, that make 'The Thin Man' films significant in the study of the detective series because the series' pastiche of styles helps to establish the dominant comedy thriller mode of other crime series of the 1930s and 1940s. Prior to *The Thin Man* (W.S. Van Dyke II, 1934), murder mysteries had generally been sober affairs, such as the surviving early 'Charlie Chan' films, *Behind That Curtain* (1929) and *The Black Camel* (1931), despite occasional moments of humour. Early 'Sherlock Holmes' films provided melodrama, in *Sherlock Holmes* (1932), or suspense and a 'pervasive feeling of fear' (Taves, 1993: 340) in *A Study in Scarlet* (1933) while the 'Philo Vance' mysteries of the early 1930s are solemn, rather ludicrously so in the locked-room mystery *The Kennel Murder Case* (1933), because of the passions and jealousies aroused among a circle of suspects drawn from people obsessed with winning a dog show.

Creating 'The Thin Man' style

Although 'The Thin Man' series ran for a period of 13 years, it retained a stable comedy thriller format through its six entries, focusing on the modern domestic situation of Nick and Nora Charles, their bantering relationship, slapstick sequences, and the self-conscious awareness that the series inhabited a textual world that was a by-product of the humour. Despite another recurrent motif, Nick's reluctance to return to detection, the films all have a whodunnit narrative, drawing together the worlds of bourgeois respectability and the criminal underworld while deploying the latter to divert suspicion away from a criminal originating in the former (Glitre, 2006: 81), and usually conclude with the entertainment Nick provides in the denouement scene. This format is established in *The Thin Man*, based on Dashiell Hammett's novel of the same title, and the following three films are generally faithful to the style, even though by the third film (*Another Thin Man*) a son has arrived (Nickie Jr) and the reference to 'The Thin Man' has shifted from one of the victims of the first film (the eccentric businessman Wynant) to the figure of Nick Charles. The defining feature of the series, however, is the intersection between the modes of comedy and tough thriller present in Hammett's novel and the screwball conventions that the film of *The Thin Man* helped to define.[2] The interfusion of styles not only helped to create the comedy thriller mode that was much imitated by other detective crime series, but also confirmed a vision of the United States found in Hammett's original novel which softened the hard-boiled style by rendering it within the form of the whodunnit to focus attention on criminality within the bourgeois world. The addition of screwball comedy in the film adaptation softens the style further, but also has the effect of emphasising the corrupt and immoral actions of the wealthy. By using humour to present the rich as screwballs rather than respectable members of society, the film makes the wealthy seem peculiar. It then attaches the signs of peculiarity to both their ridiculous behaviour and their pursuit of money by any means to make the latter also seem aberrant.

Nick Charles' entry into the world of the wealthy thereby becomes a means to explore the immorality of the rich when his past as a retired detective brings him into the circle of the New York elite to pursue an investigation involving the father of a wealthy family (Wynant), for whom he has previously worked, who has been implicated in murder. Nick is a complex amalgamation of amateur and professional detective who is also a man of wealth, having married into money, and a working man because he manages the businesses Nora has inherited. He is, however, coded differently to the bourgeois society with which he comes into contact as a result of the Wynant case, even though he is removed from the world of labour by the Christmas vacation in New York and engages in the same purposeless pursuits of the wealthy with Nora (characterised by their drinking sprees), because he is represented within populist discourses that code him as 'of the people' in opposition to society's elite.[3] His dual identity as working man and member of the elite is significant because it not only has ideological significations in figuring Nick as not of the corrupt world of the wealthy that the film investigates, but also represents him as an Everyman figure who can move in all strata of society because he has come up from a working class occupation (detective) to enter the upper class (by marriage) even while he still labours within the world of white-collar management. As an Everyman he is able to converse or connect with all parts of society while his previous role as a professional detective allows him to both straddle the worlds of law and crime and to fit in among the criminal underworld, many of whose members appear in the series to announce that they are old acquaintances he has previously sent to prison. His marriage to Nora also compounds the sense that Nick is part of all worlds within American society, because it places him within the private domestic sphere as well as in the public spheres of work, business and the law. Nick thereby becomes an unusual version of the 'unusual man', who is also 'a complete man and a common man', that Raymond Chandler describes as the embodiment of the American detective in 'The Simple Art of Murder' (Chandler, 1995: 992) because he seemingly exists within all spheres of American society in the 1930s.

Nick's completeness as a man able to exist in all social strata is a product of the combination of hard-boiled and whodunnit forms in the creation of the 'soft-boiled' detective thriller offered by *The Thin Man*. The film version of *The Thin Man* places Nick and Nora Charles in a situation that brings together a cross-section of society from the wealthy upper classes, as a product of the whodunnit conventions, to underworld and criminal figures, drawn from the hard-boiled style, with Nick as mediator (Harvey, 1998: 181), and offers a consideration of American class, society and crime within a setting that owes as much to the conventions of the screwball comedy as it does to the detective genre. Screwball codes significantly affect the textual world represented in *The Thin Man* and other films in the series because of a recurring refrain that everyone in Nick and Nora's world is 'nuts' or 'screwy' except for the couple themselves, even though they are not obviously part of the everyday world of domestic normality. Not only is Nick and Nora's relationship based on a pleasure-seeking lifestyle (dining, drinking and attending parties) and animated by their affectionate verbal interplay, described by Young in an analysis of their first scene together as 'creating a song out of their bantering' for their own 'private delight' (Young, 1994: 266), but they also live in hotel rooms when many of the cases take place. They thus exist in a transient intermediate world in opposition to the stability of the home, even in *Shadow of the Thin Man* which, although it is set in their home-town of San Francisco, still sees them staying in a hotel suite. Nick and Nora are already therefore drawn into the 'screwy' world of people such as the Wynant-Jorgensens in *The Thin Man* because they share a similar lifestyle even if they manage to maintain their distance because they don't live within this world. Much of this is the result of the screwball aspects of the film, where 'the leisure life, often in "high-society" style' (Gehring, 2002: 29) is typical, and the series as a whole often uses its portrayal of a world full of wealthy screwballs and comic buffoons to provide textual pleasure in onscreen antics for the audience to enjoy rather than to offer comment on 1930s American society.

The Thin Man's focus on upper-class society and its eccentricities does, however, have some wider concerns with American society in the Depression and New Deal years of the 1930s, particularly through showing the family of Wynant as being 'on the make'. Mimi Jorgensen, Wynant's ex-wife, is key in establishing wider political reference because she is constantly demanding money from Wynant to support her lifestyle. She is represented as a parasite, therefore, in opposition to Wynant who, as a hard-working businessman, is the kind of person valued by the New Deal ideology of reconstruction that will rebuild and remake the United States. Mimi is represented in order to imply that everybody in American society is 'on the make', expecting money without labour. Not only does she make constant demands of MacCaulay, who manages Wynant's money during his absence, but she also thinks that her discovery of Wynant's watch-chain by Julia Wolf's body will allow her to extort money out of Wynant because it appears to incriminate her ex-husband. That it is planted by MacCaulay, the killer, who is also engaged in the corrupt acquisition of Wynant's wealth by stealing bonds set aside for Dorothy, also implicates the apparently respectable members of society as the main criminals, murdering or blackmailing to maintain their life of ease. Significations of criminality among the wealthy are also figured through the connections of MacCaulay and Wynant, through Julia Wolf, with the underworld figures of Nunheim and Morelli, whose criminal ambitions are also predicated on the acquisition of money without labour in order to suggest that venality is not the preserve only of the wealthy. Nunheim's violent and dysfunctional relationship with his moll Marion, for example, is used to reflect the Jorgensens' failed family, albeit with implications that Wynant is partially responsible for the latter situation because he is, in Nick's words, 'screwy' like everyone else in his family except for Dorothy and thus another disruptive force in this world. In this context, the screwball world of cocktails and verbal games has complex significations. It reproduces the 'screwy' world of the Jorgensens that Nick and Nora encounter, provides an appropriate textual world for an amateur detective to operate within, and reflects on the web of connections stretching from the world of the privileged into the criminal world, which in the hard-boiled novel signifies not only that corruption has infected the world of the ruling class, but that they are its producers.

Although Nick is now seemingly a part of the 'screwy' world because of his marriage to Nora, he is still outside its value system, partly because he evades getting involved with the Wynant investigation for a long time, but also because he is content to inhabit the little domestic world he shares with Nora and Asta. In this, the hotel room takes on different meanings to the transient life it suggests for Nick and Nora in later films in the series, because it becomes a sign that his world has drawn into domesticity, even if it is a pleasure-seeking version common to the screwball genre. However, Nick and Nora's hotel room is also invaded and disrupted by the public world of wealth and crime during the Christmas party scene in which Nick draws together assorted police officers, underworld contacts, ex-cons and members of the sporting world. The party also brings several of the Jorgensens as well as a telephone call from Nunheim, Julia's underworld acquaintance, all of whom either bring the case or their dysfunctional family relationships to disorder Nick's world, most obviously when Mimi slaps Dorothy in front of Nick and Nora because she believes that Dorothy has revealed information that thwarts her plan to blackmail Wynant on his expected reappearance. Although the party degenerates into an anarchy of tuneless singing, drunken disagreements and maudlin sentimentality after the Jorgensen clan are ushered out, it is implied that they cause the disorder by bringing their world of crime, venal desire and pathologies to the hotel room to disturb the small world of Nick and Nora. Thus, when Nora surveys the scene and announces ironically, but with a sense of affection, that she loves Nick because he knows 'such lovely people' (a statement repeated in *Another Thin Man* and varied in *After The Thin Man* when she refers to Nick knowing 'the nicest people'), her comment applies as much to the Jorgensens and people like them as it does to the working class and underworld figures from among Nick's acquaintances who are still present. Nora's comment resonates through the series therefore to judge the pettiness and criminality of the upper classes negatively in relation to the underworld figures and working Americans Nick and Nora come across in the investigations. This is most obvious in *Another Thin Man* when the crimes of a wealthy heiress are judged against a backdrop of comic chaos caused by the baby party thrown by Nick's old criminal friends who are shown to be harmless by comparison.

Nick and Nora are still not quite of the 'screwy' world that comes to them and this is suggested by the fact that they are entwined together standing outside the chaos as observers when Nora makes her comment. Nick's refusal to take on the Wynant case thereby becomes a way for him to remain outside bourgeois society, evidenced by his response to a question at the party about why he doesn't take on the investigation: 'Haven't you heard the news? I'm a gentleman now'. Although Nick's reply suggests he is of bourgeois society, the self-irony of his comment also signals that he is different. He has self-knowledge about his own social status as only a facsimile member of the privileged elite because he is still a 'common' man underneath. His remark also contributes to the series' self-consciousness about its transformation of Nick from hard-boiled private eye to 'gentleman' detective and *The Thin Man* is very playful in this regard, reflecting on its own status as a text of the amateur detective variety by including 'amateur detectives' in the form of Gilbert and Nora, even if their main purpose in this role is to provide comic relief. Both Nora and Gilbert are easily misdirected, either because Nick sends Nora off on a wild goose chase by one trick or another (for example, ushering her into a cab to go off to Grant's Tomb), or because Gilbert is sidetracked by irrelevances such as pseudo-psychology or phrenology. In a very New Deal way, the need for professionalism and understanding of the real world are shown to be important, rather than distant library learning or the enthusiasms of the amateur dabbler. Although Nick displays seeming amateurism before he takes on the case (coded by his flamboyance), his professionalism and application once he is involved sets him against the world signified by the Jorgensens because he is not solving crime either for money or, like Gilbert, simply to occupy his time.[4] That he also works, in running the enterprises Nora inherited from her father, also puts him among those working for the betterment of American society although it is in his alternative role as a detective that he performs the greater service to New Deal America. By unveiling and punishing corruption and criminality among the wealthy Nick helps to clean it of some of the parasites who, in New Deal ideology, not only drain America of its vitality but also provide obstacles to its progress towards wider prosperity.

Nick's contribution to the social ordering of the United States, however, involves a problematic reassertion of the status quo. Sean McCann (2000: 91) notes that Hammett's novels generally provide an ambiguous return to the social contract. The film of *The Thin Man* follows this line in punishing the wealthy even as it fulfils the premise of the detective narrative by reasserting the legitimacy of the State and its institutions in dispensing justice, albeit requiring an outsider to do so. This latter trope is an important element within the detective film in the 1930s, however, because it suggests that the established order of the privileged is still guaranteed by vested interests, with the forces of law still at their service. 'The Thin Man' series often shows the police investigating 'the usual suspects' from the criminal underworld, ignoring the possibility that the crime might be from within the world of the elite, while Nick – the outsider looking in – sees where the real corruption lies. The outsider as detective has been a prevalent trope throughout the detective genre (Field, 2009: 29), but this becomes particularly important in the 1930s and 1940s crime series which are full of such figures whether in the form of the aristocratic outsider (The Saint, the Falcon, Sherlock Holmes and The Lone Wolf) or the detective who is an outsider because of his ethnicity (Charlie Chan, Mr Wong and Mr Moto). In each case it is the disinterested eye of the outsider, who isn't served by established social and economic apparatuses, that is important, and this extends to the maverick detectives with their roots in the hard-boiled tradition. Nick Charles, as both 'gentleman' detective and hard-boiled private eye is doubly coded as an outsider in American society, but this also doubles his disinterested concern in detecting aberrational activity within it. His amateur status as a gentleman guarantees his integrity (and economic independence from bribery), while the tough code of the street generated by his hard-boiled roots guarantees that he has no interest in perpetuating the self-serving interests of the privileged because his personal loyalties, as indicated in the party scene, lie outside this domain.

Throughout the series Nick's underworld acquaintances are represented as more trustworthy and reliable than most of the characters he encounters among the apparent world of respectability and, in mingling with them, Nick is associated with their 'common' decency. Nick is not therefore a distant upper-class detective, but a man of the people who moves within different circles across society to unite them by his presence. That he is also coded as something of an innocent, despite his professional knowledge of criminality and the underworld, is also important, and his pleasure-seeking lifestyle, even though it is in pursuit of the next drink, configures him as a child-like person with no malice. He is, in Gehring's view, a 'child-husband' to Nora's 'mother-wife' (Gehring, 2002: 41) and this is illustrated when he shoots balloons with his air-rifle in a variety of positions on Christmas Day and adopts a look of mock-guilt under Nora's tolerant but disapproving parental gaze when he breaks a window. The innocent is an important ideological figuration in an American context, particularly in the 1930s when such a figure becomes a sign of the innocence America has lost because it has become a world of corruptions created by big business and vested interests in economics and politics, although here it is in the social world where the corruptions are on show.[5] As significant is the way in which Nick's innocence rubs off on Nora who, as someone from the world of inherited wealth, needs to be ideologically differentiated from the greedy and eccentric world of the Jorgensens and the privileged elite they represent. Although the world of Nick and Nora has some of the same eccentricities, Nora is nevertheless shown to be innocent of its particular brand of venality and this is signalled by the implication that it is she who gave Nick the air-rifle which draws her into his way of seeing the world. Her eagerness to join in the detection, therefore, is not of the same category as Gilbert's because it is innocent enthusiasm rather than meaningless book-learning, while her sharing of Nick's drunken lifestyle is, like the couple's verbal jousting, a sign of their 'companionate relationship' (Glitre, 2006: 85).

From screwball crime to comedy thriller

The interplay between Nick and Nora provides the gloss for what is still effectively a B-Movie narrative in *The Thin Man*, even if their relationship takes up a good part of the narrative. This emphasis also makes the film more comedy-thriller than traditional whodunnit or hard-boiled detection because as Glitre notes, in discussing the juxtaposition of the couple's relationship with the mystery plot, 'their happy moments do not advance the story, but function as a form of spectacle, arresting – even supplanting – the causal chain of events' (Glitre, 2006: 84). The remaining films in 'The Thin Man' series remain consistent with this pattern, although the gloss of the screwball comedy is increasingly replaced by farce and slapstick so that later entries align more closely with the cinematic vaudeville of the B-Movie as a result of the pervasive intrusions of cross-generic material into the texts. There are some variations, particularly in the last two films, created by the small-town setting of *The Thin Man Goes Home* and the *noir* inflections of *Song of the Thin Man*, but the textual and narrative world established in *The Thin Man* generally holds sway. This textual world is mainly produced by thriller conventions over the course of the series rather than screwball comedy and it is here that the whodunnit and suspense forms prevail, in producing characters (the wealthy, underworld criminals and clumsy police officers) to perform a function according to narrative demands. The relative lack of ordinary, honest Americans outside those involved in detection is not simply a product of generic parameters because there are also other factors that determine the textual world's focus on the apparently respectable wealthy elite, drawn from the whodunnit, and the criminal underworld, identified with the suspense thriller. One of these is to create narrative mystification through the inclusion of recognisable criminal types to divert the audience away from crime among the wealthy and to create some of the obstacles to detection (red herrings or misplaced suspicions) that generate the narrative itself by providing the excess to the crime that makes up the investigation. There are, however, two criminal underworlds in 'The Thin Man' series, one of which provides conventional character types to service the narrative requirements for mystery in the parallel narratives of crime, all of whom are engaged in crime of some form in the text, and who are associated with an aberrant version of modernity because they use its freedoms for immoral purposes. The other, mainly harmless, comprises ex-cons and petty criminals from among Nick's acquaintances, who are present either for the comic criminal antics they generate or to offer a representation of the decent common American man with whom Nick consorts. Most of this latter group of criminals are shown as honest or reformed and only possess the signs of criminality as a self-conscious facsimile to code them as not of respectable society.

This is indicated in an early scene in the second film in the series, *After the Thin Man* (W.S. Van Dyke II, 1936), when Nick and Nora are being driven home after Nora has had her purse taken by one of Nick's old criminal acquaintances, 'Fingers', at a train station. Fingers' act of purse-snatching forms the preamble to a montage in which Nick is greeted by various people (news hawkers, a boxer and various onlookers) who, through a symbolic elision, as a result of the narrative contiguity with the theft and return of Nora's purse, allies Nick's criminal acquaintances with the working class people who greet him. These scenes also code Nick once more as a man of the people, even though he is being driven home by a chauffeur, especially because once the car has been halted, the various people crowd around him on the street. Although Nick is regarded here as a celebrity, and therefore not one of the crowd, he is nevertheless of the crowd and of the street, even if he doesn't step down from the car to mingle among those like himself. The ideological imperative of the series is to confirm the egalitarian and populist discourses of the first film, the result of which is that the criminals, as signs of working class ordinariness, provide an everyday normality that is valued as an alternative to the corruption of the wealthy. *After the Thin Man* is particularly concerned with establishing this separation of social classes, even if it also wants to code Nick as someone who stands above the crowd while still being part of it. Nora is used more clearly as a code for the world of respectability at the outset of the film, particularly in the form of the dinner with her Aunt Katherine, although such associations become muted as the film progresses. Nick and Nora's displaced world, signified by the wild party in their home when they return, is increasingly used as a counterpoint to the sombre solidity of Aunt Katherine's house, where the age of Nora's relatives suggests permanence in opposition to Nick and Nora's world of screwball modernity. Everything is slightly upside down in Nick and Nora's world, as had already been shown in *The Thin Man* when Asta remained standing after being told to lie down and sat after being told to stand up. Nick and Nora's inversion of the norms of respectable society is, however, regarded positively because it means they are not of the venal high society in which they move and such images continue in *After the Thin Man* when, for example, Nick and Nora eat breakfast in the evening, wearing pyjamas, when others are sitting down to eat dinner.

The murder case in *After the Thin Man* begins the night of the dinner at Aunt Katherine's when Robert, the husband of Nora's cousin Selma, is murdered. The events move quickly from a night-club scene after the dinner, when various suspicious criminals and accomplices are introduced, through the set-up to the murder, during which an old beau of Selma's, David (James Stewart), delivers bonds to Robert in order to effectively buy Selma from her husband, before moving on to the execution of the murder. This is followed shortly after by the arrival of the police at the night-club where two of the suspects (Dancer and Lum Kee) are interrogated, during which Dancer escapes, a sequence in which Nora visits David before being detained in the pen and then released on Nick's intervention just in time to witness the interrogation and arrest of Selma, all before completing the first evening. The case is wrapped up soon after, once Nick and Lieutenant Abrams have visited the apartment of Polly, a night-club singer, discovered the recording equipment leading to a room upstairs, and found another body. The conclusion, as in *The Thin Man*, takes place on a train, a circle that suggests Nick and Nora's constant sense of movement, even if the ending also hints that they will settle down because it is revealed that Nora is expecting a child. This seems to associate Nora more overtly with her wealthy relatives, because she is now more firmly within the world of the family. The representations of the wealthy are toned down in *After the Thin Man*, partly for this reason, but also because the 'screwiness' of Nora's family becomes more like that of Nick and Nora's. Although there are dysfunctional elements within the world of the wealthy similar to those of the Jorgensens in *The Thin Man*, these tend be individual or circumstantial aberrations rather than signs that the privileged elite are morally bankrupt. Selma's hysteria, characterised by the taking of pills and the appearance of her psychologist, are the result of Robert's disappearance and even though the murderer (David) is from among the people of this world, he is revealed to be unhinged in the denouement, particularly when he shifts suddenly from outward composure to raving anger when his plan has been disclosed by Nick.

The wealthy elite are mainly criticised for being impotent or redundant in the world of modernity, not only in Aunt Katherine's affected pronunciation of Nick's name as 'Nicholaas,' which codes her as part of a world of outmoded formality in opposition to modernity's informality, but also in the way in which the aged male relatives fall asleep after dinner, forcing Nick to have a satirical imagined conversation with them. Satire forms the film's main attack on the bourgeoisie because the representations of the wealthy also suggest that they are under threat from different places. Robert, for example, is shown as a dupe of the forgery racket marshalled by Dancer and Polly, a threat from outside which again suggests that the working class, like the rich, want money without labour. There is also the threat from within in the form of the psychological disturbances of the wealthy (Selma and David) which are signs of rupture within the world of the privileged as a result of its own failings. The world of the rich is fractured, torn between maintaining a false formality (Aunt Katherine) and embracing the opportunities made available in modernity (Nick and Nora). Selma, David and Robert want both, but the film suggests that such a desire creates psychological or criminal disturbance and makes the wealthy susceptible to the venality of aberrant modernity that is now associated with the working class criminals with which they come into contact, as suggested by the way that both David and Robert treat Selma as a commodity to be bought and sold. The film offers a fractured representation of both the privileged and the working class, although the criminality of the latter also derives from the need for suspicious characters to provide generic mystification. The working class are nevertheless, despite the venality of those involved in the forgery racket, a relief from the world of respectability that Nick refers to as having a 'stink' about it when he leaves Aunt Katherine's. Indeed, the subsequent visit to the Lychee Restaurant offers a simpler world in opposition to the tensions and histrionics encountered at Aunt Katherine's. Here, Nick and Nora find themselves at ease among the ex-cons who join them (to indulge in champagne and whisky chasers) and although the club is the centre of a scheme to defraud Selma, it is not the site of murder which occurs instead outside Aunt Katherine's home.

Another Thin Man (W.S. Van Dyke II, 1939) returns to a clearer focus on the privileged as those most guilty of corruption in its concern with the improper fiscal dealings of Colonel MacFay. The narrative of *Another Thin Man* ostensibly revolves around the attempt by an old associate of MacFay's, Phil Church, to take revenge for having been the fall guy in an unspecified illegal utilities deal which he negotiated while MacFay and his associate Dudley Horn remained in the background untouched by the fraud even while they profited from it. Church's return after his time in prison to extort money from MacFay through a fake mystic act reveals the dishonest dealings while also resulting in the punishment of all those involved. The victims, murdered by MacFay's daughter Lois, are the three men involved in the utilities fraud, MacFay, Horn and Church, and their deaths are an act of social and ideological policing of financial corruption among the wealthy, even if their murders also seem consistent with the narrative of deception and concealment emanating from Lois. The motive for Lois' murder of her father is financial independence so that she can escape the family home in the country in order to more fully live her pleasure-seeking urban life under the alias of

'Linda Mills', while the other murders are to conceal her secret identity and actions. The film thereby shows the wealthy as having succumbed to the seductions of modernity, willing to sacrifice values in favour of profit or desire for pleasure, although it is also much concerned with deceptions and the ways in which society provides the means to commit fraud in other guises. This is particularly shown in the emphasis on alibis in the plot, not only in the elaborate mechanical device Church creates for Lois so that she can claim to be elsewhere when she murders her father, but also in the mystifying fixation Church and his associates (Dum-Dum and Smitty) have with both establishing alibis and then concealing that they have them. The film suggests that modernity has created different ways for deception to occur, either through technology or through the anonymity of the city, both of which allow Lois to live her double life, to articulate an anxiety over whether reality can be guaranteed. This is highlighted by the way in which Smitty uses the police lieutenant, Guild (who returns from *The Thin Man*), to provide her alibi, emphasising the fragility of truth if the institutions of the State can be made complicit in deception, but also by Lois MacFay's use of a monogrammed handkerchief so that the initials on it ('L.M.') become part of the fabrication of reality in standing for 'Linda Mills' in her double life.

Although it is this latter deceit that helps return reality to stability when Nick, as a policeman of reality and illusion, reveals the nature of the deception, the uncertainty of reality has wider effects, particularly in the implication that Nora's father might have been involved in MacFay's utilities fraud. Nora's father is ultimately exonerated because of his ignorance of MacFay's dealings, but there are nevertheless doubts as to the legitimacy of Nora's inherited wealth to suggest that everyone is under suspicion of fraud in modernity. This is the dilemma of the modern whodunnit and its very form and narrative drives towards a concern with the fraud of reality even if the detective is present to restore confidence in the end. In *Another Thin Man* this concern is pushed to its limits by exaggerating narrative mystification to create emptiness at the heart of the text because the Church–MacFay narrative, which seems to form the main plot, is actually a mystifying sub-plot used to divert suspicion from Lois. While mystification is necessary to the whodunnit to confound the investigation, in 'The Thin Man' series it has other functions such as creating a view of modernity as a problematic reality. The mystification also veers away from simply perplexing the detective because there is so much of it and it is mainly unnecessary or illogical, not only in Church's obsession with establishing an alibi for a murder he didn't commit, but also in the extortion of money from MacFay, which has no relevance if the actual plan is for Church to aid Lois in his murder. This mystification effectively forms the narrative of *Another Thin Man*, which is so full of diversions that it is almost all excessive padding, its components less concerned with motive, methods and procedure than with providing mystifying delays to defer the denouement. One of the ways in which it does this is by using conventional types such as Vogel the gangster, who has a spurious narrative function as a watchdog for Smitty's husband, but whose main function is to provide mystery as a recognisable criminal type. Vogel is not alone in *Another Thin Man* because MacFay's chauffeur and Dorothy, the nurse for baby Nickie, also provide mystification just by their suspicious presence, with the diversion provided by Dorothy lasting through to the denouement to generate excessive convolution. Although much of this is necessary to the whodunnit form, the mystifications become so excessive in 'The Thin Man' series that the sub-narratives they create contribute only to the cinematic vaudeville which produces narrative bafflement. These features interrupt the narrative to delay the denouement and although they are driven by the genre, they increasingly become conflated with cross-generic forms of deferral to provide diversions to the narrative of investigation.

A scene in *Another Thin Man*, in which Nick and Nora separately visit the West Indies Club, highlights the mingling of the generic and cross-generic forms of narrative diversion. Nora heads there to talk to an informant she has come across in her own attempt to become a detective, and Nick follows after finding a matchbook from the club at Smitty's apartment. The only narrative purpose of this scene is to produce an unnamed man, who appears by accident from the table at which Nick is sitting with Dum-Dum, to reveal that Church's real girl is Linda Mills (Lois' masquerade) and to almost reveal where Church was at the time of the murder of MacFay. However, as Church's concealment of his alibi is mystification, it is the fight that Dum-Dum starts in order to conceal this narrative redundancy that becomes more important, not because it contributes meaningfully to the narrative of crime and detection, but because it provides a vaudevillian interruption in a scene that is effectively all cinematic vaudeville anyway. Although some minor information on Lois' other self and Vogel's ownership of a casino is revealed, the scene is primarily concerned with providing different forms of entertainment and spectacle. These are offered firstly by the dance performance, then the various forms of farcical or slapstick humour that follow Nora as she tries to find her mysterious informant (her masquerade as 'Bella Spruce', her inability to see the man in the band openly waving to her, and her capture by a gigolo who ushers her around the dance floor), then the fight, and the final joke of the switch of partners once the lights come up after the fight is over and Nora is seen to be dancing with Nick. Although Nora's masquerade as 'Bella Spruce' is a reflection on Lois' double life (as is her masquerade as a new tenant at the apartments where Lois has her secret retreat), it becomes merely a comic interlude, rather than a meditation on the deceptions of society, because Nora has used the name of one of Nick's old flames and openly invited him to join her under this alias. The whole scene is therefore a narrative interruption designed to baffle the linear trajectory of the plot by delaying its movement forward in providing non-generic spectacle for the audience.

Such narrative interludes become pervasive as the series progresses and there is an increased use of musical performances in the films (Polly's two performances in *After the Thin Man*, the dance already mentioned in *Another Thin Man*, and a series of jazz performances in *Song of the Thin Man*), while in the particular case of *Another Thin Man* the mystical discourses associated with Church allow the intrusion of an occasional shock scene associated with horror, such as the fake body with a knife stuck in it which causes the appropriate generic response when the chauffeur flees in panic. Comedy, however, provides most of the cinematic vaudeville in the film's variety bill of entertainment, shifting from the verbal interplay of *The Thin Man* to farcical or slapstick interruptions in later films, such as the little sub-narrative of sexual infidelity provided by Asta's jealousy of Mrs Asta in *After the Thin Man*. The series increasingly incorporates B-Movie styles by providing something for everyone in the audience so that even if narrative of detection is baffling there is still simple humour to enjoy. Thus, when Nick and Nora receive a message attached to a rock in *Another Thin Man*, there is enjoyment provided by the interlude in which they chase Asta to retrieve it from his mouth, even if its function in the narrative remains unclear. This is also the case with the denouement, which is set against Nickie Jr's baby party so that the convoluted nature of the deduction is alleviated by both the enjoyment of hardened criminals playing at being children and the slapstick chaos they produce. The cinematic vaudeville also, however, helps to highlight Nick's superiority to others, most obviously in a scene at Smitty's apartment when Lieutenant Guild and an Assistant D.A. chase Dum-Dum in a speeded-up slapstick manner leaving behind a fight between Smitty and Vogel in which the former gets much the better of the latter for comic effect. Nick meanwhile demonstrates an air of composure as he endeavours to get a drink from a bottle he has spied on the table which allows him to notice the matchbook that leads him to the West Indies Club. The vaudevillian elements are not only used to reflect on Nick's pleasure-seeking lifestyle and his professional composure as a riot goes on around him, enhancing the comedy as he saunters through the scene, but also provide a distraction within the film so that Nick can find the matchbook that will move the narrative of investigation forward.

Although the fourth film in the series, *Shadow of the Thin Man* (W.S. Van Dyke II, 1941), remains consistent with the template created by the previous three films, it becomes more of a cinematic vaudeville not only in its use of cross-generic material, but also in its reiteration of familiar routines and heightened self-consciousness about their performance. The narrative itself begins with the apparent murder of a jockey suspected of throwing races for a Syndicate operating in the sporting world and develops through the killing of a corrupt journalist (Whitey Barrow) working for the two supposed Syndicate bosses (Macy and Stephens) when he discovers a crusading journalist (Paul Clark) searching their offices for evidence and the arrest of the latter because he was at the scene. This event involves Nick in the investigation, which he uses to prove Paul's innocence and to reveal that Major Sculley, a politician working for the State Commission appointed to clean up gambling, is the real Syndicate boss. The film offers a variation to the series formula by placing the action within the sporting world, as *Another Thin Man* offered a country house variation for part of its narrative, and as the final two films offer different settings, a small-town in *The Thin Man Goes Home* and the world of jazz in *Song of the Thin Man*. By the time of *Shadow of the Thin Man,* the series had developed a recurring pattern and the film uses this as the basis for a playful self-parody whose emphasis on humour makes it more comedy than thriller. Where the previous films in the series had manoeuvred the mystery plot to create spaces for comic or musical interruptions, now the comedy provides room for the whodunnit investigation, most of which is mystification, particularly the accidental death of a jockey and a piece of jewellery used to pay a debt, neither of which have any relation to the main murder plot. The revelation that Sculley is the murderer comes somewhat out of the blue as a result of a narrative contrivance in the conclusion which incriminates him despite no other clues pointing in his direction. The denouement, indeed, is primarily comic entertainment, provided by Nora-turned-heroine as she grapples with Sculley (who is in possession of a gun that turns out to have no bullets) and repeatedly screams "Run, Nickie, run."

This is merely a self-conscious exaggeration of the format used in the previous films, which showed Nick as an entertainer marshalling evidence and theories in the denouement until he arrived at the correct solution, except that now Nora becomes a partner in providing the entertainment. The detective as entertainer, for a gathered company acting as an audience much like the one in the cinema watching the film, is self-consciously foregrounded in *Shadow of the Thin Man* when Nora first urges Nick to reveal the identity of the killer because the tension is killing her and then asks, for comic effect, whether she did it. Such self-consciousness is emphasised in recurring comments in the film about how certain events seem familiar, as when Nick and Nora get caught up in a rush of police at the stadium, which replicates the way in which they were corralled into the race track by a police motorcade at the beginning of the film, after which Nora comments: 'Either I'm dreaming or I've lived through this before'. The entry into the race track is itself a playful moment, however, because it serves as a comment on Nick's previous unwillingness to get involved in various investigations by having him stampeded into it against his will right from the start as he is unavoidably caught up in the police motorcade that conveys him into a murder mystery. His reluctance to become part of the investigation is still placed at the forefront but this becomes part of the playful humour because wherever Nick goes he finds that the case is either already there or that it soon finds him, although this is also a self-conscious comment on the mode of the whodunnit in which the detective is always in the right place when things relating to the crime occur. The film also lightly parodies the role of the detective and the whodunnit narrative by having Nick on the edges of the investigation, observing without being fully involved, and watching and directing the comic police attempts to impose order on the confusion.

The film also involves Nora more fully in the role of a detective, although she becomes a focus for humour in this part, most notably when she is placed in situations where her air of superiority can be mocked, such as a visit to the wrestling match for which she dresses as if she is going to a formal dinner. This is most evident when she follows Nick to the race track on one of his now standard night-time examinations of a crime scene and she gives away her presence very noisily as she falls over in the darkness to be revealed when the lights come up straddling a bench with her hat askew. Indeed, Nora's hats form a focus for jokes in the film, particularly in being mocked or knocked out of line to give Nora's dignity a battering, and, because the hats serve as signs of her upper class status, such moments are used to show that Nora is out of place in the working class world that Nick moves through. Nora still functions as a chorus figure and she often comments self-reflexively on the narrative proceedings or mocks the follies and idiosyncrasies of the world around her, such as the brawl Asta sets off in Mario's Grotto when he trips up a waiter, after which Nora calmly surveys the carnage Asta has created to comment that 'For the two dollar dinner, you get machine-guns'. Even Nick isn't immune from her gaze and he also becomes a butt of slapstick jokes, particularly within the domestic world in the care of Nickie Jr, as when his son forces him to drink milk rather than alcohol under Nora's scornful regard. Nick takes on a dual role in the film, split between narrative emphases on the domestic sphere and the world of crime and its investigation, being shown as out of place in the former and completely at home in the latter. As a consequence, *Shadow of the Thin Man* creates more centres for comedy and more openly resonates with the B-Movie comedy thriller formula that the series helped to create by increasingly emphasising vaudevillian entertainment.

The domestication of Nick and Nora

The pursuit of comedy is heightened in *The Thin Man Goes Home* (Richard Thorpe, 1944), although this film is also characterised by a shift that many crime films were subject to after the United States entered the war in 1941 because its whodunnit mystery is displaced by espionage motifs. Such cross-generic coding is also a product of the pastiche of genres that many crime series developed as they aged and looked for ways to vary the formula, which also involves placing Nick and Nora in a small-town setting in *The Thin Man Goes Home*, as opposed to their usual urban location. The film is thus whodunnit, small-town drama, and espionage thriller (in its denouement) while the comedy associated with the series adds satire of small-town life to the modes of farce, slapstick and comedy of manners that had appeared in earlier films. There are many easy laughs at the expense of the eccentric behaviour of small-town characters, such as Laura-Belle's histrionics, Crump the shop-keeper's pedantry, or the general craziness of Hilda the maid and, it goes without saying, 'Crazy Mary'. The narrative follows Nick and Nora as the pair return to Nick's home town, Sycamore Springs, revealing beforehand that Nick's father, a small-town doctor, was never impressed by Nick's choice of detection as a profession, to set up the possibility that Nick can do something to make his father proud.[6] The investigation that turns up on Nick's doorstep to help him out involves the murder of a local artist, Peter Berton, who is shot almost imperceptibly as he is about to confess to Nick his part in the theft of top secret weapons plans from the local factory, which he has concealed by using the plans as canvases for his paintings. The paintings are sold through a local art shop, one of which Nora buys as a birthday present for Nick after which it serves as a MacGuffin for people to chase after. This provides a diversion from the mystery of the murder, although the hunt for the painting implies espionage motifs in retrospect once the denouement has revealed that the murderer of Berton is the spy ring's local boss, Bruce Clayworth, another small-town doctor, even if sundry other mystifications (the secret of 'Crazy Mary' being Berton's mother, mysterious goings-on at the factory and Nora's perplexity in relation to the character of Brogan) hinder the conclusion.

For much of the film, the narrative is driven by the traditional whodunnit form and the tropes of espionage only become clear in the denouement which produces a rabbit out of a hat in revealing that the murders are related to the acquisition of secret plans. This revelation more closely aligns the film with the contrivances of the B-Movie because it creates generic inconsistencies (at the same time that gangland and urban crime are suddenly produced with the arrival of two criminal associates of Nick's), not only by drawing in a set of textual parameters that haven't been prepared for, but also by providing the iconography of espionage in the fluoroscope that Nick's father just happens to have which allows the plans to be seen beneath the paintings. Within moments, many of the narrative shortcuts associated with the B-Movie are displayed in the happenstance of the presence of the fluoroscope, the sudden introduction of information (the plans under the paintings), and the rapid transformation of Clayworth's character from bumbling country doctor to calculating spymaster to desperate criminal not only to put on show his guilt, but also to openly display his psychology. The denouement is only a confirmation of the playful vaudeville of the whodunnit that the film has already offered in its deployment of a comic detection, familiar from B-Movie series, to parallel Nick's narrative of investigation. A fair amount of screen time is given to Nora's suspicions of Brogan, Nick's sidekick, whose very presence in following Nick to Sycamore Springs is a B-Movie inconsistency, because when he is introduced on the train going to the town there is no reason for him to be accompanying Nick, who doesn't have a case there that requires an associate. The film adopts a playful approach to his seemingly providential presence as Nick's assistant by having Nora discover him in the bushes outside the family home talking to Nick on several occasions, as he suddenly appears from off-screen, but with the humorous implication that he has simply been waiting there all the time until he is cued in. Nora's suspicions and investigations of Brogan form a second narrative of detection in the film, albeit a disappointed detection played for humour at Nora's expense as she once again fails to be a detective. This is highlighted in a long sequence in which Nora follows Brogan, during which she finds herself the subject of advances and cat-calls and then accidentally starts a fight in a pool room as a result of Brogan doubling back on his circuit round town.

The format of *Song of the Thin Man* (Edward Buzzell, 1947) appears at first to shift back to the pattern established in the first four films in the series, but the film is very different again. This is partly a product of the fact that Nick and Nora are now a middle-aged couple (reunited with little Nickie after his absence from the previous film), but it is also the result of a new post-war setting which draws Nick and Nora into the worlds of *noir* and jazz. This has several consequences, not least in suggesting that Nick and Nora are out of place in this new society where they look old-fashioned or obsolete. In creating a world of compromised morality consonant with *film noir* the film provides an incongruous setting for Nick and Nora because of the seeming incompatibility between the film's post-war *noir* inflections and the pre-war comedy thriller form in which the couple originated. This is despite the fact that the film opens in a seemingly familiar social setting aboard a gambling yacht where a charity function is taking place to provide a milieu of drinking and pleasure within which Nick and Nora can feel at home. The opening scene also provides familiarity in the form of two comedy gangsters talking in underworld slang about the "dames" and "cultured tomatoes" aboard the ship which also has the effect of placing the film in the recurring world of the wealthy at play by connotation. This is then seemingly confirmed when the two gangsters bump into Nick, revealing they are more of his criminal acquaintances, after which Nora offers the standard comment that thanks to Nick's acquaintance with the hoods, Nickie Jr can crack a safe in fifteen minutes to imply that she is among another group of Nick's 'lovely people'. *Song of the Thin Man*, however, quickly shifts away from this format by sidelining both the comedy lugs and the usual mix of crime and wealth in its revelation that the 'lovely people' in this new world are very different from the characters Nick and Nora encountered in previous films. This is foreshadowed when the scene focuses on the singer with the band accompanying the charity event, Fran Page, one of characters later to become a victim of the murderer Mitch Talbin, whose low-key ballad acts as a sign of a more ambiguous and subdued world, in opposition to, for example, the lively song and dance routines of *After the Thin Man* and *Another Thin Man*.

The film makes a good deal of the ways in which this new society is pervasively compromised morally and criminally, by revealing a number of betrayals very quickly. Some of these are sexual or romantic, such as Fran having left the clarinettist Buddy Hollis for the band leader Drake, Drake's subsequent abandonment of Fran, and Phyllis Talbin's sexual betrayal of her husband, while others are personal, such as Mitch Talbin's presumed betrayal of Drake in not helping to pay his gambling debts to a gangster, or financial, such as Drake's breach of contract with Phil Brant, the owner of the gambling ship. Within this are also seemingly minor betrayals, such as a band member implicating Buddy Hollis in Drake's murder, when the band collects their instruments from the ship later on, as a sign that this is a society of everyday betrayal and thoughtless duplicity where people are prepared to inform on others in order to protect themselves. It is also a world in which criminals and the wealthy elite are apparently no different, and the sign of the permeation of the world of the wealthy by crime is less the socialite Janet Thayer's marriage to the gambler Phil Brant than the fact that her father, a rich philanthropist, is carrying a gun aboard the ship. The film also provides an obvious *femme fatale* in the form of Gloria Grahame's Fran Page, although, as is the case with many of Grahame's roles in this category, her version is both alluring and innocent and she dies tragically as a result of her loyalty to Buddy Hollis. The *femme fatale* figure is doubled in the form of Phyllis Talbin, not only in the iconography of furs and jewels that adorn her, with one of her necklaces forming an important clue that helps to reveal her husband as the murderer, but more significantly in the vengeful killing she inflicts on Talbin in the denouement scene in which she is a betrayed woman senselessly killing out of desire even though Talbin has confessed in front of an audience of witnesses and is about to be brought to justice. This final act completes the destabilisation of the ordered world of the comedy thriller that Nick and Nora have previously inhabited, although the way has been prepared by the presence of the underground world of jazz music and its implication of drug use. Nick and Nora find they are in an alternative cultural and criminal economy in which different values are in operation, although these values, driven by personal desire, are unstable, as signified by both Buddy's madness and Mitch Talbin's malicious encouragement of it in order to make Buddy think he is the murderer. The values of this world also lead to Phyllis Talbin's murder of her husband in revenge for his killing of her lover Tommy Drake, an act representing the overturning of moral and legal categories because she avenges her illicit lover by killing her legally bound husband, a seemingly radical inversion of stable ideologies of heterosexual union. This is compounded by the fact that not only is she not visually punished, but also by the fact that her first shot doesn't kill Talbin and she is allowed to finish him off as the forces of law look on impotently and as he passively accepts his fate.

Although the crimes of Mitch and Phyllis Talbin are comprehensible as crimes of passion within *noir* discourses, they have the effect of disrupting the ordered structure of the whodunnit, with Phyllis' crime offering an excess of criminality beyond what is usually allowed. The denouement has already been disordered, however, even if it more overtly draws out the codes of the detective as entertainer because the scene takes place during a performance by Buddy Hollis and the jazz band during which Nick more obviously takes on the role of MC by interrupting the performance to say how the crime was effected and to ask Buddy to name the murderer. However, Nick's plans are forestalled in another destabilising moment because it is neither he nor Buddy who names the murderer, but the murderer himself as Mitch confesses before being identified. Although Nick has deduced and explained the crime, it is the world of crime that produces the name of the killer and then exacts justice when Phyllis shoots her husband, thereby turning the institutional structures of law on their heads because crime has not only produced crime but also its own policing. Rather than the narrative being closed off by a restoration of the ordering structures of law, the denouement is the occasion for another murder to be committed, so that a fractured and unstable *noir* world seems to outlast the apparent emphasis on the triumph of normal society signified by Nick and Nora's return to the stability of the domestic sphere in the final scene. Nick and Nora have a radically changed role in this world, acting as a moral centre, an unusual position for them in the context of their previous pleasure-seeking lifestyle. Their fidelity to each other seems old-fashioned in the light of the romantic and sexual merry-go-round involving Drake, Fran, Buddy and Phyllis and their return to the home at the end is significant in suggesting that they represent the traditional values of solidity and respectability they challenged in the earlier films.

Nick and Nora become 'other' to themselves in *Song of the Thin Man*, transformed into what they opposed in the pre-war films. This is shown by their entry into the jazz world, within which the solution to the mystery appears to reside, where they are bemused onlookers rather than active participants in the world of pleasure it offers. This is apparent when Nick and Nora try to gain entry to an early morning jam session at Talbin's apartment for which they have to try to masquerade as 'hep-cats' in order to be accepted. To do so, they have to master the language of this underground world, something Nora signally fails to do when she is unable to remember that she is meant to be a 'canary' (a singer) and tells Talbin that she is a 'mud-hen'. Nick has already been categorised as a 'rooty-toot' (a square) by the jazz musician, Clarence, who accompanies them, and although Nora begins to comprehend the argot later on, they are still strangers in the jazz world because they look like an upstanding couple who are more comfortable at home than in the world of crime and pleasure. In this regard, they are used as ciphers for the audience because an important part of the film, which contributes to a continuing cinematic vaudeville, is the sheer number of scenes given over to the performance of jazz music. Although the discovery of Fran's body, and the lead it provides to the whereabouts of Buddy (which ultimately helps reveal the murderer), seems to motivate the exploration of the jazz world, the non-narrative musical performances more significantly serve as interludes showing an exotic world for the audience to supply both topical entertainment and comedy at the expense of the language and excessive behaviour of the musicians. *Song of the Thin Man* creates an interesting conclusion to 'The Thin Man' series by providing many of the expected components while also baffling them by placing the narrative among the disorders of the *noir* world. This confuses the discourses of the series, so that in the same way that Nick and Nora become their 'others' as they are increasingly signified in domestic terms, even gaining a surrogate 'teenage' son in Clarence, the narrative also flips over by turning the series from a screwball version of the hard-boiled format into a *noir* version of the screwball comedy.

3
Between Law and Crime: The Chivalric 'Criminal' Detective

An important strand within Hollywood crime series of the 1930s and 1940s focuses on the figure of the criminal detective whose roots are less in the classical detective mode than in the strain of criminal-centred fiction that had emerged out of it in the United Kingdom and France at the end of the nineteenth century. Criminal adventurers such as E.W. Hornung's Raffles, Maurice Leblanc's Arsène Lupin and Allain and Souvestre's Fantômas provide the background types for the emergence of Jack Boyle's Boston Blackie, Louis Joseph Vance's Lone Wolf, Leslie Charteris' The Saint, and Michael Arlen's Falcon, all of whom subsequently became Hollywood criminal detectives.[1] Hollywood's representation of these figures makes them either reformed criminals or dubious in their motivation, but also depicts them as honourable and selflessly chivalric, albeit in a rough-hewn form of gallantry in the case of Boston Blackie, to allow them to become detectives. Because of residual associations of criminality, they inhabit a world of peril that provides excitement and suspense, even if the threat of arrest and imprisonment is only ever simulated in order to open up a criminal space within which they can operate. This is particularly the case with Boston Blackie and the Lone Wolf whose adventures are predicated on a repeated false accusation of crime and their continued pretence that they are still criminals in order to facilitate their detection. As both of these series tend towards an iteration of the cops-and-robbers format, in which the criminals are revealed early on, there is actually very little detection involved and very little variety. In the case of 'The Lone Wolf' films, the departures from the cops-and-robbers format are sometimes only provided either by the ways in which the Lone Wolf and his valet, Jamison, orchestrate the arrival of the police to arrest the criminals and acquit themselves (on a ferry in *The Lone Wolf Strikes* [1940] or by intersection of boats and cars in *The Lone Wolf Keeps a Date* [1940]), or by the farcical misadventures and pranks the pair get up to in their attempts to avoid arrest. The 'Boston Blackie' films have even less variation and *Alias Boston Blackie* (1942) and *Boston Blackie and the Law* (1946) even use the same situation, a convict who takes advantage of a show put on by Blackie as a cover to escape from prison to seek revenge on old associates, the only change being the gender of the criminal.

'The Saint' and 'The Falcon' series are more varied, despite the similarities between the two criminal detectives, because the two protagonists have a more mutable relationship with both law and crime, and this chapter focuses on these series as a consequence. Boston Blackie and the Lone Wolf are both conformist figures and their main concerns are to recuperate other criminals (Boston Blackie in *The Chance of a Lifetime* [1943]), extricate implicated innocents from the criminal world to reinstate their reputations, and to restore the status quo by proving that 'the odds are all on the side of the law' (*Secrets of the Lone Wolf* [1943]). The Saint and the Falcon, on the other hand, represent continuing signs of crime as disorder because of their ambiguous status between law and crime. Most 'Lone Wolf' films, for example, involve attempts to curb Jamison's recurring larcenous tendencies by channelling them towards respectable ends while individual films also deal with similar matters of rehabilitation or exoneration of blameless characters who are under suspicion (an heiress in *The Lone Wolf Meets a Lady* [1940] or an accused kidnapper in *The Lone Wolf Keeps a Date*). Boston Blackie and the Lone Wolf exist in a world in which law and crime are clearly differentiated, despite their seeming criminality, whereas The Saint and the Falcon inhabit a textual world where law and justice are not necessarily identical, thereby raising ideological questions about the nature of law and its enforcement. The latter two figures also retain the sense of excitement about crime, misbehaviour and transgression found in the Raffles and Lupin stories, but which in the other two series only exists in the relish Jamison's unrepentant rogue takes in the possibility that the Lone Wolf might return to a life of crime. Boston Blackie's non-conformity, for example, is confined to goonish pranks at the expense of Inspector Faraday (most obviously in the slapstick of *After Midnight with Boston Blackie* [1943]) or clowning with disguises (*Boston Blackie Booked on Suspicion* [1944], *Boston Blackie Goes Hollywood* [1942], *Boston Blackie's Rendezvous* [1945]), often involving racial stereotypes (*Trapped by Boston Blackie* [1948]), while the

Lone Wolf, after Warren William took on the role, is a conventionalist who enforces class hierarchies (*The Lone Wolf Keeps a Date*) and supports the social and political establishment (*The Lone Wolf Spy Hunt* [1939], *The Lone Wolf Takes a Chance* [1941]).

'The Saint' as racket-buster

As a criminal detective 'The Saint' (Simon Templar) exists on the borders of crime while working for the restoration of law and order. The Saint, however, is a disruptive figure who threatens disorder by his very presence in the narrative because he signifies the taint of crime, even if he also provides the reassurance that the disturbances that either follow him or that he creates through his activities will ultimately be resolved by the restoration of the law. Because The Saint has no home other than the hotel rooms he occupies, the streets he walks, and the crime scenes he examines, there is no fixed place for him within the social order he reproduces in re-establishing the effectiveness of the law. The Saint occupies a world of disequilibrium and although he brings equilibrium through his investigation, his position at the end of each narrative forebodes further disequilibrium as he either walks off into the street (*The Saint Takes Over*), stands watching it (*The Saint Strikes Back*), or moves on to a new destination on the promise of new adventure (*The Saint in New York*). The Saint can be regarded as a narrative disturbance in the plot-space, bringing disruption because he causes events to occur instead of simply observing them. This is not peculiar to 'The Saint' films and many other detectives both observe events and generate narrativity, but The Saint is a paradigm of the fictional detective in general, and the detective in B-Movie crime series in particular, because he represents the demand for constant action and narrative movement in signifying the disorder that is a predicate of the fictional world of the detective. While the detective is someone who returns narrative and society to order, he or she also acts as a metonymic sign of the presence of crime and disorder in society who reveals the presence of detection's necessary 'other': criminality and transgression. While The Saint restores stability to society, he emphasises the sign of the detective as someone whose very presence indicates that the narrative and society are in a state of disorder or rupture.

Resolution of the ruptures to society and the narrative do not occur, however, through the process of detection, because unlike most other detective series of the 1930s and 1940s, 'The Saint' crime series involves a different process by which crime is eradicated. Although The Saint is called upon to solve mysteries, he is not a detective who follows the traces of a crime from inception through to its solution, collecting clues and gathering evidence in the manner of the 'clue-puzzle' style (Knight, 2003: 77). This is partly because in several of the films the mystery is either solved very quickly (*The Saint Takes Over*) or tacked on to provide a denouement (*The Saint in New York* and *The Saint Takes Over*), but also because some films reveal the identities of the criminals at the outset (*The Saint in London* and *The Saint's Double Trouble*). The Saint takes on a different role to the classical detective because, until the series softened into a comedy mystery format in the later films, he is more like the 'racket-buster' figure Porter identifies with the hard-boiled detective (Porter, 2003: 105). In 'racket-buster' mode, The Saint is very like the 'cleaner' of assassin movies, who cleans up the mess that has been created when a hit has gone wrong, not only because he started out life as a judicial assassin in *The Saint in New York*, but also because most of his cases involve cleaning up the 'mess' of a society gone wrong according to the ideologies of the films. In four of the six 'The Saint' films made by RKO in the United States, *The Saint in New York*, *The Saint Strikes Back*, *The Saint's Double Trouble*, and *The Saint Takes Over*, The Saint is called upon to eradicate the operations of organised gangs whose activities have threatened the stability of social structures and confused the signifying relationships within society. *The Saint in New York*, for example, deals with the cleaning of gangs from the city and the rooting out of corruption in official society by discovering the identity of the secret gang boss there, a pattern replicated in *The Saint Strikes Back* in the search for the mysterious mobster, Waldeman, who is once again a seemingly upstanding member of society.

By uncovering the identity of secret masterminds within the inner circles of power, The Saint returns order to the social hierarchy, by eliminating corruption in official society, and restores stability to the signifying order of society. In re-establishing law and crime as distinct meaning systems he repairs the relationship between signifier and signified so that it is possible to identify who is honest and who is criminal. The Saint becomes the arbiter over appearance and reality but this important trope within the series also affects The Saint who must clarify the meaning of his own identity because of his dubious reputation. It is fairly standard in each of the films for one character to name The Saint as a 'dangerous criminal' (a member of the Citizens Committee in *The Saint in New York*), a 'crook' (Anne Bitts in *The Saint's Double Trouble*), or as someone who robs people 'right and left' (Mrs Fernack in *The Saint Strikes Back*), while others defend him by stating that 'they couldn't pin a thing on him' (Inspector Fernack in *The Saint Strikes Back*) or by remarking that he has 'never been convicted of a crime' (Professor Bitts in *The Saint's Double Trouble*). These views express some doubt about his motives because implicitly he is only innocent because he hasn't yet been proven guilty, even while they enunciate a conviction that he warrants trust even so. This latter position is most clearly stated in the views of The Saint as Robin Hood (Valcross in *The Saint in New York* and Penny Parker in *The Saint in London*), a view that frames him working for the public good and in support of the legitimate social order as well as helping the 'underdog', even if it is parodied in *The Saint in Palm Springs* when The Saint replies to a hotel clerk's announcement that he is a 'modern Robin Hood' by replying that he is 'a remarkably bad shot with a bow and arrow' and that he has 'never eaten venison' in his life.

The ambiguity of The Saint's position derives from the original novels by Leslie Charteris, who conceived of The Saint as a figure between law and crime who provided the justice that the legal system could not deliver. Julian Symons notes of Charteris' Saint that 'he is a self appointed agent for terrorizing criminals against whom no evidence justifying arrest can be secured' (Symons, 1972: 203), while T.J. Binyon refers to his literary persona more positively as 'a gentleman-adventurer rather than a gentleman-thief' (Binyon, 1989: 131). These views, which emphasise justice and social status, inform the figuration of The Saint within the RKO crime series because he is never represented as a vigilante (even though his actions amount to the enforcement of law within the United States by a private citizen, and one who is not even American), but as an aristocratic Englishman. His aristocratic status gives him a protected position and grants him licence to act against criminals, which is often confirmed when it is revealed that he has been acting as a special operative for the authorities (*The Saint in New York*, *The Saint Strikes Back* and *The Saint in London*).[2] The Saint's ambiguous status seems to be meaningless in this situation because he is always on the side of the law and his 'criminality' becomes merely a plot device either to obscure his motives or to place him in situations where he is required to evade or best the police in order to retard the narrative. Nevertheless, his ambiguity still affects meanings relating to class and social ideology because as an aristocratic freelance undercover operative with licence to eradicate crime by any means, he embodies a fantasy of the free-willed individual who is willing to respond to the calls of civic duty without being assimilated into society and its institutions.

The Saint's criminal ambiguity is further nuanced by his development into an Everyman figure by the time of *The Saint in Palm Springs* although he is still outside, beyond or above the law. He is a subject who has escaped social bonds because of his aristocratic status but because he occupies a more hard-boiled world than most of the series detectives, he is also inside the world of crime. This makes him both a subject-outside-history and a subject-inside-history, although he is always able to move on to a new adventure and thereby escapes confinement by social law as well as criminal law. As a fantasy English aristocrat, produced in the imagination of an English writer and then modified in an American context, he not only articulates the ability to take control of society while being in control of his own actions, but also becomes a sign of freedom and high-minded fair play. Although this produces a sense of paternalistic responsibility for 'inferiors', while also providing an easy recognition of such principles at play within the B-Movie format (in which the aristocratic English outsider becomes an uncomplicated sign of chivalry, fair play and honour), The Saint also becomes a curious upper class Everyman, not only because he defends the underdog, but also because he either becomes the underdog as a result of having to constantly defend himself from false accusations or because, in *The Saint in Palm Springs*, he is as mystified by the crime as Pearly Gates, the American criminal Everyman. When the series removed to England (with Hugh Sinclair in the role), such complexities disappeared and The Saint became a trusted figure drained of criminal associations to allow him to hunt out Nazis in *The Saint's Vacation* and clean an English village of crime and corruption in *The Saint Meets the Tiger*.

The Saint's incarnation in the final British films returns him to the revenger figure of *The Saint in New York* (Ben Holmes, 1938), the film most closely based on Charteris' source material. In this film, The Saint (played by Louis Hayward) is primarily a judicial assassin who has no apparent social concerns as he picks off gangsters, either by shooting them (Jake Irbell, Maury Yule, Hutch Rellin, and Red), or by causing them to be undone by the suspicions or actions of other gangsters (Pappy and Hymie). He is, however, also a mischief-maker, disrupting the gang's plans with malicious glee, and the restitution of law and order seems secondary to the pleasure he takes in creating chaos in the gang by turning one criminal against another. Punishment of crime is an aristocratic game for Hayward's pleasure-seeking adventurer, rather than a judicial or moral matter and this lack of a deeper meaning to The Saint's actions turns him into a cold assassin, adrift from society he protects, even though it is his service to society that provides moral purpose, without which he is simply an aristocratic murderer unwittingly in the employ of a criminal mastermind. At the same time, however, The Saint's trajectory through the film, polishing off gangsters, seems to make him the embodiment of Chesterton's idea of the detective as an 'original and poetic figure' (Chesterton, 1983: 4). He travels on an Orphic journey through the criminal underworld, emerging to find truth and justice when Valcross is revealed as the criminal mastermind before being shot down in the sunlit street by Fay Edwards, his secretary and The Saint's romantic interest, an event which symbolises the cleaning of the city.

The film, however, is more suspense than whodunnit because its mystery only emerges late on when Fay reveals the rather contrived situation by which the members of the gang have agreed to share out the proceeds of their criminal activities on a given day, at which point it becomes clear that The Saint has been killing off the members of the gang so that one of them can seize all the money. The Saint is unaware of this scheme and he is also ignorant of the identity of 'The Big Fellow' until Fay points out Valcross in the street, and his lack of comprehension means that he is therefore not an 'original and poetic' detective figure (even though one of the gangsters constantly refers to him as a 'genius'), nor someone who displays 'the aristocratic ideal of superior understanding' that Thompson identifies with Poe's Dupin (Thompson, 1993: 44), but a 'racket-buster' or 'cleaner'. This makes him very similar to the Continental Op in Dashiell Hammett's *Red Harvest*, for whom solving the murder that sets the narrative in motion is secondary to his role in cleaning Personville of criminal corruption. Like The Saint, the Continental Op arrives from outside and serves a seemingly upright member of the community (Elihu Willson) who turns out to have caused the criminal activities in the town. Similarly, Valcross, like Willson, presents himself as an altruistic servant of the city while looking after his own economic well-being in using The Saint to perform the same dirty work of cleaning the city undertaken by the Op. One key difference between the Continental Op and The Saint is that the Op is a professional working detective, a member of the labouring classes, and although he might represent the same fantasy as The Saint, of the non-alienated, fully-fledged individual able to operate outside social and political forces, he is still bound by both the operations of capital and forms of authority.[3]

The Saint is of the 'bourgeois dilettante' type of detective described by Ernest Mandel (1984: 28) and this allows him to operate without restrictions to his 'licence' as an English aristocratic outsider who isn't restricted by the laws to which the police are subject. He appears to be a knight errant come to rescue a fallen society, stepping out of the realm of the whodunnit to become Binyon's 'gentleman-adventurer' in a hard-boiled world, cleaning up the criminal 'mess' the police cannot deal with and engaging in an act of ideological cleansing which makes him an enforcer of the existing social hierarchy and its values. Stepping into an urban environment very similar to Personville, which McCann describes as 'a stateless milieu that demands a heroic effort to reestablish civil order' (McCann, 2000: 80), The Saint's presence suggests that, to put its house in order, the United States requires an outsider with values that are very different to its own. The 'stateless' city and its mapping of the fallen condition of American society (the corruption of public officials and the failure of the law) is measured against the The Saint's aristocratic values which provide a symbolic hierarchical order to fill the vacuum he creates as he disposes of one gangster after another. In the process, Hayward's Saint disciplines corrupt figures within official society (Valcross and Nather), provides structure for a fragmented world where boundaries between law and crime have become indistinct, and puts the working class in its place to ensure that the wealthy retain power. The criminals in Valcross' gang are working-class men who, through criminal acts, are on the verge of becoming capitalists able to rival wealthy members of official bourgeois society such as Valcross until The Saint eradicates them. In this context, Hayward's Saint becomes a charmless, reactionary figure, expecting and receiving deference to his social position,[4] while meting out punishment to those with the impertinence to believe they are his superiors. While he retains his distance from the hard-boiled world he encounters because of his aristocratic disdain, he nevertheless lacks the virtues of decency, integrity and 'fair play' associated with the ideological construction of the English aristocrat that the film wants to recruit to its cause.

From rogue to everyman: George Sanders' Saint

There is a significant shift in the representation of The Saint with the arrival of George Sanders in the role in the second film in the series, *The Saint Strikes Back* (John Farrow, 1939), because Sanders' persona imbues The Saint with effortless aristocratic style and sophistication to transform him from enforcer to charming rogue. Unlike Hayward's Saint, who has no sense of the total picture until the conclusion of *The Saint in New York*, Sanders' Saint also has the same access to knowledge possessed by the classical detective. He is introduced appearing out of the misty shadows of San Francisco, already knowing most of the situation with which he is faced, having briefly been shown displaying an all-seeing gaze inside the Colony Club while one murder is foiled through the execution of another. When he confronts Val Travers (Wendy Barrie's first appearance in the series) outside the club by questioning her involvement with underworld affairs, he reveals in a few moments that he knows who Val is, where she lives, the identity of the dead man (Tommy Voss), and the reason for his murder. The Saint is already an omniscient figure, able to understand the totality of the situation even before the mystery plot has begun and he remains one step ahead of everyone else for the entirety of the narrative. The film may only reveal that Val's closest friend, Allan Breck, is Waldeman, the secret mastermind, in its conclusion, but Sanders' Saint seems to have woven the various strands together well before then. In the denouement, he produces a pair of spectacles belonging to Breck that were found at a murder scene, harking back to his jibes about Breck's short-sightedness at their first meeting which, in the hindsight of the conclusion, reveal that he has known all along that Breck used glasses in the guise of Waldeman in order to conceal his criminal identity.

Sanders' Saint has a totalising knowledge which gives him complete control of the situation throughout, so that he can even find time to suddenly appear sitting in an armchair in Inspector Fernack's home in New York without being noticed, having travelled there overnight from San Francisco in order to absolve himself of the Colony Club murder. That he then places himself under suspicion firstly by suggesting to Fernack that he could be Waldeman and then by revealing to the Inspector on the flight back to San Francisco that he flew the other way the day before is only a ruse to prove his ability to dominate events and to exercise his superior insight. Fernack, like Val, only has a partial understanding of the situation, which is signified when he is shown running around an airport in only his pyjamas having been outwitted by The Saint, and both he and Val function within the film to show how those within its textual reality are constrained by the forces that control them. Because these forces are marshalled by corrupt figures within official society they are both subject to misdirections. The skewed images of society create distortions which neither Val nor Fernack can recognise, a situation most obviously shown in the way in which they both believe in the false sign of The Saint as an untrustworthy criminal. Sanders' Saint is beyond these forces and he can therefore exonerate Val's father, who has been wrongly accused of corruption, and uncover the identity of Waldeman in a matter of days, even though these distortions have frustrated Val and the police for far longer.

Sanders' screen presence is particularly important as a sign of his superiority because it provides The Saint with a cool distance from events that allows him to portray the omniscient man of mystery more effectively than Hayward's Saint. Sanders' dress also signals that his Saint is a different figure, his dinner jacket, white bow-tie and matching scarf in his appearance outside the Colony Club, for example, indicating that he is a debonair or urbane figure as opposed to Hayward's 'urban' Saint. It is as much Sanders' voice and control of language that codes his Saint as superior and untouchable, however, as he puns on the way in which Voss was 'potted' among some pot-plants before he 'potted' someone else, to display his roguish charm and insight. Sanders' voice also codes him as an outsider, because he is clearly not only not of the underworld, but also not of American society. He does, however, still retain some aspects of the persona of Hayward's Saint in his air of superiority and in his pranksterism, but these are refigured to give The Saint a more casual aristocratic superiority. His aloofness is tempered, for example, by his self-knowledge, so that his dismissal of Val's 'sweet suburban pretensions' when he first meets her in her home is tempered by his admission, after he forces a kiss, that he is regularly a cad and that he is often guilty of 'maudlin sentimentality'. This self-awareness suggests that Sanders' Saint has no pretensions of his own, to make him more like others, except that it also has the opposite effect, proving his superiority by distinguishing him from those, like Val and Breck, who succumb to pretension. The Saint's pranksterish behaviour also helps define his superiority, as when he slaps Breck with a tennis racket or gives the pyjama-clad Fernack the run-around in an airport and then locks him in his office. The latter pranks are part of the film's comic vaudeville, drawing upon standard images of police incompetence, but they also align The Saint's wit and intellectual superiority with class status to suggest that the upper class are upper class not because they are born to it, but because they are able.

The Saint's relationship with Zipper Dyson (Barry Fitzgerald), an underworld safe-cracker, seems to confirm The Saint's social status as proof of his superiority when he uses physical power to exercise class power in blacking Zipper's eye to prove that the latter was forced to help The Saint break into a house. Zipper is not the only one subject to The Saint's games, however, and the aristocratic lawyer, Eastman, also finds himself on the receiving end when The Saint, Val and her accomplices move into his house after the killing of one of Val's underlings, without his knowledge until The Saint reveals himself at Eastman's bedside the morning after, joking about how he has renamed his butler. This pranksterish persona is also a product of the B-Movie format, however, created to provide entertainment because there is very little mystery after The Saint reveals early on the machinations by which Cullis, a corrupt criminologist and associate of Breck, framed Val's father. The Saint's playfulness becomes a way of filling the narrative, substituting games for mystery so that although the magic tricks The Saint exchanges with Cullis seem to reveal that Cullis was capable of the sleight of hand that could plant evidence incriminating Val's father, they also serve other functions. The tricks create an excessive game to provide entertainment in the manner of cinematic vaudeville, fulfil the visual demands of putting cognitive processes and intellectual puzzle-solving on show, and display the detective's superiority for the audience. *The Saint Strikes Back* is effectively a trivial game to keep The Saint and the audience diverted, so that Allan Breck is important less as a criminal mastermind to be brought to justice than as an opponent who will provide The Saint with the opportunity to play games that aren't merely aristocratic exercises in power. Breck is also used as part of a narrative opposition because he can be seen as the 'anti-Saint', not only as a criminal masquerading as a respectable member of society (to The Saint's aristocrat masquerading as a criminal), but also in his fake gallantry, lack of wit, and inability to play games. This contrast accordingly frames The Saint's superiority as merely a narrative device even while it uses The Saint's class, intellect and charm as displaced codes to prove the moral superiority of law and honesty over crime.

'The Saint' crime series thus plays a confidence trick by using the appearance of aristocratic superiority not as a sign of class power, but as an empty aesthetic code to signify style and wit. The ambiguity over The Saint's apparent criminal motives is a game thereafter and Sanders' Saint effectively becomes a parody of the aristocratic amateur sleuth, able to exercise intellectual control while divesting his superiority of any class connotations, even if the films often play out class concerns through the use of an underworld assistant. This is the case in *The Saint in London* (John Paddy Carstairs, 1939) where The Saint strikes up a relationship with a criminal called Dugan in which the latter acts as a working-class, American mirror of The Saint. The shift of the series from the United States to Europe produces a suspense narrative with espionage motifs, applying codes of subterfuge to the new setting and allowing Dugan to be a safe figure who represents the no-nonsense American common man in opposition to the European skulduggery represented by continental agents working to subvert their government through the printing of currency for personal profit. With the help of Dugan and the aristocratic Penny Parker, The Saint sets out to thwart the mastermind behind the scheme, Bruno Lang, and his cohorts in a foreign embassy (Kussella and Stengler) in a setting that alternates between country houses and a seedy London of faded respectability that is redolent of Graham Greene's 'entertainments' of the 1930s. The film is a pacy affair, a product of the Charteris' story on which it was based ('The Million Pound Day'), and this produces less narrative vaudeville than is found in *The Saint Strikes Back* as the film establishes the plot immediately after The Saint has befriended Dugan by introducing Blake, a friend of Templar's working in the Secret Service, who then persuades him into investigating Lang's operation. The action immediately cuts to a country party where The Saint meets Lang, issues a challenge, meets Penny, with whom he shares a chaste relationship when she takes on the role of Girl Friday, and encounters Teal, the usual foil for The Saint in Charteris' stories and a replacement for Fernack while The Saint is in England, to bring all the principles together very quickly.

The pacy narrative also modifies The Saint's persona so that in *The Saint in London* he is more athletic (albeit with some use of stand-ins), hurdling fences and climbing walls to add more action to the narrative. The pace of *The Saint in London* makes it typical of the B-Movie, offering some humour and pauses in narrative, but even when the pace slackens, as when Penny and The Saint have a drink after The Saint arranges with Teal to escape police custody, The Saint decides to interview Kussella almost as soon as they have placed their order. More importantly, the pace of the film and the fuller narrative, which avoids much of the game-playing of the previous film, help to develop The Saint as an extremely competent action hero. There are still elements of his pranksterish persona, as when he leaves a calling card at Lang's home after cracking his safe announcing that he has won the first round of their struggle, or when he masquerades as Teal in an attempt to elicit information from Kussella, but these are used more as a device to show The Saint's nerve, rather than merely to provide entertaining interludes. The speed with which The Saint has to deal with events and react to threats to himself and his assistants from different quarters – in which he rescues Penny twice at the same time as fending off Teal's enquiries, evading arrest, and escaping death at the hands of Lang's hired hand, while he accumulates information about Lang and his associates in a round of action that twice takes him from

London to the country and back again – contributes to an overall sense of The Saint's deftness in handling whatever is thrown at him, while also compounding the sense of The Saint as an omniscient figure who is one step ahead of others and therefore in control of the situation rather than at the mercy of it.

The pace of the narrative and its demand that The Saint befriend Dugan very quickly also modifies The Saint's aristocratic signifiers because he is represented as someone who can mix across classes with ease. He also gathers together a community of helpers (Dugan, Penny, Mother Buckley, a doctor friend called Jim, Blake, and, on occasions, Teal) so that he is no longer aloof and distant. This also democratises him so that his relationship with Dugan offers a more balanced signifying pattern in relation to class than previously shown because both Dugan and The Saint are seen to mirror each other. There are several scenes in which they perform similar actions, most notably when they each casually play a game of Patience while they are being interrogated by Teal, using their pre-occupation with the game to deflect questions and conceal the knowledge that they possess. A more telling example of the way in which the pair mirror each other is when Dugan comes to the rescue of Penny and The Saint after the former has been taken hostage at a tobacconists and the latter has been forced to accompany her abductors in the hope of forcing an escape for them both. Dugan appears out of the shadows in the back room, after bluffing the tobacconist that he has a gun, in the same way that The Saint bluffs his way out of trouble with Teal, and clubs Kussella to the ground, after which Penny embraces him as if he were a gallant knight riding to her rescue. He also appropriates a cigar from the tobacconists as they leave, an image that mirrors The Saint's appropriation of a glass of scotch after he has cracked Lang's safe. The film suggests that Dugan is a working-class version of The Saint, someone who is also able to perform tricks and use his wits while demonstrating an experienced understanding of the world, in opposition to Penny, whose naivety is used to display the lack of knowledge, and possibly innocence, of the English upper classes. This mirroring also reflects on The Saint who becomes a mediator between two worlds, sharing the same innocence as Penny while having the same streetwise understanding as Dugan, a combination that that makes a more democratic figure while still allowing him to retain the charm and sophistication of the upper classes. In transferring traits and attitudes on to The Saint, Dugan also takes on some of The Saint's virtues in reflection to become a Runyonesque knight who still provides comic interludes, but who more importantly embodies the sense that the American common man has the same virtues as the aristocratic Saint.

The return to the United States in *The Saint's Double Trouble* (Jack Hively, 1940) develops neither the concern with community nor the attempt to value Americans as highly as The Saint. Instead, the film emphasises comedy to offer a diverting potboiler with contrived situations rather than deepened understandings of The Saint. The film takes place within the criminal underworld of Philadelphia and has Fernack returning to the series when he visits the city, while The Saint is given another chaste relationship with Anne Bitts. *The Saint's Double Trouble* is a farce first and foremost, played for humour and action in a narrative of mistaken identity and disguise that involves a plot concerning the criminal activities of Boss 'Duke' Gates, also played by George Sanders, who is smuggling diamonds from Egypt inside a mummy delivered to an old tutor of The Saint's, Professor Bitts. Although a mystery is provided by an initial murder, for which The Saint is put in the frame, the narrative has very little time for investigation because the emphasis is on The Saint as prankster when, instead of denying his involvement, he strings along Fernack, Anne, and Gates' associates to play games with his ambiguous criminality in order to infiltrate Gates' gang. Although there is a sub-text around The Saint's ability to remove doubt and restore trust, concluding with Anne's renewed faith in his mastery of events, the film emphasises narrative vaudeville in several sequences. The first of these involves Gates' associates being deceived by The Saint's appearance for the purpose of comedy, but there is also a series of action routines involving the rescue of Anne from a speeding car and The Saint's escape from a sinking boat. With no mystery, the film substitutes vicarious suspense and the minor puzzle over whether it is The Saint or his underworld double, Gates, who is onscreen at any given moment before ending in a convoluted disguise routine when The Saint visits Gates (who the police believe is The Saint) dressed as 'Mrs Bitts' to regain his identity. He then disappears with his reputation as a man of mystery restored, once more a loner, having again resisted the romance narrative in order to stay free of the bondage that the series increasingly ascribes to relations with women.

The Saint Takes Over (Jack Hively, 1940) plays with the possibility that romance will finally incorporate The Saint into society with the reappearance of Wendy Barrie as Ruth Summers. It is effectively a remake of *The Saint Strikes Back*, except that Barrie's character is now on the trail of the mobsters who killed her brother, rather than the criminal mastermind who framed her father, killing her way through them to gain revenge. She is a female version of The Saint, in the manner of his representation in *The Saint in New York*, cleaning up a 'stateless' city while The Saint, having quickly established his usual omniscience by deducing she is the murderer of the gangsters (some rose petals at the scene of one of the killings giving away her identity), concentrates on exonerating Fernack, who has been accused of corruption. Throughout the series, Fernack acts as a touchstone to indicate The Saint's superiority to the judicial authorities and to indicate the different kinds of fallibility to which the police are subject. In *The Saint in New York*, Fernack is a dependable but ineffectual onlooker, becoming more involved as a detective in *The Saint Strikes Back*, albeit only to provide a comic false detection. By the time of *The Saint Takes Over* and *The Saint in Palm Springs*, Fernack has become more like a flunkey, signified through moments when The Saint asks him to do up a tie, to signal that the law is at the service of The Saint. Although Fernack becomes a trusted aide of The Saint in *The Saint Takes Over*, the police force is still represented as only marginally more effective than the Keystone Kops. There is a sequence, for example, during which a boy selling newspapers ridicules a beat-cop by asking him, primed by a headline announcing that the police are 'baffled' by a murder spree that The Saint has already solved, whether he too is 'baffled'. As he asks this, The Saint, Fernack and a criminal comedy sidekick, Pearly Gates, draw up in a car which also contains one of the victims of the murder spree, so that the beat-cop's comic bemusement reflects Fernack's incomprehension inside the car as he tries to understand how The Saint has managed to place him in a position which, rather than exonerating him, indicates guilt for additional crimes. The film, however, develops a more ambiguous and compromised position for The Saint because he has little detection to do as a result of solving the case so early. This puts him on the margin of events because Ruth provides the narrative dynamic in her killing of the mobsters. The Saint ambles through the narrative, moving from one murder scene to another, apparently in charge, but when he tries to take control his plans go wrong in comic ways to incorporate him into the vaudeville of events that mainly comprise the film. He is also shown as less composed on a number of occasions, particularly in his clumsy romancing of Ruth, suggesting that he is more comfortable in the world of crime and adventure than in relations with women.

Although it is implied that it is one particular woman, Ruth, who has discomposed him in order to contrive a conclusion in which his sorrow at her death forces him to leave society behind once more, his discomposure is also used to undercut his aristocratic superiority so that he seems more like an ordinary American. The Saint as an ordinary Everyman is more fully expressed in *The Saint in Palm Springs* (Jack Hively, 1941), which is the closest the series comes to the whodunnit format, although it is also the most self-consciously playful in its presentation of The Saint persona. The film opens with The Saint apparently wanted for murder, but after the prank of handcuffing together the police sent to arrest him it is revealed that the charge has been faked in order to compel him to act as a bodyguard for a man taking some valuable stamps to the daughter of a European refugee. With the help of Pearly Gates, The Saint manages to lose the stamps on a couple of occasions once he has arrived in Palm Springs, comes under suspicion for their theft, bungles an attempt to trap the thief and murderer, falls for the mystification provided by Margaret Forbes (who is a secret agent rather than a criminal) and admits his bafflement before finally saving the day when he rides to the rescue in the mode of the cowboy. The film effectively debunks The Saint myth by transforming him from omniscient and superior English aristocrat into an American ordinary Joe, as mystified as Pearly by the vaudevillian antics in which he is involved, but with the qualities of resilience that allow him to triumph. The Saint is further Americanised when he defends the United States from slurs regarding its cupidity and violence, becoming a curious honorary American when he describes it as 'a very nice country, really' after which he offers himself as a paradigm of its 'nice-ness', all the while drawing attention to his own placelessness as well as emphasising its shortcomings if it needs someone so obviously English to act as a model citizen.

Gay Lawrence: The Falcon in trouble

In 1941 the American productions of 'The Saint' series came to an end although two further entries starring Hugh Sinclair were made outside of the United States by RKO British Productions. In its place, RKO created the 'Falcon' series, based on a character created by Michael Arlen, the rights for which were cheaper than those paid to Leslie Charteris for the use of The Saint.[5] The Falcon had only appeared in one short story, 'Gay Falcon' (1940), but RKO managed to generate thirteen films out of the character between 1941 and 1946, after which there were another three movies starring John Calvert as a different version of the 'Falcon' at the Poverty Row studio Film Classics. As Gates notes (2006: 73), the 'Falcon' series is very similar to the late style of 'The Saint' films, although Hardy comments that there is at least a difference in the way in which the Falcon operates by 'friendly rivalry with the police rather than as an outlaw vigilante' (Hardy, 1997: 123). This difference is compounded by the way in which the central character of the Falcon, in the early Sanders' entries, takes on the burden of comedy that had been provided by assistants in 'The Saint' films, even though the Falcon's sidekicks, particularly Goldy Locke, who appears intermittently throughout the series, still provide humour. The comedy surrounding the Falcon faded when Tom Conway, George Sanders' real-life brother, took on the role as Tom Lawrence, the brother of Sanders' Gay Lawrence, in the fourth film in the series, *The Falcon's Brother*, although other differences between 'The Saint' and 'Falcon' films remained. While The Saint is outside social relations because of the aloofness his outlaw status provides, the Falcon is immediately introduced in *The Gay Falcon* as not only within social relations (his engagement to be married) but also economic relations. He is presented as having given up the life of the detective-adventurer to set up an investment brokerage firm with his partner, Goldy Locke (played by Allen Jenkins in the first three films), although the early scenes also suggest that he is still located within a world of law and crime because of the gun that Goldy packs in his jacket, a sign that both Goldy and the Falcon still have a close relationship with criminals.

More significantly, the Falcon is seemingly located within socially acceptable boundaries of desiring relationships in the form of the fiancée who visits him in the opening scene of *The Gay Falcon* in the brokerage she has persuaded him to establish. However, this situation is problematised even before the audience learns her identity because the Falcon is discovered sitting at his desk staring through the window at a model, as barely clad as possible at the time, in the room opposite. The Falcon is therefore defined instead within disruptive desiring relationships, as a 'Playboy criminologist', to signal one of his key differences in relation to The Saint who was primarily defined in terms of his troublesome legal or criminal status as an outlaw-adventurer. The Falcon is still a fantasy of masculinity, albeit directed towards a self-sufficient and self-contained sexual desire, in which he is an empowered subjectivity as both a desiring male and as the recipient of female desire. In 'The Saint' series, *femme fatales* or mysterious women provide much of the narrative complexity as The Saint tries to penetrate the mystery of figures such as Val Travers in *The Saint Strikes Back* or Margaret Forbes in *The Saint in Palm Springs*. However, in the 'Falcon' series such women are rare because the Falcon is less a masculine fantasy of the active adventuring hero and more a fantasy of the desirable hero, with the result that all women, even those with a modicum of mystery such as

Iris Fairchild in *The Falcon in Danger* or Gwynne Gregory in *The Falcon Strikes Back*, are attracted to Gay or Tom Lawrence. This means that the mystery narrative often becomes a sideshow or hindrance to the sexual narrative, although there is always some intersection between the two, not only because the Falcon is often prevented from pursuing the investigation either because of the attentions of women or because of his desire to pursue them in turn, but also because the sexual narrative allows him to display the same mastery over situations and people, in this case women, that he applies to detection.

A further key difference in the Sanders' period of the series is that whereas The Saint is above the petty machinations and worries of society in the main, the Falcon tends to be dropped into them and has to work his way out of a conundrum or misunderstanding. Only in *The Saint's Double Trouble* is The Saint enmeshed within a criminal problem that he has to resolve for his own continued freedom, rather than someone else's, but in the 'Falcon' series, Gay Lawrence is almost constantly under threat from criminals or from the authorities. In *The Gay Falcon* he is suspected of the theft of jewellery and of murder, in *A Date with the Falcon* he is kidnapped or captured by a gang of criminals on three occasions (while also being pursued by the police), and in *The Falcon Takes Over*, because Goldy is discovered at the scene of a number of crimes, he is presumed to be involved as well. In addition, because of his promiscuous gaze after other women, he is constantly performing a dance of contrition in order to mollify his fiancées while creating further entanglements for himself because he still continues in his sexual advances elsewhere. Sanders' Falcon (Gay Lawrence) is in a comprised situation, for example, in *The Falcon's Brother*, the film in which Conway took over the role as Tom Lawrence, because he is suspected of murder again, having been discovered at the scene of a killing. It is Tom who extricates him from trouble by solving the case to become the Falcon in the process when Gay is killed after sacrificing his life to save a South American diplomat from a German spy ring.[6] After finding himself in similar circumstances in his first solo outing in *The Falcon Strikes Back*, Conway's Falcon becomes a peripatetic loner who studies muddled affairs while remaining outside of them as a watchful presence who knows exactly where to be at any given moment. Unlike Sanders' Falcon, Conway's version is detached from slapstick contrivances and farcical misunderstandings and he is also rarely called upon to fight or even run, most often strolling through the various landscapes into which he is placed as an observer with all the time in the world.

The transformed motivations, roles and narratives created for the Sanders and Conway incarnations of the Falcon are also a result of the B-level production of the series. While the transformation of the Falcon from farceur to casual *flaneur* derives from the changed persona of the central figure, it also results from the need to vary the formula of the series, so that by the time of *The Falcon's Adventure* (William Berke, 1946), the last of the Conway Falcons, the re-use of a plot concerning a gang of criminals trying to obtain a formula for industrial diamonds, originally used in the Sanders' film *A Date with the Falcon*, can be made fresh simply by having a different Falcon persona to whom different kinds of narrative motivation or problematics can be attached. In *A Date with the Falcon*, it is the entanglements that enmesh Sanders' schlemiel-like Falcon, as he shuttles between capture by criminals and arrest by the police, which drive the episodes within the film. Even when the Falcon evades his captors, his escapes are presented in slapstick sequences that indicate not his control of events, but his inability to avoid awkward situations. On one occasion, he escapes the police by climbing through a window to calmly smoke a cigarette on the ledge outside, but his fiancée, who is characterised as a recurring romantic entanglement, draws attention to his presence and causes a crowd to gather, the result of which is that the police find and detain their man despite the Falcon's efforts to evade them. In *The Falcon's Adventure*, Conway's Falcon is more clearly in control of situations so that although he is detained for murder he evades the police in a very simple manner by getting into a squad car through one door and then stepping out of the door on the other side before coolly returning to the place of his arrest, where the police are still present, to help the film's damsel in distress. The Conway Falcon's persona also drives subsequent events and although there is a slapstick sequence, in which Goldy impersonates an alligator to scare information out of one of the criminals chasing the diamond formula, and although the Falcon takes a couple of beatings from the criminals, his control of events allows him to forestall attempts to steal the formula before he takes revenge in swashbuckling manner by swinging aboard a yacht at the film's conclusion to defeat the criminals with only his fists.

Conway's Falcon is much more like the figure envisaged by Arlen and although *The Gay Falcon* (Irving Reis, 1941) draws on the plot of Arlen's only 'Falcon' story in its narrative about insurance fraud run by a female mastermind (Diana Temple in the story and Maxine Wood in the film) with a denouement in which she kills her partner (her husband in the story, Manuel Retana in the film) by administering poison through a concealed hypodermic needle in order to conceal her criminal identity, its version of the Falcon, played by Sanders, is less in command of affairs. Sanders' Falcon is contained by social, economic and sexual relations and although he struggles against them, his difficulties arise precisely because he attempts to escape the confinement deriving from his office-based career and impending marriage. The restrictions are immediately made clear when his fiancée, Elinor, says that she is taking him to a society dinner hosted by Mrs Gardner, which he resists, by suggesting a dinner for two instead, not to signify his commitment but to assert his autonomy. This desire to control his own life is made evident when Helen Reed (Wendy Barrie, reappearing from 'The Saint' series), asks for the Falcon's help in investigating a series of jewellery thefts that have taken place during society parties organised by Maxine Wood, for whom she acts as a secretary, by attending Mrs Gardner's party that evening. Attending the party now becomes a way for him to assert his will while appearing to cede control of his life to Elinor, and his flirtation and dalliance with numerous women at the party (including Helen), during which he conceals his relationship with Elinor to press his amorous advances, signify his attempt to regain independence, but also the fragility of his freedom as Elinor, acting as a watchdog, follows him to keep both his sexual and investigative impulses in check. The society party results in the murder of Mrs Gardner and this gives the Falcon licence to return to his life as a detective by dropping a case in his lap so that although there are entanglements when Goldy, having witnessed the murder, is held by the police, the Falcon seems able to achieve self-sufficient masculinity. He gains an important piece of evidence (Mrs Gardner's ring), outwits his fiancée and the police (by planting the ring on Inspector Waldeck before retrieving it), frees Goldy to use him as bait while he plays the active investigative hero, woos Helen and flirts with Maxine.

One of the important elements of the Sanders' films, however, is to display a fantasy of active and desirable masculinity above petty complications, before revealing it precisely as a fantasy by putting obstacles in the way of the Falcon achieving a condition of self-control. When Goldy is found by the police at the scene of a second murder and reveals the Falcon's possession of the diamond ring under interrogation, the Falcon finds himself under threat of containment once more, this time by the forces of legal authority. He still manages to evade his complicated predicament, plays more games with the police by masquerading as a tramp, breaks into the apartment of Maxine's still-living partner, Retana, discovers the location of his safe by means of a stratagem, escapes being killed and clears himself with Waldeck by entrapping Maxine as the criminal mastermind. He then establishes his dominance over Elinor by chastising her for inadvertently helping Retana and frees himself from having to choose romantically between Elinor and Helen to suggest that he has thwarted attempts to contain him. His apparent freedom seems to be confirmed by his return to the role of detective when a new case arrives in the form of a distraught woman asking for his help at the end of the film. However, the helter-skelter pace of events, although partly derived from the need for pace in a B-picture, suggests that not only is he just keeping one step ahead of his problems, but also that for much of the time he is frustrated by the obstacles placed in his way. The conclusion also shows that the Falcon isn't a self-sufficient masculine subject, despite having broken free from impending marital containment, because not only does he submit to his sexual urges in offering his help to the damsel in distress, but also because it is implied that the breakneck pace will continue in the new investigation.

Although *A Date with the Falcon* (Irving Reis, 1941) begins with a different situation to the one suggested by the conclusion of the previous film, opening instead with an impending marriage to Helen, his new fiancée, the Falcon is soon mired in a case without having any choice in the matter when a gang of criminals seeking to acquire a formula for industrial diamonds decides to prevent him interfering with their plans by persuading him to join their enterprise. Although he refuses and then intentionally allows himself to be abducted, he is soon inserted into a narrative in which he shuttles between capture by the criminals and arrest by the police while also being continually flustered by having to balance the attentions of the female characters he encounters. The Falcon's continuing troubles suggest that he is more like the characters around him, contained or frustrated by their lot, whether it is Goldy failing to find the quiet life for which he yearns, Helen becoming increasingly jealous, or Inspector O'Hara lamenting the buffoonish subordinates with whom he is saddled as he chases in the Falcon's wake. Goldy, in particular, is used as a measure for the Falcon's predicament, refracting the Falcon's struggle against containment in exaggerated form by stumbling from one arrest and incarceration to another. Goldy has a degree of control in *A Date with the Falcon*, but in *The Falcon Takes Over* (Irving Reis, 1942) he is constantly found at the scenes of crimes to place him under police interrogation, a situation that leads to a running joke in which whenever he is addressed by the Falcon he goes into a patter beginning with 'I was sitting in a chair ...' before tailing off when he realises that he is not being questioned by the police again.

The Falcon Takes Over is based on Raymond Chandler's *Farewell, My Lovely* and although changes were made to streamline the plot so that it fitted into the running time of a second feature, it emphasises mystery more fully than the prior films. *The Falcon Takes Over* draws out the reflected relationship between the Falcon and Goldy by making the latter more of a comic stooge after Moose Malloy, the giant ex-con searching for his old flame, Velma, puts him in fear of his life at the beginning of the film. Thereafter, he is presented as a comic coward subject to wisecracks made by the police, particularly O'Hara, whose hard-boiled jokes at his expense ('It's sing or Sing Sing', for example) highlight Goldy's powerlessness. The Falcon also becomes a passive object of events because, like Goldy, he continually has to dodge Malloy, although his lack of control is signified more by the fact that he only evades death at the hands of Marriott, a member of the blackmail ring headed by Velma in her new identity as Diana Kenyon, because Marriott's gun has been loaded with blanks as part of a double-cross to kill him in the Falcon's place. The film also makes the Falcon a vaudeville comedian, adapting Chandler's novel to suit the comic mode despite the opening menace provided by Malloy and the use of atmospheric lighting to make him more frightening when the Falcon encounters him at Mrs Florian's house and at Amthor's den. These moments, however, are alleviated by comic sequences, such as the Falcon repeating his feigned drunkenness from *A Date with the Falcon* or pretending that he thinks Moose is a party guest called 'Herman" on meeting him outside Mrs Florian's where Goldy hides under the car to be revealed when Moose drives off. Despite the hard-boiled wisecracks, the Falcon and Goldy are turned into a vaudeville double-act which emphasises their likeness to establish that the Falcon has the same weaknesses as others, albeit with the ability to remain calm when placed in a difficult situation, unlike Goldy, who panics under similar conditions.

The Falcon is still a trickster or a hoaxer, like The Saint, and often his function is not to solve mysteries or to become a chivalric hero for the multitude of damsels in distress he encounters, but to remain composed so that he can wriggle out of difficulties. Detective fiction has often been seen as a series of games (Mandel, 1984: 48) and critics have, as Marcus (2003: 262) comments, drawn on the work of Roger Caillois (1983: 1–12) to either discuss the ludic nature of detection narratives or the games writers play with their readers (Knight, 2004: 93). The detective is also a player of games within the narrative, taking on disguises or creating stratagems in order to trap the suspect, but few take on this role as overtly as the Falcon.[7] Games and tricks extend across the series and involve both Falcon personas in burlesque charades, disguises and masquerades, such as Tom Lawrence's pretence of being a waiter and a wax dummy in *The Falcon's Brother*. Sleights of hand are particularly prominent, such as handcuffing police officers together (*The Gay Falcon* and *The Falcon Takes Over*), slipping incriminating evidence into the pocket of Waldeck in *The Gay Falcon* or framing a hotel detective in *The Falcon Strikes Back* by palming money from him before planting it again when he is searched. There are also psychological or emotional games such as a phoney telegram to get rid of a fiancée in *The Falcon in Danger* or the numerous games the Falcon plays with attractive female suspects by wooing them to gain information. This latter game is complex charade of 'romance' in which the Falcon separates his professional persona (detective) from his romantic persona (potential suitor) to play with a woman's affections in order to elicit information while also implying that his reason for being romantically interested in the woman is because, as a detective, he believes she is innocent. However, the charade leaves unspoken the fact that the Falcon's desire is empty and only part of a game of 'love' that he is playing, without any commitment other than to confirm his continued desirability to women. The game is therefore somewhat masturbatory because it is based upon a narcissistic sense of self-worth, albeit one that requires reciprocation from others to produce self-fulfilment. As a way of articulating the Falcon as a fantasy of the desirable hero, these moments are unnecessary because the Falcon's charm, wit and composure (in both the Sanders and Conway versions) provide an enviable image of masculine confidence that is expressed most clearly in *A Date with a Falcon* when an old girlfriend learns that he is about to be married and announces that 'It's a crime' to which he replies: 'Yes, and I can't solve it. It's the perfect crime.'

This comment, however, is also one of the many games that the series plays, in this case linguistic games involving flirtation, which are supplemented by other verbal games of banter, wisecracks and malapropisms, although the Falcon isn't always the centre of the series' verbal invention. Goldy and the police quip freely while the former, or the Falcon's other sidekicks, are the main purveyors of malapropisms. The films as a whole can be seen as a set of games as part of the vaudeville of routines that the series offers for entertainment in its quickie B-format. This makes the 'Falcon' films more playful, self-conscious and narcissistic than many other B-crime series, although 'The Thin Man' series offered something similar in its self-parody. The 'Falcon' series is also characterised by numerous self-conscious textual games that play with the conventions of the amateur sleuth and whodunnit forms. *The Gay*

Falcon draws attention to its form as a whodunnit in only the second scene when Helen Reed is discovered at the Falcon's apartment in the act of ransacking it, not as an act of theft, but to look for the button that opens the secret passage she knows all detectives have because she has read about such things in novels. That the Falcon is revealed to have a secret passage only doubles the metafictional resonances created by Helen's search for it and places the series in a self-consciously fictional world. Such playfulness can be found throughout the series, whether it is the parody gangsters of *A Date with the Falcon* or the knowing way in which the scripts have Detective Bates set up a quip for Donovan by asking an innocuous question with an obvious answer (such as in *The Falcon Strikes Back* when after being told to get the squad car to investigate a crime scene he asks 'Why, chief?' to prepare the way for Donovan's response: 'Because there's too much tread on the tyres and I'd like to wear some of it off'). There are also specific moments of self-consciousness such as the fictional contrivance of having a kitten playing with a baby's rattle to terrify Detective Bates just after he has expressed a fear of rattlesnakes in *The Falcon Out West* or comic echoes or iterated jokes from one film to another such as the Falcon reading the funny papers in *The Falcon Strikes Back* in a reference back to the mortician doing the same thing in *The Gay Falcon*.

Tom Lawrence: The Falcon's smarter brother

In part, such games are articulated in order to disguise the programmatic nature of the narratives because they suggest that plot contrivances and lack of verisimilitude are not the result of low quality B-production. The films, however, always look like filler material, even if they try to make light of their lesser production values, although this does not prevent them from providing enjoyable fare for second feature entertainment. The series is therefore always meant to be 'fun' and after its one intervention into the America-versus-the-Nazis cycle that dominated Hollywood production in the years after Pearl Harbor, in *The Falcon's Brother* (Stanley Logan, 1942), the films continued in a breezy manner even if the slapstick and burlesque elements gradually faded away. *The Falcon's Brother* deals with the discovery and neutralisation of a spy ring which uses a fashion magazine to pass messages to agents in the United States. The film typifies the espionage style that was common among the B-series which, according to Schatz, provided 'easy reformulations of low-grade crime formulas' so that detectives, G-men and police could fight Nazis rather than criminals (Schatz, 1997: 241), and even manages to turn Sanders' desire to leave the series into a patriotic act typical of such films by having his version of the Falcon die heroically for the war effort. The film maintains its patriotic credentials up to its conclusion when, after receiving a telephone call threatening revenge for his exploits, Tom Lawrence becomes the Falcon out of a sense of duty instead of heading off to South America on holiday. Besides the espionage-related plot, the film differs very little from the previous entries in the series except that the comedy is more focused on the wandering eyes of both Lawrence brothers, particularly the way in which each brother is seemingly distracted from his task of investigation by every attractive woman who comes into view.

The Falcon's Brother, despite having a stylish gloss that is lacking in similar B-grade Nazi-hunting films such as *Meet Boston Blackie* (1941), is more clearly a programmer than the previous films. There are loose ends aplenty, such as the reason for the two deaths that set the narrative in motion or the fashion designer who is arrested on suspicion of being a spy but who is then forgotten because her narrative purpose has been served. Indeed, the film is instrumentalist in the way of B-Movies in using events or characters merely to provide mystery and suspense on a temporary basis, without placing them within the totality of the narrative, such as two dancers who provide mystery until they are revealed to be Mexican agents, at which point they are discarded from the plot because their function, to provide mystification, has been fulfilled. B-Movie plotting becomes more evident during subsequent films in the series, although Conway's first solo outing, *The Falcon Strikes Back* (Edward Dmytryk, 1943), is one of the more tightly constructed Falcon entries. It seems at first to be just another potboiler about spying, signified by a gang creating a cover for their activities behind the front of a wartime charity (the Volunteer Knitters of America) and the use of foreign characters such as the aged European exile, Mr Steffen. The film, however, artfully deploys these as deceptions until the denouement reveals that the gang are just criminals engaged in bond fraud (rather than enemy agents) and that the murders of the members of the gang are not part of nefarious espionage activities but an entirely unrelated set of crimes committed as an act of revenge by one of their previous victims, Dugan the puppeteer. The espionage tropes, rather than being causative narrative devices, are turned therefore into mystification but, because the plot deals with fraud, the film's playful concealment of its own trickery helps to maintain their continued relevance. By sleight of hand, the film turns its plotting inside out once the criminal genius, Mrs Lipton (previously seen as the head of the charity group), reappears towards the end of the film and the gang's real activities are revealed, but this does not invalidate the prior events, which still retain their consistency within the new narrative focus.

The Falcon Strikes Back establishes the Falcon as a detective in the ratiocinative mode in his pursuit of Dugan, but this is dissipated in *The Falcon in Danger* (William Clemens, 1943) even though the film initially offers an ingenious whodunnit conundrum concerning the crash of an unoccupied airplane. The narrative shifts to farcical contrivance as the Falcon tries to balance the needs of the detection narrative with his romantic involvement with both his fiancée and one of the suspects, although it is the sexual entanglements and comic escapades that dominate. The rest of the films in the series tried to vary the format by locating the Falcon in new settings, beginning with *The Falcon and the Co-eds* (William Clemens, 1943) which sets the action in a girls' seminary. The film uses hints of espionage (in the form of a European teacher, Mr Graelich) as mystification, provides comic antics in the form of the caretaker's daughters (the three 'Ughs'), who help and hinder the Falcon's investigation, and offers musical interludes, but the emphasis is on the female Gothic in the creation of the mystery plot. The mode seemingly derives from the psychic abilities of one of the pupils (Marguerita) and her identification with nature through her alignment with the elemental power of the sea. This concatenation of meanings as a sign of feminine sexual repression, however, is misdirection to conceal the insane jealousy of the meek Mary Phoebus, whose pent-up hatreds and suppressed desires lead to a murderous spree. The Falcon's role, once he has gone through an early trickster routine masquerading as a psychologist is to become a detective-psychologist (indicated by both his reading of the personality of a murder victim from clues in a room and by his control of his own desires so that he can avoid sexual competition with Graelich) to impose masculine ratiocination as a way to interpret feminine psychology. He thereby saves Marguerita from being compelled to commit suicide by Mary Phoebus in the denouement, although it is masculine activity, as he races along a cliff-top, and an ideologically constructed feminine mental instability, as Mary takes fright at his appearance and jumps out of her skin and into the sea in the place of Marguerita, that rescues the situation.

The Falcon Out West (William Clemens, 1944), *The Falcon in Mexico* (William Berke, 1944), *The Falcon in Hollywood* (Gordon Douglas, 1944) and *The Falcon in San Francisco* (Joseph H. Lewis, 1945) all advertise their attempts to create variety through their settings in order to dress up plots about a scheming woman murdering for money, a bankrupt art-dealer killing to protect his investments, a producer sabotaging his film to cover a fraudulent sale of shares, and a gangster returned from the dead. The first film emphasises the variation provided by the setting, throwing in all the trimmings of the B-western, such as ranch-hands providing a welcome by firing guns in the air, a runaway stagecoach, a bucking bronco, singing cowboys, a posse ride, Native Americans and associated mystical beliefs, and a gunfight to conclude the film. Some variety is provided by Vanessa Drake, a *femme fatale* who murders her fiancé after he has signed over his estate to her, which produces an interesting dissonance between figure and setting, although her character is also simply part of the pastiche of generic references characteristic of the B-Movie. Although *The Falcon in Mexico* resolves into a standard whodunnit, its real investigation involves the mystery that follows from the misdirection created by a Gothic style deriving both from its setting and the apparent reappearance of an artist thought long dead. *The Falcon in Mexico* generates most of its action out of mystification, but provides some complexities because of the variety of styles that complement its comedy and mystery, including musical and carnival sequences as well as a contrast between *noir* America and Gothic Mexico. After a routine narrative in *The Falcon in Hollywood*, which emphasises comedy through the introduction of a Girl Friday in the form of a taxi driver who follows the Falcon's every move, *The Falcon in San Francisco* presents more depth and complexity in drawing together an intrigue involving a crime ring, smuggling, a dead gangster returned to life in a new identity, and the mystery of two sisters kept in apparent captivity. The film ends with a conventional revelation of secret identity when the returning gangster is shown to be the father of the two sisters, but its use of gangster and *noir* motifs (in its convoluted scheming and villainous *femme fatale* not averse to using brutal methods) raise its generic pastiche above the comedy vaudeville provided by Goldy planning to marry to reduce his income tax payments.

The final two films at RKO are both remakes of earlier films with *The Falcon's Alibi* (Ray McCarey, 1946) reworking *The Gay Falcon* and, as discussed, *The Falcon's Adventure* revisiting *A Date with the Falcon. The Falcon's Alibi*, however, is a nuanced affair because its thread involving insurance fraud is not only subsidiary to the main criminal narrative, but also acts as mystification or misleading motivation to suggest that the most significant crimes (a series of murders) derive from itself. In fact, it is the murderous jealousy of a disc jockey, Nick (Elisha Cook Jr), and his attempts to win back his unfaithful wife, Lola (Jane Greer), by stealing jewels in the hope of preventing Lola from leaving him for her manager that is the focus for crime in the film. The *noir* inflections of the doubled narrative provide a complex investigation for the Falcon, not least because interventions from a gang of thugs trying to genuinely steal the pearls involved in the insurance fraud help to muddy the case by supplementing the twists of the Nick and Lola narrative and the deceptions of the fraud narrative. The complexity created by the *noir* narrative provides a different landscape for the Falcon in the later stages of the series so that, even though the film uses a variation of the automated puppet show from *The Falcon Strikes Back* in the form of Nick's pre-recorded programmes (which provide him with alibis), the film provides variation to the format. Conway's Falcon, despite suffering the usual accusations of involvement and suspicion from an insurance investigator, manages to see his way through the labyrinth in which he is placed, understanding the relationships, schemes and secrets in each of the different strands. He also avoids the farcical misadventures that affected Sanders' Falcon in the earlier version of the insurance fraud plot, not least because he and Goldy are both mainly outside the comic interludes that are provided by an insurance investigator. In this way, the Falcon's superiority in transcending the *noir*-inflected discourses surrounding him and in avoiding the snares set for him suggests his self-sufficiency, although it takes a reversion to an action format in the conclusion, during which the Falcon rescues the damsel in distress who brought him into the case and defeats Nick in a fight, for him to be able to fully extricate himself.

4

Englishness and America: Basil Rathbone's Sherlock Holmes

The 'Sherlock Holmes' series of films, originally produced by Twentieth Century Fox for two period versions in 1939 (both released as headlining movies), and then by Universal, after the series was revived and updated to the contemporary period in 1942, are a curious example of the detective genre. Although the films mainly have a mystery detection format and feature the most famous detective in modern culture, they are also the most variable of the detective series films in their marshalling of generic codes. At times, Holmes is a classical detective engaged in hermeneutic activity, but at others he is a spy-hunter, an active male hero in the manner of the investigative thriller, or a special agent (like Dick Tracy or Bulldog Drummond) in the B-thriller mode, often shifting from one role to another within films as the situation demands. Holmes is as variable in his function as The Saint and encounters a wider variety of criminal types and narrative forms, even if the series also requires him to move through the vaudeville of styles as if he were the unchanging figure announced in the pre-sequence titles of *Sherlock Holmes and the Voice of Terror* so that he can be used to embody values of permanence and stability in order to tame a shifting and uncertain world. The films often seem to emphasise the relationship between the onscreen personas of Holmes and Watson, as performed by Basil Rathbone and Nigel Bruce, with a focus on the comic incomprehension or blustering buffoonery of the latter, and this also deflects away from the classical form of the detective narrative of ratiocination to create a music-hall or vaudeville version of the detective format in which the mystifications associated with the whodunnit are supplemented and displaced by the comic diversions that Bruce provides. Although the series seems focused on the mystery and ratiocination characteristic of the whodunnit, the films are often therefore characterised by an influx of iconographies, narrative patterns and ideological inflections from other genres, most notably the Gothic, but also the *noir* suspense format, espionage and comedy.[1]

Sherlock Holmes at Twentieth Century Fox

This is even the case with *The Hound of the Baskervilles* (Sidney Lanfield, 1939), which is generally faithful to Conan Doyle's novel, including Holmes's absence from the narrative when Watson accompanies Sir Henry to Baskerville Hall, as well as retaining the disguises and deductions that Holmes performs, although it does add a romance between Sir Henry and Beryl Stapleton, the sister of Henry's would-be murderer. The film offers the same kinds of Holmesian detection that Conan Doyle's novel provides, most significantly the mystification of the subplot concerning the escaped murderer, which occupies much of the narrative and absorbs Watson before Holmes makes his appearance to immediately reveal that it has nothing to do with the threat to Sir Henry. Holmes' deductions also reveal his omniscient gaze as he offers resolutions to clarify the confusions that Watson endures by seeming to pluck explanations out of nothing, suggesting that even in exercising rationality to explain otherwise incomprehensible or supernatural cause, there is something uncanny about his abilities which make him not only superhuman, but inhuman. The film, however, veers away from the detection narrative into Gothic motifs because the visualisation of the mystery offers an iconography that is more in harmony with the Universal horror films of the period. The credits, for example, are played against the backdrop of a misty moor and the first scene shows Sir Charles Baskerville running across the same landscape, with a dog howling in the background, Sir Charles' movement cross-cut with shots of a mysterious bearded figure, who then bends over him when he collapses, after which the scene concludes with Mrs Barryman holding a lantern in the darkness to compound the Gothic imagery.

In terms of iconography, the only visual identifiers that the film is a detective rather than a supernatural mystery come in the few scenes in London when Holmes and Watson are introduced and when Holmes agrees to Dr Mortimer's request to offer Sir Henry his protection. The signs of the murder mystery occur in the form of several tableaux shots which attempt to mimic Victorian literary illustrations in order to give the impression that this is a Holmesian world of detection, although the staging and lighting of scenes such as Sir Henry's first meeting with Holmes, in which the latter appears in profile, with Mortimer and Sir

Henry balancing him on either side, or the interview with the cab driver, which is lit to create a flatness of effect, also evoke illustrations by Phiz to create a Dickensian effect. It is the events that frame these scenes that mainly provide the ideology of rationality associated with the detective form, in Holmes' deductions of the character of Dr Mortimer from his walking stick, the mystery of the missing boot, and Sir Henry's levity at the idea of a family ghost. There are, however, also suspense motifs in the B-thriller mode that are incongruous in the context of the Holmesian detection narrative, such as the sequence in which Holmes saves Sir Henry from being shot, which has no obvious narrative purpose if Stapleton has stolen Sir Henry's boot in order to kill him by the same means used for Sir Charles. Further action sequences disrupt the intellectual pursuit of the mystery, particularly a long sequence before the denouement during which Holmes and Watson rush across the moor as the hound attacks Sir Henry and Stapleton traps Holmes in the hound's lair to produce tension associated with B-Movie thrills. This sequence is followed by a final nick-of-time rescue when Holmes suddenly appears to prevent Sir Henry drinking the poison given to him by Stapleton and it is only then that Holmes offers ratiocination to explain events, although the mystery has already been solved for the audience by Stapleton's actions.

This confusion with regard to the film's generic parameters is compounded by a long section after Watson accompanies Sir Henry to Baskerville Hall, during which Holmes' detection is absent from the screen, replaced by Gothic signifiers in a pastiche of styles very typical of the B-Movie. The Gothic codes are highlighted in the arrival of Sir Henry and Watson at the estate, where the use of shadows on the walls inside the hall are used to create haunted house motifs and these tropes are continued in the images of the Grimpen Mire, the misty moors and the mysterious figure haunting them, while a dinner at the Stapletons also introduces the Mortimers' interest in the occult and provides the opportunity for an impromptu séance. Watson's confused detection is the only sign of the whodunnit mystery in this section, although it is curtailed by the insertion of a romance narrative between Sir Henry and Beryl Stapleton. The film, without Holmes, looks nothing like a detective mystery at all, although the cross-generic confusion allows it to mediate on discourses of history and modernity, using Gothic and romance as signifying components to serve the detective form's ideology of rationality. Baskerville Hall, for example, is not just a site of likely supernatural activity, but a sign of history, its shadows coded as the darkness of the past to be dispelled by the enlightenment provided by Holmes' rational deduction. This is developed in one of the romance sequences when Sir Henry and Beryl visit the ruins of a prehistoric village and the former expresses his love, dismissing old-fashioned courting customs which prevent him from saying outright that he loves Beryl before concluding that as a result of such strictures 'we can't even be ourselves when we want to be'. In his desire to end conventions justified only by tradition, he not only implicitly criticises superstition (belief with no evidence except a history of acceptance), but also symbolises modernity (and an American version of it) in speaking the ideology of the individual as of primary importance in justifying an action.

In spite of the Gothic motifs and the use of tableaux to suggest a world of the past in the staging and concerns of the film, *The Hound of the Baskervilles* is therefore already an updated version of Sherlock Holmes, offering twentieth-century ideas that align with the rationality of the detective mystery. Even fusty old Watson is brought into this modernising vision, even if at first he is rather bashful when he happens across Sir Henry and Beryl's very open display of love, because he not only accepts it, but displays his happiness at their union. The characterisation of Watson by Nigel Bruce in the film is important in representing the triumph of modernity because although he is represented as of the past in his dress and manner, he is also still ready to embrace the modern world. The film, indeed, seems more concerned with the characterisation of Holmes and Watson than with the mystery itself, in order to enact the triumph of the modern over tradition. As Amanda Field has noted (2009: 133–4), Holmes is comfortable with modernity and its technology in the series, although the conception of the detective in Conan Doyle's stories was always of someone familiar with the rational systems of modernity and its modes of organisation. Rathbone's incarnation provides a drier wit and more humour, in part because *The Hound of the Baskervilles* and other films in the series place him in situations out of his control or offer a visualisation of his disguises as part of the films' vaudeville, but he still invests Holmes with the same fascination with science that, when the films are updated, suggest an embrace of modern technology. The films, however, also want to retain the values and solidity of the past that Holmes also represents, but it is in the displaced form of Watson that these are found, even while his cinematic version desires to be part of modernity.

One significant aspect of *The Hound of the Baskervilles*, although it is unremarkable in its formulation because it appears as a coda to the detection narrative, is Dr Mortimer's enunciation of the detective as protector of society. Although this idea returns when Universal revived the series, it is dropped in the other Fox entry, *The Adventures of Sherlock Holmes*, which is more concerned with the concept of crime and its detection as a puzzle or a game. The character of Moriarty expresses this early on when he says that Holmes is someone who needs 'toys', after which he provides him with two, a letter threatening the theft of an emerald called the Star of Delhi and another threatening the murder of a member of the Brandon family. Thereafter, *The Adventures of Sherlock Holmes* puts the clue-puzzle on show although it conceals Moriarty, who becomes a puppet-master until his plan to steal the Crown Jewels is eventually put into effect in the final reel. Based on *Sherlock Holmes*, an 1899 play by William Gillette, the film is almost entirely made up of riddles and games to offer a paradigm of the clue-puzzle mystery in the almost complete emptiness of anything of significance to the real crime, thereby revealing that the detective mystery in its enigma form is mainly narrative subterfuge, padding, diversion and deferral. The Brandon case occupies much of Holmes' attention, and most of the film's running time, although it is a diversion away from the main crime and includes its own smaller narrative diversions, such as Watson jumping to the wrong conclusion when he sees Moriarty visit the offices of Jerrold Hunter, Jerrold's unexplained mysterious activities, and the flautist who plays an Incan chant of the dead outside Ann Brandon's window, who, though he is the murderer, has no reason to be there except to deepen the suspense and mystery of the diversionary narrative.

None of these are pivotal narrative events, although as an accumulation of episodes they create the 'elephantiasis' of 'hermeneutic activity' (Fowler, 1994: 353) that fills up the film's running time until Moriarty's real crime is revealed.[2] Holmes' deductions in the Brandon case have no relevance to the main crime, therefore, and they are revealed to be merely entertaining routines, taking their place among the other routines in the film so that the deductive performances, or 'supererogatory demonstration[s] of method' (Fowler, 1994: 357) in which Holmes displays his seeming omniscience by, for example, predicting the appearance of an elderly gentleman 'with a touch of gout in his right leg' immediately before Sir Ronald arrives, are merely diverting entertainments, even if their apparent purpose is to display Holmes' insightful mind.[3] Because they are simply one set of discrete diversions among others, rather than fundamental to narrative or textual meaning, these deductive performances are equivalent in value to the moments of comedy, action and music that are provided elsewhere. Although some of these moments move the action forward, such as the race through the streets to stop Moriarty's plans for the Star of Delhi, most other such incidents are inconsequential to the narrative. A chase through the streets to try to save the life of Ann Brandon's brother provides a facsimile of narrative momentum in the apparent speed of the hansom, but has no narrative purpose because Holmes and Watson arrive too late to help. Comedy routines provide similar unmotivated interludes, including a scene in which, apparently to aid Holmes' examination of the crime scene, Watson is required to lie down in the street. This prompts an exchange with a bemused passer-by and provides comedy of misunderstanding, but has no purpose except as a humorous interlude because Holmes calls Watson to him without explaining why he was required to lie in the road. Rathbone is also part of this vaudeville of diversions when, as Holmes, he disguises himself as a music-hall performer to introduce an actual moment of vaudeville into the film by performing 'Oh, we do like to be beside the seaside' at Lady Conyngham's party. All of these moments suggest that the narrative subterfuge that is a fundamental feature of the whodunnit is, in *The Adventures of Sherlock Holmes*, less a matter of providing mystifying threads for the detective and audience to interpret than a way of providing interludes to divert the audience away from the fact that much of the narrative is inconsequential mystification.

Into the 'Bs': Holmes the spy-catcher

While the game-playing Holmes of *The Adventures of Sherlock Holmes* is in accord with Conan Doyle's conception of his detective, for whom detection was often more a matter of art than morality, this conception does not fulfil the needs of the character when he is updated in Universal's revival of the series in 1942 as 'strong programmers' (Haralovich, 1979: 57). The changed political landscape of the United States, which had by now entered the Second World War, required a more actively ideological Holmes, even if the wartime spy-catcher films still include the ludic elements of the whodunnit and provide entertainment by incorporating more fully the action-based elements of the B-Movie thriller. The ideological focus is most obvious in *Sherlock Holmes and the Voice of Terror* (John Rawlins, 1942),[4] while entertainment is emphasised in *Sherlock Holmes and the Secret Weapon* (1942), which resembles an action thriller in the style of Dick Tracy despite its English setting. The films in the Universal 'Sherlock Holmes' series tend to oscillate between the clue-puzzle form where the villain is only unmasked at the end (*Sherlock Holmes Faces Death* and *The Scarlet Claw*) and the thriller mode in which Holmes takes on Moriarty or a Moriarty-like figure (*Sherlock*

Holmes and the Secret Weapon, Spider Woman or *The Pearl of Death*). In the latter case, the narrative patterns tend to the cops-and-robbers format, as Langman and Finn describe *The Pearl of Death* (1995b: xii), in which an agent of the law (Holmes) takes on a criminal mastermind and his or her 'gang'. Here, the focus is less on the identity of the criminal, which is usually revealed very quickly, and more on the battle of wits between the two protagonists.

Sherlock Holmes and the Voice of Terror is both espionage whodunnit and B-action thriller because it introduces the 'gang' as Nazi spies working for Sir Evan Barham, the top Nazi agent, who operates from within the British Intelligence Inner Council. The film is very similar to other Nazi-busting films of the period in which various heroes battled against Fifth Columnists which means that Sherlock Holmes takes on a more overtly political representation as a defender of democracy. Although Holmes is shown protecting Britain in these films, with the exception of *Sherlock Holmes in Washington*, he draws in American inflections because he is acting against the tyranny represented by the Nazis in the name of values at the heart of American ideology. Such values of freedom and democracy are attached to Britain, because it is fighting the same enemy of democracy, and Holmes' defence of Britain makes him the guarantor of American ideology and society, while also by an act of displacement making Britain into the United States in the values it espouses. Curiously, therefore, an English gentleman detective, who represents a class system rejected by American society, becomes the emblem of freedom, combining a Hollywood notion of British fair-play, decency and honour with American values of freedom and democracy to become a protector of the latter while he is at work in Britain. Holmes also takes on the role of Churchill in the spy-catcher films in the series, speaking some of his words, for example, at the end of *Sherlock Holmes in Washington*.[5] Field notes how Holmes embodies English Victorian values (209: 118–9) in the films, through which he implicitly signifies stability and integrity, but these are also combined with more modern attitudes associated with the United States, to place value on the ordinary people that the films see as most threatened by the Nazis. Holmes voices American concerns about the 'common people', for whose benefit the United States was created in its own discourses, while the films use the iconography of the Nazis-as-mobsters in order to show what the 'common people' will look like if they are stripped of the decency and sense of honour Holmes' Englishness represents and the freedom and democracy that American values provide.

Holmes is not just a defender of democracy, therefore, but someone who helps to strengthen it by providing an example for others to follow, such as Kitty, who takes on the role of an enemy of Nazism at Holmes' prompting. The Fifth Columnist narrative has wider ideological meaning because it represents, in the defeat of enemy agents, the larger victory of the values and the spirit of democracy that the representation of a military triumph can only imply. An enemy at home is required, therefore, without necessarily suggesting that there ever was a host of traitors actually working in Britain and the United States, in order to symbolically show how ordinary people can combat Fascism and contribute to its defeat simply by rejecting its values in favour of those that are represented by Sherlock Holmes. By another displacement, ordinary British and American citizens become associated with Holmes, who is even more superior and composed than in the Fox films, where the action elements of the narratives required discomposed urgency on occasions. The denouement, in particular, displays this persona because after revealing Barham's true identity Holmes calmly announces that he has arranged things so that Britain is properly defended where it needs to be protected. This pronouncement is followed by footage of Spitfire airplanes returning after defeating the Luftwaffe and shots of commandos on the beach, appearing in the narrative seemingly at Holmes' command. Such control of events is also depicted when Holmes arrives at the Intelligence Inner Council to take on his case at the beginning of the film. Here, he finds the Council in a state of confusion, responding in the narrative to the preceding montage (in which the Voice has spread its message) to display fear, tension and anger. His calm in applying deductive reason without anxiety and then in assuring the Council that the British public won't be panicked by the Voice's messages (unlike the Council) not only serves to help compose its members, but also expresses a propagandistic confidence in the ordinary people of Britain which also aligns Holmes with them because he displays the same calm he claims they will show.

Kitty serves to prove Holmes' claims in showing how an ordinary person can become exceptional like Holmes, and does so in exaggerated form because she is not only working class, but also a prostitute and therefore, in Hollywood's moral codes, below the ordinary worker because she is outside ideologically legitimate forms of 'labour'. Her transformation from anti-social pariah to pro-social model is, because of the pace required by the B-Movie, fairly speedy and it takes only one speech by Holmes, emphasising that the war is a struggle between civilisation and 'barbarism' for her to become the embodiment of both the Blitz spirit and the spirit of democracy, thereafter demonstrating her new-found exceptionality by inspiring apathetic drinkers in a pub to renew the fight against Nazism. In so doing, she repeats Holmes' statement that 'England is at stake', but then voices what this version of England is by stating that there is only one side to be on in the war – 'England, no matter how high or how low we are – to offer a vision of a very modern England that transcends class to make everyone within it both ordinary and extraordinary if they join the fight. Her death is significant in this regard because it illustrates the differences between Nazism and the Anglo-American ideology of egalitarian decency that follows on from an earlier debate between Holmes and the Nazi agent Meade, during which the latter proposes that 'only the powerful are worthy of respect' to prove that Watson's life has no meaning. Holmes' response, that 'to our stupid British minds, every life is of consequence' speaks to the ordinariness of Britain, not only in emphasising that everyone is equal, but also in the use of the word 'stupid' to suggest that the British are ordinary and undistinguished. The word also implies that the British do not want to be superior (implicitly in opposition to the Nazis), but this has ironic effect in suggesting that the British are actually exceptional in valuing all life.

In her death, giving her life for democracy, Kitty becomes like Holmes, an exceptional person, simply by making the same sacrifice made by many ordinary people during the war. Yet, in honouring her, Holmes becomes a more egalitarian figure, someone as 'stupid', and therefore as ordinary, as the rest of the British, for whom valuing life is the normal mode of thinking. In the updating of Holmes to the war years, Holmes takes on an ideological role as a defender of equality to become an ordinary person and, in this regard, Bruce's performance of Watson is important because, in his dullness, he represents 'ordinary people', so that Holmes' fondness for him is transferred to millions of others. The formulation is yet more complex because in Holmes' updating and ideological recreation, along with the mixing of the generic codes of the espionage and detective forms, he becomes a model of the unflustered, commanding, all-knowing and all-seeing detective that had been Conan Doyle's conception of him, but this is only the accidental product of a concatenation of ideological and textual discourses that the series had previously lacked. While *Sherlock Holmes and the Voice of Terror* creates the model of Holmes the detective, *Sherlock Holmes and the Secret Weapon* (1942) sets the narrative tone for the rest of series even as it simplifies the ideological discourses present in the former film because Holmes oscillates between extremes of brilliance and bafflement, a trope that recurs from film to film, so that in *House of Fear* he seems to have found the solution well in advance of the denouement, while in *Pearl of Death* he appears perplexed throughout, even if he knows from the beginning the identity of the criminal genius he is after.

In *Sherlock Holmes and the Secret Weapon* the plot is provided by the Swiss scientist, Tobel, who has brought a new bomb-sight over to the allies, and Holmes is initially given little room to display his brilliance except in disguise and in his strategy of concealing the parts of the bomb-sight inside two hollow editions of Dickens to outwit the Nazi agents trying to spirit Tobel from Switzerland to Berlin. Once in Britain, in order to provide Holmes with a mystery, Tobel, rather than simply handing his device over to the military, comes up with a plot as elaborate as his apparently fantastic invention is simple in order to manufacture the bomb-sight by giving each of its four different parts to four other Swiss scientists in London, after which he promptly disappears, as does the code he has entrusted to his girlfriend, Charlotte, who also happens to be in London. The narrative then turns to Holmes' pursuit of Moriarty, who he identifies from Charlotte's description, and his cracking of 'The Dancing Men' code when he discovers its imprint on a sheet of paper, allowing him to track down the one Swiss scientist Moriarty hasn't murdered. Much of this is only viable within the generic verisimilitude provided by the textual world of the B-thriller, not least the presence of four Swiss scientists in London at the same time, to which textual reality the narrative and setting also contribute, particularly Moriarty's stronghold, with its soundproofing, unbreakable glass, and secret escape route, which also conveniently has its own hospital to allow Moriarty to act on Holmes' proposal that the most ingenious way to kill a man is to drain him of his blood. Such things are not only creations of the B-thriller because there are also resonances with the radio or B-action serial not only when Holmes is placed in perilous situations that require others to race to his rescue on two occasions, but also in the use of ingenious ideas such as the luminous paint dripping from Moriarty's car to provide a trail for Watson and Lestrade to follow in order to save Holmes from being drained of his blood. The B-Movie forms also extend to the representation of Moriarty, not only in his mutability as an all-encompassing villain who shifts from calculating criminal mastermind to cold-hearted killer to mad scientist (as when he taunts Holmes over the last drops of blood leaving his body), but also in the way he is represented as being driven by financial gain, not by ideology, to simplify character motivation. The film therefore loses much of the focus on the egalitarian discourses and wartime ideology that had been developed in *Sherlock Holmes and the Voice of Terror* and becomes more clearly B-Movie entertainment which doesn't need its wartime setting to generate the spy-chasing narrative.

Much of this is down to the generic confusion of the B-thriller which mixes espionage and whodunnit forms simply to ensure different ways of providing suspense, action and thrills. The film, for example, begins in espionage mode with the spiriting of Tobel to England by means of a stratagem involving decoys, disguise and diversions and maintains this style in Tobel's mysterious assignation with Charlotte, only incorporating whodunnit principles once Tobel has disappeared and Holmes has taken up the detection. Even here, however, his actions are inflected with espionage connotations, particularly his cracking of 'The Dancing Men' code, even if it is drawn from a Holmes story of the same title. This generic confusion is all part of the strategy used by the B-Movie to deploy multiple forms of material to fill the plot and to hold back its resolution. For example, Holmes' confinement in a chest with a false bottom is motivated more by requirements to provide suspense and danger in the action-thriller mode than it is by the classical detective story, for which it acts as a delay. Because the film is also of the espionage mode, this sequence is naturalised within its generic conventions, as are many of the other moments of cinematic vaudeville because of the multiple generic parameters within which the film operates. Such is the case with Holmes' impersonations of a Swiss bookseller, a lascar and a Swiss scientist, which are motivated by both the Holmesian detection and espionage modes. The use of disguise is also, however, one of the most overtly vaudevillian elements in the 'Sherlock Holmes' films, not least because it becomes unclear whether the spectacle is of Holmes in disguise or Rathbone's performance of the character that Holmes has adopted, especially in the first impersonation in which Rathbone plays Holmes playing a Swiss bookseller at the same time that Holmes the bookseller is playing a Nazi spy, which of course is also Rathbone.

The generic confusion of *Sherlock Holmes and the Secret Weapon* is multiplied in *Sherlock Holmes in Washington* (1943) which not only offers espionage and detective modes, but also comedy and the B-thriller again as well as Hitchcockian suspense and police procedural forms. Many of the codes from different genres overlap, however, because while a body wrapped in a carpet and another nick-of-time rescue for Holmes are primarily associated with the B-thriller, the use of hidden intercoms (in antique vases) and the secret hideout of the Nazi agent, Hinkle, behind the front of an antiques shop can be found in both the B-thriller and the espionage films. Codes from espionage films can also be found in the suspense thriller, which is also on show in the enemy agent who is an upright member of society, in the Hitchcockian device of passing a match book containing microfilm from one person to another at a party (and through the hands of the British official who should have delivered it to Washington) in a cinematic version of 'Find the Lady', and in Holmes' 'false' MacGuffin when he leads Hinkle to believe the microfilm is concealed under a stamp on a letter which he then exchanges for the matchbook that Hinkle has had, without realising it, since his abduction of Nancy. The relationships between genres are complex in *Sherlock Holmes in Washington* and the whodunnit element within the film almost becomes lost among the compendium of multiple and overlapping crime fiction forms that are deployed, particularly the espionage motifs and procedural forms of detection that drive the narrative. In its first phase, the film offers espionage as its form in following the British agent Pettibone (travelling as a lawyer called Grayson), who is carrying some secret plans on microfilm to the United States. He is abducted before he can deliver them, but in the crowded club-car of a train between New York and Washington he transfers the microfilm concealed in a match-book into the purse of a Washington socialite, Nancy Partridge, under the noses of the Nazi agents before they overpower him.

The rest of the film follows Holmes as he investigates the missing plans, but although there are moments of deduction typical of the ratiocination of the classical detective, as when he asks an FBI agent how many of the people on the club car have been assaulted (having inferred that the Nazis will visit each one until they discover who has the plans), the detection has a scientific basis that derives from the procedural form. This includes Holmes' examination of Pettibone's rooms in London, his examination of the club-car, his discovery of a sliver of wood from an antique chair in the blanket that wrapped Pettibone's body, and the legwork applied by Holmes and Watson when they do the rounds of the antique shops in Washington to find the Nazis' secret headquarters. Deductive investigation is replaced by the 'method' of scientific procedure, so that Holmes' examination of the club-car is narrative padding because the police reports have already provided the information he needs. The club-car sequence has most significance in providing a propagandistic moment when the steward, an African-American, proudly announces that his son is going to be an Air Force pilot in order to show American democracy in action, even though in the segregated American military of the 1940s this is more probably ideological wish-fulfilment. Much of the narrative, however, is simply cinematic vaudeville, provided not only by comedy deriving from the incongruities of Watson trying to be American (chewing gum, drinking ice-cream sodas or speaking American slang), but also by the pastiche of genres which provide different kinds of narrative entertainment, within which even the traditional Holmesian disguise appropriate to his brand of detection (this time as an eccentric art-collector) is played by Rathbone more for its humour, even if it is also narratively motivated to allow him to get into the secret areas of the Nazi headquarters. The use of pastiche, however, prepares the way for the diffusion of detective codes by an array of different styles in the later films because, as in *Sherlock Holmes in Washington*, it is the entertainment provided by the thriller narratives and the vaudeville of generic intrusions that becomes paramount.

Gothic mysteries and closed circles

The Gothic mysteries in the 'Sherlock Holmes' series develop outside of the wartime settings of the propaganda films, taking place in Holmes and Watson's 'own ahistorical time zone' (Field, 2009: 154), even though the first of these Gothic stories, *Sherlock Holmes Faces Death* (1943), is set in Musgrave Manor, an ancestral home being used as a sanatorium for convalescent officers, where the mystery begins with the apparent stabbing of Sexton, a doctor helping Watson. The narrative proceeds through the murders of the two Musgrave brothers, Geoffrey and Phillip, and the butler, Brunton, after the arrival of Holmes at Watson's request, before revealing that Sexton is the murderer and that his crimes are motivated by his discovery of an ancient document granting the Musgraves great wealth through land which he hopes to claim on marrying Sally Musgrave. This first film after the spy-catcher movies continues the diffusion of genres found in *Sherlock Holmes in Washington* by returning to the Gothic motifs of Fox's *The Hound of the Baskervilles*, although it also embeds Holmes' ratiocinative deductions more clearly within the detection narrative. Despite some implicit references to Anglo-American relations, through Sally's romance with an American officer accused of the murder of Geoffrey Musgrave, and Holmes' protection of both ideological and romantic relations in taking up the investigation to prove the latter innocent, the wartime setting is 'incidental' (Field, 2009: 150). The film opens in a local pub where the landlord is prompted to speak of the suspicious and unnatural happenings at Musgrave Manor before the scene shifts to the gates and house of the manor, where wind whips up the undergrowth and the landlord, in voiceover, mentions 'corpse lights' in the greenhouse and 'wailing, like lost souls, in the lime walk' to emphasise Gothic tropes. As the images show the interior, suits of armour are picked out to suggest a concern not only with history, but also with history as a place of repressed horrors, a motif developed when Watson appears and converses with Brunton about the ghosts that inhabit the manor in a room evoking these spirits because of the smoke billowing from a backdraft in the fireplace.

Gothic imagery is developed to parodic excess when the windows blow open, when Brunton picks up a black cat and when the clock strikes thirteen, but immediately the scene moves to London, which stock footage shows as a sunny place to both dispel the darkness of Musgrave Manor and to create a metonym for Holmes as the person who will bring enlightenment to Gothic darkness. Although Gothic and supernatural tropes re-enter the film, during Holmes' arrival in darkness with the wind gusting about the manor once more, as well as in the body in the hidden crypt and in the storm that sends lightning to strike a suit of armour when Sally is reciting the Musgrave Ritual, these are moments of parodic playfulness to enliven the narrative with thrilling suspense. Unlike *The Scarlet Claw* there is no debate between science and the supernatural and the narrative is solidly based on detection, which is signalled when Holmes arrives at the manor and, ignoring the Gothic motifs swirling around him, he immediately deduces something mysterious about a pile of leaves and produces the empirical fact of Geoffrey Musgrave's body beneath it. Holmes' role is to visually dispel the supernatural and he often achieves this merely by his presence as, for example, in a scene in which Watson plays caring father to Sally, which firmly places Holmes at the centre of matters. A lengthy shot holds him in focus as he scrutinises Watson and Sally, who are talking offscreen, and then, when they are onscreen, he is still there in the corner of a mirror to not only suggest his offscreen presence and apparent watchful omniscience, but also to display and privilege the invisible processes of his logical detection. His deductions are also, however, put on show as visualised routines that contribute to the film's entertainment, as with the chess-board sequence in which the Musgrave Ritual is revealed to be a cipher rather than a curse through its playing out on the chess-board of the hall floor using the characters as pieces. While such deductive routines are diffused among comedy (Watson being distracted while on watch or Lestrade becoming trapped in the secret passages) and Gothic routines (the reciting of the Musgrave Ritual), detection still triumphs over Gothic principles in visual form by subordinating the latter to the former in sequences such as Holmes' discovery of Geoffrey's body, the chess-board scene, and the pursuit of the raven to find Philip's body in the rumble-seat of Sally's car.

The Scarlet Claw (1944) offers another pastiche of generic conventions by deploying the Gothic address alongside the detection narrative, although the former is more inflected by the horror created by Ramson's criminal activity than by the supernatural motifs that pervade the film. Supernatural images are dressing for the narrative to provide a chilling atmosphere and even though the film is premised on an opposition in which rationality and logic triumph over the supernatural, the film effectively dispenses with this textual discourse when Lord Penrose, the representative of the supernatural within the signifying structure of the film, disappears from the plot after he has provided Holmes with the information that points only in the direction of human agency in the murder of his wife.[6] By this time, the film has already become a detective suspense thriller with Gothic undertones, although the pleasure the film takes in setting out its supernatural and Gothic signifiers (misty marshes and graveyards, dark streets, a rotting hotel that signifies the moral decay of its occupant, Ramson, and eerily tolling church bells), and the use of language to describe them ('ghosts and monsters' or 'goblins'), also helps to provide complementary and appropriate images for the activities of the murderer Ramson, an actor whose ability to not only impersonate others but also to outfox Holmes is presented as being uncanny as he sets about taking revenge for his rejection by Lady Penrose. The fear he continues to spread even after his identity is learnt halfway though the film creates an invisible threat that is similar to that of the ghostly monster he mimics, but because his current identity as Potts the meek postman integrates him into the community even while his murders make him an outsider, he is uncanny in the Freudian sense of being simultaneously *heimlich* (homely) and *unheimlich* (unhomely).

Much has been made of the film's resonances with Expressionist style (Field, 2009: 163–8), and although some of the shooting in this regard has more to do with the B-Movie's economy of composition to allow for multiple pieces of visual information to be conveyed in one shot,[7] nevertheless the use of such modes of visual expression are still present. They either serve as misdirection pointing toward a supernatural explanation of events or complement the connotations of the uncanny that surround Ramson as a ghost moving through La Morte Rouge as a member of the community in the form of Potts and Tanner. Through such visualisations, Ramson becomes a force of un-nature, outside the bounds of legitimate society, his murder of Marie Journet a sign of his abnormality because she is a sign of innocence in the film. Even though Marie's murder is unseen, Holmes' deduction that her murderer was someone well known to her further enacts the *unheimlich* or uncanny nature of Ramson in disguising himself beneath the homeliness of the friend, in this case Potts the meek postman, whose very name suggests the homely, but who, as Ramson beneath, transforms the friend into the stranger and the homely into the unhomely, as he does in his use of a garden weeder as a murder weapon that replicates the ripping of throats by a wild animal. The community of La Morte Rouge has similar iconographies, its name (and the origin) suggesting unnatural deeds and motives, although its visualisation is fractured between the nostalgic and cosy and the uncanny or strange. Cosiness is represented by Journet's hotel where the check tablecloths, roaring fire and stove connote pleasant comfort on many occasions. The village draws on other less homely iconographies, such as the Gothicism of the church, misty marshes and Penrose Manor, while the setting of Journet's hotel also draws on frontier imagery in order to suggest that La Morte Rouge is in the deepest wilderness despite the twinkling lights of its introduction and the fact that it is only twelve miles from Quebec in order to place the community as an outpost outside society both historically and spatially.

Within this, Holmes also plays a part because his rational deduction is treated as incongruous within the world of the supernatural that the villagers live by, with the result that he becomes an unhomely presence in the community. While Watson is associated with the homely, Holmes is, like Ramson, an outsider, so that when Watson shares a celebratory drink with Thompson, Holmes breaks into Penrose Manor as an intruder in search of evidence. The conventional form of the series (in which Watson's comic interludes provide interruptions to Holmes' detection) is overturned because the cinematic vaudeville of the former is integrated into the film by providing comforting and cosy familiarity, through, for example, the repetition of Watson falling into a bog, which is not only an expected and fitting occurrence for Bruce's Watson, but also reassuring in its iteration. Holmes, on the other hand, is a rather unsettling figure in *The Scarlet Claw*, the calm composure of the previous films replaced by an unscrupulous and supercilious persona, so that he not only resorts to house-breaking, but also demonstrates a smiling condescension to Lord Penrose because of his belief in the supernatural and shows more sarcasm in his treatment of Watson. Although Holmes is on the side of law and rationality in opposition to Ramson's criminal insanity, he creeps around the village in the same way or sneaks off to the marshes to witness the glowing figure who acts as his double. His ambiguous status is signified by two moments, one when he finds Journet hiding at Brisson's and he stands in a column of light apparently cast through the doorway with darkness on either side, joined with Journet, who is shortly to commit a revenge-killing himself, as a figure of light *and* dark, and the other when he and Ramson are shown to be doppelgangers when they remove each others' fake moustaches in the final scene in the marsh, establishing their similarity as they reveal the true identities underneath their disguises of Journet and Potts.

The last of the Gothic films in the series, *The House of Fear* (1945) offers a more comfortable landscape, even if, like *Sherlock Holmes Faces Death*, it is set in an isolated ancestral manor. The film also provides a more playful approach in its mobilisation of Gothic signifiers despite the gruesomeness of the reported crimes (a car plunging over a cliff, incineration in a furnace, a body destroyed by an explosion, and another whose body is discovered without head or limbs), as each member of a club of middle-aged men called The Good Comrades is apparently killed after receiving an envelope of orange pips as a warning of their impending doom. However, this is visual trickery using obtrusive Gothic cinematic effects as misinformation while also deploying such signifiers to complement both the fraud played by the Good Comrades in faking their deaths and the mystifications provided by the narrative. *The House of Fear* is more like a house of mirrors, whose inward-looking involutions become apparent late on when Watson, left to his own devices in Drearcliff House, is subjected to the kinds of Gothic psychological torture typical of thrillers in which human agents inflict on their victims inexplicable and apparently supernatural occurrences in order to induce insanity. Some of the frights in this sequence, as Watson goes looking for two characters who have apparently disappeared from their rooms (Merrivale and Alastair), are the result of machinations of the Comrades (a door slamming shut apparently on its own, a French window suddenly coming open, the rapping of the door knocker and a mysterious figure hiding behind some curtains), but the shadowy light, stormy night, appearance of a cat and the whistling wind are beyond the Comrades' control because they are matters of editing, mise-en-scène and camerawork. The visual style of the film's presentation of the ghost story creates narrative misdirection much in the same way that the Comrades use the signs of the ghost story to confuse Watson and the devices of the whodunnit to try to confuse Holmes, thereby, however, providing the mystification he needs to construct a narrative of detection which ultimately brings them to justice.

The House of Fear is the last of the Gothic-inflected mysteries in the series, perhaps because, in taking the visual and narrative signs of this format to parodic extreme, it reveals that the film is merely a cinematic vaudeville of mystifications and diversions. The film, however, can be seen to be the perfect incarnation of the B-Movie murder mystery because it also reveals that interludes and textual divagations between the crime and solution are the basis of the murder mystery, not only because there is no murder to set off the investigation in the first place but also because the narrative of investigation is created out of distractions that are precisely designed to conceal that no murder has occurred. Those films in the remainder of the series that have more of a basis in the whodunnit format, *Pursuit to Algiers* (1945) and *Terror by Night* (1946), are like *The House of Fear,* films that focus on hermeneutic activity within closed circles and enclosed spaces, although unlike the Gothic inflected whodunnits they avoid rural settings in being set aboard a cruise ship and a train, respectively. They are also very much programmer material, with the former offering a suspense thriller following various shipboard attempts on the life of the fictional King of Rovenia, interspersed with musical numbers, red herrings about the unrelated theft of some jewels (a case that Holmes almost incidentally solves along the way) and Watson's comic interludes, while the latter is a more conventional murder mystery involving the theft of another fabulous jewel (the Star of Rhodesia) set within the cosy confines of a couple of train carriages. *Pursuit to Algiers* shares some of *The House of Fear*'s playful narrative of distractions by providing misdirection in the form of a night-club singer with a secret and two archaeologists whose half-heard conversations suggest that they are the secret agents trying to kill the King of Rovenia, but the narrative mainly derives from the B-Movie thriller as Holmes thwarts a gang of assassins before being overpowered and apparently defeated at the end in order to provide some suspense in a routine plot.

Terror by Night makes more use of comic distractions than *Pursuit to Algiers*, as well as using some action stunts (a brawl and Holmes hanging from the train), having to do so to delay the investigation in order to provide a sufficient narrative to fill the running-time. Watson's humorous interlude with a middle-aged couple who confess when he questions them, albeit only to the crime of a stolen teapot rather than the murder he has been set to solve by Holmes, is particularly notable in this regard because it provides a crucial postponement of the search of the baggage-car which at that moment (less than halfway through the film) would reveal the secret assassin and bring the narrative towards conclusion.

Despite the emphasis on Watson in comic mode, *Terror by Night* is more conventionally within the whodunnit as signified by its setting, which not only allows for shots of close-knit groups, for suspects to wander past compartment windows and for cuts or pans from one suspicious character to another, but also gathers the suspects close by and allows the narrative and investigation to move quickly because there is no need for establishing shots of new locations. The film is of most interest, however, in putting on display class relations more overtly than in the previous films in the series. Despite lauding democracy in the propaganda films, Lestrade had previously been shown as a working-class fool, but here, although he is still subject to lampooning for his stolid incomprehension, he becomes more of a partner to Holmes even while the film lays bare the hierarchical relationship between the pair. This is partly because Watson enters a temporary partnership with his 'old friend', Major Duncan-Bleek (Sebastian Moran in disguise), which in itself points to concerns with class as the pair cosy up in their world of privilege, leaving Holmes and Lestrade to form a new partnership. The new partnerships generate a set of contrasts and oppositions because while Holmes uses Lestrade as a foil so that he has the same function as Watson in previous films, Moran manipulates Watson so he can be used as a decoy to divert attention from his crimes. The relationship between Holmes and Lestrade more clearly reveals that Lestrade is in a subservient role, something that is emphasised after the murder of Carstairs and the apparent theft of the Star of Rhodesia. First of all, Lestrade is shown eating in the compartment next door and although his presence here is needed in order for him to overhear suspicious noises, the film also draws attention to the fact that he is a working-class man unable to afford the luxury of eating in the dining-car where Holmes and Watson have their meal. Although this may appear incidental, when Holmes arrives he immediately takes charge and Lestrade, now outside his jurisdiction, has to defer to him, after which Duncan-Bleek and Watson arrive to emphasise Lestrade's inferior status by excluding him from their world of privilege. The film, however, allows Lestrade a moment of triumph because, although it is Holmes who exposes and detains Moran, he is the one who, by his own efforts, detains the fake police serving as Moran's henchmen.

The Spider Woman and other arch-villains

The other major strand in the later 'Sherlock Holmes' films has very little to do with the whodunnit because the mystery is less about the identity of the villains than about the suspense created by the battle of wills between Holmes and the criminal arch-villains he encounters. The films have *noir* inflections, although they still use the 'day for night' techniques that were usual before film noir's substitution of 'night for night' shooting (Palmer, 1991: 144), but these discourses are ambiguous or indicate only a nascent incarnation of the style. However, ideologically and narratively, the 'Spider Woman' films do have tropes associated with *noir*, even if, as Field notes (2009: 186–7), the representation of the *femme fatale* in the series lacks the sexualised criminality that frames her ideologically in *film noir* as a deviant woman outside official heterosexual and economic discourses. The female criminals in the 'Spider Woman' films do nevertheless live according to an economy of desire associated with the *femme fatale*, although because they are more like the vamp (or female sexual vampire) in their articulation, the 'Spider Women' are involved in murder in order to fulfil the economic desire that feeds their penchant for a life of luxury. This is most obvious in the figure of Lydia Marlowe in *The Woman in Green* (1945) who, though not involved directly in the killing of young women, is nevertheless complicit with the framing of wealthy members of society in order to earn money by blackmail, thereby feeding her desire for wealth and consumption not only by destroying the lives of young women but also by feeding parasitically off Moriarty and Dr Simnel who organise and perpetrate the murders. Within this more urban and modern world, Holmes also begins to look more like the figure of the private eye of the investigative thriller analysed by Frank Krutnik, who 'proves himself by his ability to withstand any challenges to his integrity – and to his very status as the active hero' (1991: 92–3). Thus, where, in the Gothic films, Holmes' figuration is designed to guarantee the rationality of modernity against the superstitions and corruptions associated with the past, in the 'Spider Woman' or criminal vamp films, he polices the morality of money and sexuality.

It is less his own masculinity that he upholds than masculine dominance of economic and sexual relations by, for example, removing Adrea Spedding's destructive femininity from society in *Spider Woman* (1944) or by reining in the feminising influence she and Hilda Courtney, in *Dressed to Kill* (1946), represent through their reduction of the men in their gangs to subservience. In this regard, Holmes is very like hardboiled or *film noir* heroes such as Sam Spade in *The Maltese Falcon* or the insurance investigator, Riordan, in *The Killers*, who eliminate the threats to masculine power posed by women. Holmes as an active hero is tested within the criminal vamp films by being put in tight corners from which he escapes by his ingenuity or strength of will in order to confirm his masculine authority. While the 'close shaves' that Holmes survives are part of the narrative dynamics of the thriller, they also symbolise the male hero's resolute will and refusal to submit. In escaping the fairground shooting gallery in *Spider Woman*, or resisting Lydia Marlowe's hypnotism in *The Woman in Green* or escaping the elaborate set-up by which he is suspended from a beam in a garage filling with poisonous fumes in *Dressed to Kill*, Holmes not only escapes death, but also submission to female will. Noteworthy in these desperate predicaments is Holmes' skipping dance along the ledge of a balcony several storeys up in *The Woman in Green* to prove that Lydia Marlowe hasn't forced him to her will, an act of male bravado that Moriarty is unable to replicate when he falls to his death as he seeks to escape by jumping from the same ledge. Holmes' escape from being shot by Watson as he is bound behind a target in *Spider Woman* is also significant because it represents Holmes' rescue not only of himself, but also of Watson, who would have been reduced to condition of one of Adrea's stooges without being aware of it had he killed Holmes. The insidious quality of the machinations of the criminal vamp does align therefore with the *femme fatale* of *film noir*, even if there are variations within this format so that, as Steinbrunner and Michaels point out, Adrea Spedding is more like the '*femme fatale* of the old-fashioned gothic romance' (1978: 118) in the 'feline' cruelty Holmes attributes to her in naming her a 'female Moriarty'.

The Spider Woman causes fear and anxiety within masculine society, most notably in *The Woman in Green* where the murders of young woman (albeit not by Lydia Marlowe's hands) for the purpose of blackmailing wealthy members of legitimate society not only poses a threat to masculine economic control, but also to the official sexual order. Lydia Marlowe may be a sexualised figure but she is represented as someone outside of sexual and reproductive relationships because she is part of a scheme that destroys women within the reproductive order, although this is further complicated by the representation of female victims as child-like in their description as 'young slips'. Lydia Marlowe represents a deviant sexuality that is not only sterile, because she has directed her sexual drives towards the acquisition of money, but also 'unnatural' because she preys on women who are represented as 'children'. Adrea Spedding's perverse sexuality is represented more by the implication of an incestuous relationship with her half-brother, Norman. Although she is primarily shown as a cold schemer, her introduction, following a fade from Holmes and Watson discussing the 'pyjama murders', not only identifies her as the criminal mind behind the crimes, when the announcement planted in the newspaper by Holmes finds its target as she reads it, but also visualises her perverse relationship with Norman. Field (2009: 195) has read this scene as a mirroring of the power relations between Holmes and Watson, but the reclining pose of Adrea as Norman leans in to pass across a lit cigarette, a code in classical Hollywood cinema either that sexual relations have occurred between the couple exchanging the cigarette or that sexual desire is present in the giver,[8] suggests a refusal of authorised sexual relations in favour of those not sanctioned by society, not least because in accepting the cigarette Adrea indicates that she reciprocates her half-brother's desires. Not all of the criminal vamps are phallic controlling women like Adrea, however, and Naomi Drake in *The Pearl of Death* (1944) is more like a maid-servant to the criminal mastermind, Giles Conover, her subservience guaranteed by the fear of being made subject to the desirous attentions of the Hoxton Creeper. Similarly, Hilda Courtney in *Dressed to Kill* is a reluctant criminal vamp initially, chastising her chauffeur, Hamid, for needlessly killing Julian 'Stinky' Emery, although by the end of the film she is less squeamish and orders the death of Holmes as a smiling aristocratic assassin even if, like the other criminal masterminds, she never dirties her hands with the act of murder, but uses a henchman, Hamid, for the deed.

The variety and multivalency of meanings attached to the female villains in the criminal vamp films suggests that it is the B-Movie's pastiche of style that drives their representation in grabbing at any potentially useful textual tropes to vary the formula. This is also the case in the deployment of crime narratives because the plots of these films are derived less from *film noir* than from the cinematic suspense mode in its B-Movie incarnations. The last of the series, *Dressed to Kill* (1946), is a fairly simple MacGuffin movie with musical boxes, offering a lot of static talky scenes, varied by use of camera angles, so that it is in some ways most like a Conan Doyle story although it is also the most padded and flat of the narratives. The other criminal vamp films have more complex narratives, although in each case the criminals are identified early on so there is no murder mystery according to the whodunnit format even if there is mystery with regard to motives or the narrative destination of the criminals' desires in their search for an object. The first of these films, *Spider Woman*, identifies Adrea Spedding as the arch-villain very quickly and the mystery in the film is provided by the method used to commit the murders. Even this is solved before the narrative is half finished because after Holmes sets himself up as a decoy, he discovers very quickly that the spiders used in the 'pyjama murders' are dropped onto sleeping men who then, made insane by the poison, leap from windows to their deaths. The narrative is a series of set-piece episodes, very like a vaudeville bill, in which Holmes fakes his death, visits Adrea in disguise, receives a visit from Adrea in which she tries to kill him with toxic fumes from a candy wrapper activated by fire, takes a trip with Watson to see an expert called Ordway, and finds his way to the fairground, within which is a further set-piece involving Watson unknowingly firing at Holmes tied to the back of one of the targets at the shooting gallery.

This produces a certain lack of fluidity that betrays the film's B-Movie production as does the B-thriller roof-top shoot-out with one of Adrea's henchman after Holmes has discovered the means by which the victims are poisoned. Such tropes also depict Holmes as an active detective hero of the hard-boiled or *noir* mode, in the same way that his entrapment and evasion of death in the shooting gallery add suspense motifs characteristic of the action serial. Even the whodunnit aspects of the film involve uncomplicated B-Movie deductions because they are clearly put on show for the audience, such as the dolls that lead Holmes to the trap Adrea has set for him at the fairground or the partially burnt journal discovered at Ordway's which reveals exactly the information needed at the right time, even if this sequence also offers some complexity in the process of deduction in Holmes' use of Latin to unmask the impostor disguised as Ordway. Nevertheless, the use of the obvious clue of the partially burnt journal helps to display the simple linear relations of the B-Movie format in which cause immediately leads to effect. The whodunnit form is therefore rather marginalised among the other modes of criminal narrative that are deployed. In addition to the vamp, *noir* and suspense forms, these include tropes of the criminal mastermind format, in which the tension is created not by mystery but by the battle of wills between Holmes and Adrea Spedding as the pair engage in an ideological, as well as a criminal struggle over whose values will dominate society: Holmes' upright and active masculinity or Adrea's murderous femininity and perverse sexuality. This also brings the film closer to the ideology of *film noir*, even if the pastiche of criminal genres and the comic interludes involving Watson (such as the misnaming of a scientist called Gilflower) and Lestrade (after Holmes returns from the dead as a postman) serve to divert the film away from the more sinister aspects of the genre to turn it into merely an entertainment.

The film does, however, present a series of motifs relating to disguises and decoys that is interesting with regard to the textual privileging of masculine ideology. Field (2009: 194–6) has noted that the film is permeated by images of mirrors, in which Holmes and Adrea, for example, reflect each other in their use of disguises, but the use of fakes, deceptions and impostors that is prevalent in *Spider Woman* suggests a deeper concern with the nature of reality. Not only do Holmes and Adrea adopt disguises, but so too does one of Adrea's henchmen when he becomes an impostor for the dead Ordway, while the young boy Adrea brings round to Baker Street to confuse Holmes and divert him away from the use of the pygmy is also a deception that uses a form of imposture. Similarly, the dummy Holmes uses when he sets a trap for Adrea's murderous henchmen is a decoy, as well as being a form of disguise, while even Latin becomes part of the process, albeit as a benign imposture, when Holmes asks the fake Ordway if he has a variety of spider called the *mendex flagrante* ('flagrant liar') in order to trick him into displaying his ignorance and so uncover the truth of the disguise. The use of Latin in this case suggests hidden truths that not only exist beneath surface appearances, but which also aid in the revelation of the deceptions of the surface. An interesting involution with regard to the matter of appearance and disguise occurs when Adrea visits Holmes with the small child. In this scene, Adrea appears as Adrea Spedding, but pretends not only to be someone other than the woman Holmes has already met, but also acts as if she has never encountered Holmes before. In the matter of identities, she is being truthful, not only in appearing as herself, but also in asking Holmes to search for the Indian lancer whose persona Holmes created in order to meet her initially. However, Adrea is also in disguise in this scene, in the persona of 'Adrea Spedding', her real self, thereby creating problematised relationships between reality and deception that are in keeping with *noir* discourses of both the uncertainty of female identity and the shifting signifiers of reality. Although Holmes ultimately delivers Adrea to justice and returns truth to reality, he does so not through hermeneutic activity and the power of rationality, but through his ability to dominate as an active hero by overcoming her attempts to render him passive or feminine through captivity.

The concern with reality and concealment is developed in *The Pearl of Death* (1944), which is separated from *Spider Woman* by *The Scarlet Claw*, but in this case there is a return to hermeneutic activity to overcome the criminal mastermind. There are still nevertheless important moments when Holmes becomes an active hero, notably in the willpower he exercises to defeat the terrifying figure of 'The Creeper' and in the film's struggle of masculine intellects as he engages in a battle of wills with Giles Conover. The film, like *Dressed to Kill*, involves a MacGuffin-inspired search and, like *Spider Woman,* reveals its arch-villain very early, although mystery is generated by the attempt to discover the identity of the henchman performing the murders ('The Creeper') and the reason for the murders (a stolen pearl hidden in one of six plaster busts of Napoleon). As *Spider Woman* substituted the narrative subterfuge of imposture and deception for an overarching mystery, *The Pearl of Death* uses the motif of the 'secret cargo' for the same purpose, most obviously in the narrative of the search for the pearl, in which even the busts that are empty of the treasure act as secret cargoes because they conceal that they are not the right bust. Some uses of the 'secret cargo' motif (hidden compartments in a suitcase and Naomi Drake's camera) allow Naomi and Holmes to exercise their cunning or ingenuity in relieving owner and thief, respectively, of their cargo, but others seem merely to complement the overall motif. This is the case with the soup-plate carrying its secret cargo of a message from Conover to Naomi or the hollowed out copy of Johnson's *Dictionary* with a knife-trap concealed inside, while Watson's mouth serves as an unexpected and comic use of the motif when it conceals the Borgia pearl. Of more importance is the suggestion that the arch-villain, Conover, is a secret cargo because, according to Holmes, he 'pervades Europe like a plague' although no-one has heard of him, while the pearl itself carries a 'blood-stained history' within it.

These conundrums are incidental to the plot in many ways, although they offer a veneer of complexity to conceal the fact that the narrative is all delay and digression until the second killing reveals a pattern to prompt a meaningful narrative of detection. This investigation reveals that earlier events have a place in the mystery narrative, but much of the film is nevertheless a cinematic vaudeville of visual bluff and diversion. Naomi Drake is most significant in the first part, her shifting disguises (from fur-coated *femme fatale* to dish-washer and match-seller), providing a series of bluffs to suggest that she is a vampish figure like Adrea Spedding. However, the visual signifiers that make her look like a criminal vamp are secret cargoes of a sort, concealing that she is just another servant of Conover's, rather than a prime mover of the narrative, thereby diverting attention away from her role as narrative diversion to help delay both the search for the pearl and the appearance of The Creeper. Narrative diversions also occur in comic interludes involving Watson and Lestrade and in the suspense provided by the knife-trap and an attempt on Holmes' life, which generate B-Movie distractions to divert the audience away from the lack of detection other than Holmes' supposition over the involvement of the Hoxton Creeper. The film masquerades as a whodunnit, which could also be said to be a secret cargo concealing the fact that the film is a MacGuffin movie within a B-Movie pastiche of genres that also includes horror (when The Creeper finally appears, albeit initially in silhouette and shadow to heighten the tension) and further action elements in the confrontation of masculine intellects as Holmes, once more the active hero, defeats Conover.

The Woman in Green begins with a signally different sense of confusion and fear in its depiction of Holmes' perplexity over the horrors of the murders of young women who have a finger removed to provide a souvenir for the murderer. The film has a more stylised mode of shooting than other films in the series, using gradations of light and dark and high and low angle shots to unsettle the familiar Holmesian world so that, for example, when Holmes is first shown, descending the stairs in 221B Baker Street, the low angle shot makes it appear as if he is in an entirely different and disquieting textual reality. This stark and disconcerting style acts as a visual metonymy for the narrative of serial killing performed simply for the purpose of blackmail, in which wealthy middle-aged men such as Sir George Fenwick are hypnotised and then framed for the killing of young women, a cruel plot because it treats the women instrumentally as disposable commodities whose dead bodies can be exchanged for money, but also devious (even perverse) in the way it appears to show a fracturing of masculine structures of power by simulating the murder of society's 'daughters' by the father figures who ideologically should be their protectors. The disordering of society centres on Lydia Marlowe and in particular the bowl of water she uses to hypnotise the blackmail victims so that the film's unbalanced composition emanates from her, even though Moriarty is implied to be the plot's mastermind. A high angle shot from behind Lydia and Fenwick looking down into the bowl of water which is the centre of her power as she hypnotises him demonstrates her role as focus for the film's visual style, the effects of which turn Fenwick into a *noir* victim with no memory once she has exercised her dominance to upend masculine forms of authority, the bowl of water acting not only as a visual signifier of this inversion, but seemingly creating it in reflecting Lydia's willpower.

Holmes' role in the film is to overcome his bewilderment and revulsion at the horror of the crimes and to exercise male rationality and activity in trapping Lydia Marlowe to return legitimacy to masculine authority and to remove the scandal that attaches to it. Initially, Holmes is so baffled by the seemingly unnatural crimes that he is unable to exercise ratiocination, to the point of claiming 'brains, I haven't any', although soon after he is provided with the opportunity to affirm his brilliance when Maude Fenwick arrives to ask for his help and he analyses her and her situation (the car following her), before she has entered his rooms. His diagnostic skills are further mobilised when he interprets the scene of Fenwick's death, after which he is in his stride as he deduces that Moriarty is behind the scheme, although when the arch-villain visits him to begin their battle of wills, his deduction is rendered superfluous. It is, however, the attempt on his life by a hypnotised ex-soldier, another example of Lydia's aberrance as she transforms an ideological protector of home and polity into a murderous puppet for her own devices, that sets Holmes on the path of the true detection as he follows her trail, because Moriarty, although ostensibly the mastermind, is actually a form of mystification who conceals Lydia's control of events. Significantly, Lydia isn't named until the scheme has been fully revealed late on to signify that she is the secret arch-villain hiding behind Moriarty and Simnel the murderer. However, after Holmes has tracked her down at the Mesmer Club and Watson has offered a comic interlude by submitting to hypnotism after mocking it, Moriarty takes control once Lydia has seemingly hypnotised Holmes. Neither Moriarty nor Lydia are in charge because Holmes' hypnotised state is a simulation and, once Watson and the police arrive, he skips along a narrow ledge to both demonstrate an end to his perplexity and to establish his overall control of affairs. Although there were three further 'Sherlock Holmes' films (*Pursuit to Algiers, Terror by Night* and *Dressed to Kill*), the series might more appropriately have concluded here. At the end of the film, Holmes restores himself to omniscience and society to masculine order, sees Moriarty fall to another death and then encapsulates his role, in the film and the series as a whole, when his all-seeing gaze is literalised as he looks down on London to announce to Watson that the pair are guardians of the city.

5
Ordering the World: The Uncompromising Logic of Charlie Chan and Mr Moto

Detective series involving Asian detectives were very popular in Hollywood in the 1930s and 1940s and, indeed, the most prolific of the Hollywood detective crime series in this period was the 'Charlie Chan' series, which produced 44 films between 1931 and 1949, after two early silent films and then one sound film, *Behind That Curtain* (1929), in which Chan, played by E. L. Park, an actor of Korean extraction, appeared as a minor character. The series starred three different non-Asian actors in the main role, Warner Oland, Sidney Toler and Roland Winters, initially at Fox (Twentieth Century Fox from the end of 1935) and then at the Poverty Row studio Monogram after Toler acquired the rights to the character. The first 'Charlie Chan' films preceded the creation of B-units and were made as 'A-class productions' (Hardy, 1997: 76), with only one film being made each year until they entered B-production in 1934 when the output was increased to three or four films a year. The 'Mr Moto' and 'Mr Wong' films were both produced as Bs, the former at Twentieth Century Fox alongside Charlie Chan and the latter at Monogram where Mr Wong helped to provide the later 'Charlie Chan' films with some of its stories. All three detectives are coded in terms of Asian values, but they also enunciate Western values to control or contain their 'otherness' and this, along with their portrayal by Western actors, produces tensions with regard to both ethnicity and cultural representation. The portrayals of Charlie Chan, Mr Moto and, in part, Mr Wong are further complicated because they are often used to mediate and order a confusing world to provide understanding in accord with Western and American ideology, but they are problematic figures for the United States to incorporate into its own system of values because of both their ethnicity and the different ideological and value systems that their 'Asian-ness' represents. One of the ways their 'otherness' is contained is to locate them within worlds that are clearly defined as textual or screen worlds, the 'closed world' of the whodunnit for Charlie Chan, for example, although such strategies also help to provide comforting textual resolutions to real-world problems when the series more fully engages with cultural and political concerns, even if the persona of Mr Moto still has the capacity to create ideological disturbance until he is regulated by the move from espionage and action-based films to the conventionality of the whodunnit just as his series comes to an end.

The textual world of Charlie Chan

The first Warner Oland entry in the 'Charlie Chan' series, *Charlie Chan Carries On* (1931) is a lost film,[1] although the survival of a version in Spanish made for the South American market, *Eran Trece*, suggests that its format is the same as that on show in *The Black Camel* (Hamilton MacFadden, 1931) which was released in the same year. *The Black Camel* foregrounds Chan's humility and composure which allows him to glide through his investigation after a preamble sets up the situation involving a film company shooting in Honolulu and hints at a mystery in the past. Chan's narrative of investigation reveals not only the story of the crime (the murder of the actress, Shelah Fane), but also the pre-narrative *récit* (Shelah's killing of an actor called Denny Mayo) and its motivation of the murder Chan is investigating. A causal relationship between events creates connections between past and present to reveal that the fragment of the whole that the current crime represents, which offers only obscure knowledge of reality in isolation, can be understood as part of a totality. This is the classic form of the clue-puzzle style in which the filling in of detail is analogous to the completion of a crossword puzzle or jigsaw, but the style also works by metonymy to treat 'textual reality' as if it were the same as 'reality' in order to prove that the latter has meaning by creating meaning in the former despite the mystifications that interfere with the path to truth. In *The Black Camel*, these comprise acts of concealment by Tarneverro (a mystic) and Julie (Shelah's friend), an ex-husband confessing to Shelah's killing, the blackmail of the ex-husband by a painter (followed by the latter's shooting), Julie taking a ring from Shelah's body, and the discovery of Tarneverro's real name, none of which are directly related to the murder of Shelah by Mayo's wife, serving as her maid, but which create a pattern of tangential connections for Chan to read.

More than any other detective in the crime series, Chan is a master of the elliptical or the oblique because his deductions are based not on a knowledge of prior facts or history (as is often the case, for example, with Sherlock Holmes),[2] but on the immediate and particular evidence of the case put before him in the clues he finds and the testimony he interprets. In this regard, the investigation is reality within the textual discourses, and the world becomes the investigation, so that Tarneverro only becomes Denny Mayo's brother, for example, on the testimony of a Scottish couple that Chan questions within his focalisation of events. The impression of the world reduced to the investigation is suggested by two sequences in which the key characters gather, firstly in a long closed room sequence after Shelah's murder, prefaced by Chan's aphorism that 'Death is a black camel that kneels unbidden at every gate' which gives the film its title and suggests that there is nothing outside the murder investigation, during which Chan works through evidence and listens to testimony of the closed circle but also draws the world into the room as other witnesses or figures related to the investigation are brought in. The second sequence involves the denouement in which there is no outside world because all the principal characters and key components of the investigation are assembled in one place. In both cases, it is only the clues and phenomena specific to the world Chan has entered that are significant. A recurring refrain throughout the series is the concept articulated in the aphorism 'Little things tell story' (*Charlie Chan in London*) to suggest that the role of the detective is to make reality speak. Chan's sensitivity to the language of objects suggests that in making everything speak, he not only ensures that reality has meaning by listening to it attentively, but also builds a world by creating a narrative out of the evidence, so that the hermeneutic act of reading clues becomes an act of making.

The detective as someone who guarantees reality and creates the world within the closed circle, or who reorganises a previously existing self-contained world to eradicate disorders so that it conforms to the norms of established society, is a common trope in the 'Charlie Chan' series. This closed world format correlates narrative relations (the crime and its detection) with spatial relations (setting) in order to collapse time and space into a 'world in a bottle' for the period of the investigation before the detective and the exonerated characters emerge from the textual world to disperse into 'reality' outside. The form is not peculiar to the 'Charlie Chan' series and can be found as a structuring principle across the whodunnit, which requires a limited group of suspects to focus narrative action. Other detectives in the Hollywood crime series also find themselves in similar situations, such as the Falcon (in *The Falcon and the Co-eds* or *The Falcon in Mexico*) and Sherlock Holmes, particularly in the Gothic mysteries that take place in a closed community (*The Scarlet Claw, The House of Fear*). In the Warner Oland 'Charlie Chan' entries, the device produces a static narrative in which relationships between characters create an internalised world so that outside reality rarely intervenes. The investigation justifies the world Chan makes as he makes the investigation, a circular logic which Norman K. Denzin implies when discussing *Charlie Chan at the Opera*. Making reference to Todorov's account of the whodunnit having a story of crime and a story of the investigation, Denzin comments that '[a]s the stories come together and merge, it becomes apparent that the first could not be present without the second' (Denzin, 1995: 96) to suggest that the world of crime only comes about because of the world created by the detection.

There are many other examples of the closed circle format, particularly in the early films in the series, such as *Charlie Chan in London* (Eugene Forde, 1934) and *Charlie Chan in Egypt* (Louis King, 1935).[3] The former film places Charlie Chan in a country mansion and replicates the exclusion of the outside world when Chan gathers together all those who gave evidence at the trial of Paul Gray (who has been wrongly convicted of murder) to present evidence. Chan re-enacts the details of the trial, but nevertheless rejects anything beyond the immediate facts of the night of the murder, so that even though he re-visits the moment of the crime, he insists that any pre-history that has no bearing on it is avoided (such as the information that Gray and the murder victim, Hamilton, had not got on even before the night of the murder), which makes him a judge as well as a detective. *Charlie Chan in Egypt* also has a self-contained world among a group of archaeologists excavating a tomb (literalised in the closed space of the tomb's chambers) and although some pre-narrative history is provided by Chan's appearance investigating the theft of valuable artefacts, the internalisation of narrative action and motivation thereafter helps to place the crime in parentheses to separate it from the outside reality from which Chan has emerged. Not all of the films offer the same closed circle format although it is one of the more pervasive styles even if, on occasions, Chan finds that there is a reality already in existence for him to enter. This is the case in *Charlie Chan's Secret* (Gordon Wiles, 1936) in which Chan enters into the realm of the 'old dark house' which, with its 'honeycomb' of secret passages and entrances, literalises the closed world once more. In this case, his role is not to create reality through the investigation, but to return the 'old dark house' to everyday reality by correcting the errors of an aberrant family, although as a by-product of his investigation he also guarantees that reality *is* reality through his detection of supernatural fraud (by proving that the supernatural is the product of technology, a motif revisited during the Toler period in *Charlie Chan at Treasure Island*). Chan's purpose, however, is essentially to guarantee the 'reality' of something that only has textual reality. His aphorism in *Charlie Chan in Paris* that it is 'very difficult to explain hole in donut, but hole always there', designed to verify the ineluctable but mysterious truth of reality, seems therefore to better describe the 'hole in donut' that is his textual world which, although the only reality in existence, is still the empty hole in the middle of reality.

Charlie Chan's Secret does render some ideological reality in its emphasis on Chan's relationship with the family as one of the driving principles behind his creation of a world. This motif is emphasised throughout the series although the family is generally either invisible or represented in displaced form through the presence of one of his sons (variously Lee, Jimmy, Tommy, Charlie Jr, or Willie), who act as a metonymy for the family at the same time as they mask its absence. This becomes more pronounced as the series develops because Chan only ever makes mention of his wife and the rest of his family whereas in *The Black Camel* there is a brief scene showing Chan at home. In later entries he effectively has no home, which only appears in the films' passing references to his family, in images of the same photograph of his wife and other children and in his desires to return to Honolulu. There are occasional appearances of the family (*Charlie Chan at the Circus* or the Toler entry *Charlie Chan in Honolulu*), but the home is otherwise absent except in the use of Chan's sons as his assistants. Charlie Chan becomes a wandering exile from the home, someone who is both the world and of the world because he exists only in the public sphere. This is already implied in *The Black Camel* because society has Americanised his family (signified by the use of modern slang) which offers no refuge from the public sphere, to the extent that Chan hurries off very quickly from the family meal to 'the peace and quiet of a murder investigation' (Hardy, 1997: 77).[4] The family is still one of the key textual and ideological motifs of the series (Taves, 1993: 337) and it is implied in *Charlie Chan in London*, for example, that Chan is impelled to restore the ruptured family of Pamela and Paul Gray, a brother and sister, and Pamela's relationship with her fiancé, because of the family photograph he has been looking at fondly just before Pamela asks for his help.

Seemingly unable to provide a calming influence at home, Chan provides the order and harmony associated with idealised visions of a patriarch-dominated family within the world he creates out of detection in his unruffled presence and reminders to others to be honourable and law-abiding (such as his prompt to the Scottish couple in *The Black Camel* to remember their sense of duty). Charlie Chan transforms people into his own likeness to recreate society as a version of his family, in ideological form, by acting as the 'father' of this world in the manner of a kindly and forgiving patriarch who cares for the many charges who come within his compass, as in his feeling of regret for Nardi in *Charlie Chan in Paris*, after having failed to protect her from death, and concern for Tom Evans after he is shot in *Charlie Chan in Egypt*. There are also more overt references to Chan as a father in his games and singing for children on board ship in *Charlie Chan in Shanghai* and displacements of fatherly affection onto Colonel Tim and Lady Tiny in *Charlie Chan at the Circus*. While it might seem fanciful to argue that Chan as father becomes the god of the world made by his investigation, there is some evidence to suggest this in *Charlie Chan in London* when he is asked to produce a 'miracle' by proving a man innocent in sixty-five hours and then does so. Even if he is not the god of his own world, he is at least the controlling force within it as its father, even when he appears to be on the margins (*Charlie Chan in London*, *Charlie Chan in Paris*, *Charlie Chan on Broadway*) or threatened with ejection from the world of the investigation (*Charlie Chan in Egypt*). Not only does nothing disconcert him but there is also never any doubt that he will order his world through the investigation, even if this involves performing a magic trick in the denouement by revealing facts previously concealed, such as information about a previous relationship between murderer and victim in *Charlie Chan at the Circus* or an unfinished cablegram in *Charlie Chan at the Olympics*.

The calm and order provided by Charlie Chan is most obvious in *Charlie Chan at the Opera* (H. Bruce Humberstone, 1936) even if there appears to be another controlling force in this world in the form of Gravelle (Boris Karloff), who signifies a disordering presence in the repeated references to him as a 'maniac'. Gravelle's threat is implied in the opening scenes (before Chan has appeared) when he is introduced as the inmate of a sanatorium, his presence revealed in the background as two wardens discuss his detention as an amnesiac. He is shown off-centre through a window playing the piano, his wild song accompanied by a lightning storm outside, and this Gothic imagery invokes the danger he poses to the ordered calm of the whodunnit as it enacts the threat that Chan must contain. When the wind blows open a window it wafts a newspaper toward him and he is cured of his amnesia when he sees a story concerning his wife, Lilli Rochelle, an opera singer who has returned to Los Angeles after seven years. The wind seems to blow memory back into his mind (as well as returning Lilli to his life), but it also makes of him a chaotic and elemental force of nature because, having been no threat before, he now becomes violent, so that his first act on regaining his memory is to overpower a warden, after which he goes in search of Lilli. On finding the opera-house where Lilli is performing, he haunts its confines, creeping around above, beneath and behind the stage, dominating this closed world as he appears suddenly from behind curtains or doors to terrify old colleagues before assuming the operatic role played by the man who aided Lilli in her attempt to kill him in the past (Barelli) to go onstage to perform opposite her. After the murders of Lilli and Barelli, for which he is held responsible, Gravelle returns to the concealed rooms and passages in the margins, while Chan goes about his investigation, although he is joined by Lee Chan, who seems to act as Gravelle's textual double as he too creeps around in the shadows.

Charlie Chan, however, is the ideological double of Gravelle, who is not a murderer, but a doting father once he learns of the existence of Kitty, his daughter. In a reiteration of the collective questioning of the closed circle, Charlie Chan brings the outsider Gravelle inside his world because although Gravelle is looking down on the scene through a trapdoor, seemingly outside the circle, he is symbolically included when the camera reveals him as Kitty tells the story of her mother (Lilli) and the death of her father (Gravelle). Just by asking questions, Charlie Chan has begun the process of turning Gravelle into himself and he then completes this task, firstly by placating Gravelle through a display of rationality and composure after Gravelle's fatherly affection has terrified Kitty (because he is still the stranger and 'maniac' to her) and then by restoring daughter to father at the end of the film. The self-contained world of the opera-house is returned to order by the restoration of family bonds and by the revelation that what seemed to threaten it was inside, not outside, although it needs two outsiders to return it to equilibrium, one to uncover the concealed discord by disordering its superficial calm (Gravelle) and another to provide lasting harmony (Chan). The return of order to the 'world in a bottle' signified by the opera-house is mediated therefore by its penetration by social ideology in the reconstruction of the family once its aberrant members (Lilli and Barelli) have been punished by the actions of the murderer, Anita, the wife of Barelli. If Gravelle is Chan's ideological double (the father without a home), then Anita is his criminal doppelganger because, as the vengeful hand of ideology who exacts retribution, she masks the fact that Chan has the same function, thereby allowing him to appear in both the guise of the calming influence of the law in restoring the family, and as the legitimate agent of justice in punishing her.

Of the Warner Oland films, *Charlie Chan in Shanghai* (James Tinling, 1935) and *Charlie Chan in Paris* (Lewis Seiler, 1935) are the main exceptions to the closed world format because they involve secret gangs that have been operating before the investigation begins and crime is thereby given a textual space outside of Chan's investigation. The use of omniscient narration to show the double-crosses between members of the bond forgers in *Charlie Chan in Paris* and the communications between members of the opium ring in *Charlie Chan in Shanghai* serve to suggest a reality outside the detection, although the former film still retains the implication that Chan's intervention creates the world because it is his involvement that leads both to Nardi's death and the double-dealing within the gang that results in the implication of the innocent Yvette Lamartine in murder. Chan must still make a space for his detection in *Charlie Chan in Paris* and this is shown by the way he engages in surreptitious investigations in the shadows (when, for example, he visits the apartments of Nardi and Dufresne to find clues) as an act of assimilation or territorialisation, although this task is destabilised by Lee's parallel acts of detection, even if the narration attempts to incorporate the latter by showing them in flashback. In each case, the gangs are also given their own territories, such as Marloff's headquarters and underground base near the river in *Charlie Chan in Shanghai* and the hideout in the sewers in *Charlie Chan in Paris*, both serving to literalise the gangs as outside official society. These provide spaces for Chan to penetrate, but also signify spaces outside his control until he has completed the investigation, at which point crime and its spaces are reterritorialised by official society as a result of Chan's successful detection, although in *Charlie Chan in Shanghai* it is the arrival of the police that allows the reclamation of criminal space because Chan's primary role in the film is to restore confidence in American authority by unmasking the gang member masquerading as an American secret agent called Andrews.

It is the entry of extraneous information into Chan's investigation that most clearly breaks the closed circle format, so that in *Charlie Chan in Shanghai* it is not the alternative criminal space that causes problems, but the reliance on information that already exists elsewhere in the form of the report from the American authorities that the real Andrews has been killed. Other examples that involve the reliance upon information Chan could not have deduced himself are produced by the newspaper report of a shootout at a casino in *Charlie Chan at the Circus*, even if he finds it within the world he is investigating (in a scrap-book of one of the characters), Hamilton's invention in *Charlie Chan in London*, and the use of candid camera photographs in *Charlie Chan on Broadway* (Eugene Forde, 1937). This latter film provides a clear deviation from the closed world format, even if it must, as most murder mysteries, still use a limited circle of suspects. Its differences are signalled by the unusual perturbations Charlie Chan experiences when crime permeates his world (firstly when he finds that Lee steals towels from hotel rooms and then when Lee is held as a suspect for murder), the symbol of which is a diary detailing gangster activity and graft that has been hidden in his trunk. Although his authority and presence clear away Lee's brushes with crime, the film suggests that Charlie Chan is in a foreign land in New York, its differences from his usual environment indicated by the pacy narrative that mimics the bustle of the city. His inability to understand New York is suggested by his incomprehension of city slang, but more importantly his powerlessness to affect the city in any significant way is depicted through his displacement from the investigation narrative by Inspector Nelson whose noise, energy, cynicism and aggression dominate proceedings. Nelson's shouted attempts to browbeat witnesses are deployed to signal their difference from Chan's quiet methods which only occasionally intervene, in his kindness to a witness whose husband has just been murdered, for example, and although he still provides the final solution, for much of the film he is an onlooker who flees to the safety of Honolulu after the denouement.

Charlie Chan and the modern world

Although the films of the Oland years are self-contained within their own worlds, there are moments when the series suggests reference to political, social and economic realities. These allusions to referentiality are most usually still confined within the closed system of the text because they are designed to generate a sense of urgency or textual significance for Chan's investigation beyond his interiorised function of guaranteeing the 'hole in the donut' that is the 'reality' of his textual reality. This is the case in *Charlie Chan in Paris* in which the bond fraud that forms the cause of the crime is deemed to be sufficiently important to threaten the global economy, thereby appointing Charlie Chan as a guardian of world affairs in his investigation. This is primarily a textual effect to prove Chan's genius as a detective, although more significant concerns with an external reality are articulated in *Charlie*

Chan in London, despite its closed world, because Chan is given the role of protecting British civilisation after Pamela Gray questions the legitimacy of a nation in which the State can commit murder by executing an innocent man. By preventing a miscarriage of justice, Chan restores civilisation to the 'British Lion', revealing that the threat is not from within the ruling classes (which, within the discourses of the text, give the nation its authority) because the murderer is not an English gentleman, but a foreign European agent. Charlie Chan proves the legitimacy of the United Kingdom's claim to civilised status even if he seems to uncover reasons why it might be considered otherwise in the form of a butler's rudeness, a maid's hysterical bigotry and a stable-hand's suspicion of his ethnicity. His good humour in the face of their insults suggests that Britain is lacking in many ways in comparison to the values he embodies, but the problem is restricted to servants and this serves to scapegoat the working class in order to ideologically reinforce a class system in which the aristocracy retains power. Social policing becomes one of the functions that Charlie Chan provides as a consequence, not merely in the delivery of murderers to justice, but also in punishing characters who fail to meet the standards that the ideology of Charlie Chan's world requires. In particular, those guilty of criminal fraud (Nellie Howard in *Charlie Chan at the Circus*) or duplicity, even if no criminal act has occurred (Fenton in *Charlie Chan at the Race Track*), are disciplined, but so too are those who pursue money unscrupulously (Savarin and Evelyn in *Charlie Chan at Monte Carlo*).

There is one area where the 'Charlie Chan' films do express a persistent concern with cultural, ideological and social formations and this is in the representation of modernity. One jarring note within the insulated and serene world of Charlie Chan in *The Black Camel* is his Chinese assistant, a junior police officer, who provides comic relief either by rushing around like a whirlwind or by suddenly appearing from beyond the frame of Chan's world to announce he has found a clue. Although his manic energy is partly the result of his representation as a racial caricature, it is also created by his identification with an unthinking modern world. His role is taken up in later films by Charlie Chan's sons, beginning with Lee (Keye Luke), who also draws in the Americanised world of Chan's family to introduce modernity into the world of the detective, although the wisdom and understanding of the father are always privileged over the worldly modern knowledge of the son. Modernity is presented as a place of ignorance rather than knowledge because its dynamism, movement and action (signified by Lee's helter-skelter eagerness) are the inverse of the deeper understanding provided by Chan's invocation of tradition. Charlie Chan's wisdom provides a totalising vision whereas Lee's knowledge amounts only to fragments, as the latter discovers in *Charlie Chan at the Circus* when he rushes back to report on the results of his own detection, but finds that his father can read what he has discovered merely from his clothing. Lee is also constantly the object of jibes about his lack of understanding (in *Charlie Chan on Broadway* he is described as a 'puppy detective'), a role taken on by Jimmy Chan (Victor Sen Yung) when Sidney Toler took over the part of Charlie Chan in *Charlie Chan in Honolulu* (H. Bruce Humberstone, 1938). If anything, Jimmy suffers more for his embodiment of modernity than Lee, constantly being sent down blind alleys, finding himself overpowered and tied up, or simply walking into burlesque pratfalls, so that in *Dead Men Tell* he falls into the water on four occasions and in *Castle in the Desert* he is dropped through a trapdoor, gets knocked down the stairs, and has a cigarette pushed into the suit of armour he wears for much of the film.

Charlie Chan's sons also, however, have a narrative function because they help to highlight Charlie Chan's genius. As well as providing comic diversions, Charlie Chan's sons serve as assistants to carry the burden of the investigation narrative so that Chan never appears baffled and can intervene in the denouement to deliver knowledge of the totality of the case without appearing either to have expended any effort on detection or to have been sidetracked by red herrings. His sons, on the other hand, are submerged in mystification and bafflement, only ever having a partial knowledge because their purpose is to follow false trails (to deflect superfluous information away from Chan), offer incorrect hypotheses, and to deliver occasional significant fragments to their father (often inadvertently) so that he can follow only the pertinent clues or assimilate their discoveries into the whole. Charlie Chan's sons also contribute to the style of the films, especially on Jimmy's entry into the series when the cinematic vaudeville provided by his comic relief is emphasised, although Lee's appearance in the Warner Oland years also helped to shift the emphasis away from the closed world format. This is less the case in those films where he works as a surrogate for his father (*Charlie Chan in Paris*, *Charlie Chan at the Opera*), where he is just another set of eyes, but in most of the films in which he appears he sets out to investigate the case in his own parallel false detection. This creates a sub-plot outside Charlie Chan's purview to not only provide variety in the form of vaudevillian slapstick, but also to open out the narrative and ideological dimensions of the textual world. The presence of Lee and Jimmy therefore offers a more expansive narrative by providing a second centre for the focalisation of events, even if their adventures in detection are usually revealed to be digression.

Although Lee and Jimmy are used to articulate concerns over modern society, the series also uses them to provide a more tolerant examination of the contemporary world, not least because both sons aspire to be like their father. On a number of occasions, the haste of the sons is caused by a mix of modern values and the traditional values signified by Chan as, for example, when Lee reports his father's murder in *Charlie Chan in Shanghai* without first checking the facts, which Chan describes as a product of a 'hasty conclusion and devotion to father'. Anxieties about modernity usually reside outside both the family and the modernity of everyday life that is associated with Lee and Jimmy in their forays into modern romance, their desires to acquire expertise without labour, and their eagerness to have 'fun'. The sons are usually reproved for their embodiment of the thoughtlessness that the films attribute to modern society rather than for any leanings towards disorder, venality, violence and superficiality, which are mapped as modernity's more important failings. When Charlie Chan precipitously leaves New York at the end of *Charlie Chan on Broadway*, it is an admission that the modern world it signifies is too unstable and shallow for him to either rectify or to civilise with the values of tradition, simplicity and certainty that he embodies. The certainty of tradition signified by Charlie Chan is not, however, merely valued for its own sake in opposition to the confusions provided by modern society. In the Toler vehicle *Charlie Chan's Murder Cruise* (Eugene Forde, 1940), Chan comments that 'in China, Mah Jongg very simple; in America very complex, like modern life' but he then comments on the 'simplicity' of China where the Emperor, when faced by a murder case with several suspects, used to execute all of them, guilty or otherwise, in order to attach brutality to simplicity and civilisation to complexity.

That the comment is spoken by an American actor in the role of a Chinese character, in a script written and directed by Americans, also, however, articulates a problem around ethnicity. Norman K. Denzin argues that Charlie Chan, like other Asian detectives, is othered by being associated with Western ideals of rationality, virtue and normality to make him a 'stranger and friend at the same time' (Denzin, 1995: 91). His representation is further complicated because he is also still represented in Orientalist discourses of 'Asian-ness' to become a doubled sign, enacted in the use of Western actors (Swedish or American) to embody a Chinese figure. Charlie Chan is particularly associated with Orientalist images of the 'Asian' qualities of harmony, tradition and serenity, characteristics which the series suggests the United States lacks (although Charlie Chan discovers that the rest of the world is also seemingly missing these qualities when he goes globetrotting) because Westerners, according to Denzin, are 'irrational, depraved, childish, violent, [and] immature', traits that Orientalist stereotyping usually attributes to the 'Asian character'. Charlie Chan, however, is a restorative figure and the values of harmony, tradition and serenity are represented as just what the United States (and the rest of the world) seems to need in order to contend with the destabilising effects of modernity. In *Charlie Chan in Shanghai*, for example, it is not Chinese criminals who have produced disorder in Shanghai, but a gang boss coded as Russian (Marloff) and an American accomplice (the fake Andrews) who command a gang of Westerners. Charlie Chan is represented as 'not-American' precisely so that he can bring tradition and stability to the West in general and the United States in particular, allowing him to combat the perversions of modernity that have transformed the United States and the West from cultures of tradition and stability to corrupt, chaotic and venal places. He therefore restores to these cultures the values they have lost by embodying their persistence in the present in 'non-Western' cultures (articulating a further Orientalist discourse of the modern West and the backwards but unsullied East) by being both 'Asian' (and therefore 'other') and 'American' according to a nostalgic vision of what the United States once was.

Charlie Chan's personification of tradition as a homely discourse is particularly valued, rather than tradition invested in power structures which, in the example from *Charlie Chan's Murder Cruise*, is cruel rather than caring. This homeliness still privileges masculine forms of authority and, because Charlie Chan is an appointed officer of the law, a tension develops between benevolence and retribution in his representation.[5] This tension becomes more apparent in the early films of the Toler period when women become a source of anxiety because they appear to be unruly, having previously acceded to masculine ideology and the law in the main by both accepting and desiring their containment within the marriage narrative. There had been conniving women in the Oland years (Nellie Howard in *Charlie Chan at the Circus* and Evelyn in *Charlie Chan at Monte Carlo*), but in the Toler films women are a problem even when they are not criminal or duplicitous. There are still scheming or murderous women (Jeanne Bently and Vivian Wells in *Charlie Chan in Reno*, Lily in *Charlie Chan at the Wax Museum* and Miss Finch in *Charlie Chan in Panama*), but a number of female characters are also represented more generally as irrational or hysterical. Carol

Wayne in *Charlie Chan in Honolulu*, Eve Cairo and Myra Rhadini in *Charlie Chan at Treasure Island* and Susie in *Charlie Chan's Murder Cruise* are all portrayed as whining, emotional or uncontrolled, suggesting that femininity is an annoyance in everyday life as well as a danger when channelled into criminality. Although Charlie Chan contains these feminine threats to Western masculine authority, he is still a problematic figure for the United States to incorporate into its own system of values because of the different ideological and value systems his 'Asian-ness' connotes. The series Westernises him sufficiently, in ideology (Chinese wisdom refigured as ratiocination) and representation (the sign of the actor), so that he is also 'not-Asian', but this further displaces Asians and Asian values to imply the difficulty of incorporating them into the United States.

Charlie Chan at the Olympics (H. Bruce Humberstone, 1937) seeks to address such concerns by assimilating Charlie Chan through the transformation of detection into counter-espionage in the service of the United States government. The film focuses on the theft of the recent invention of a remote control device and although it is not a foreign agent trying to steal the mechanism, but the inventor himself because he wishes to sell it to a higher bidder, Chan's role in both returning the invention to the United States and punishing the inventor's treachery makes him an American patriot. Perhaps more significant is the setting of the film during the 1936 Berlin Olympics so that although the film only gestures towards the possibility that it is the Nazis trying to gain the invention as a mystifying device (because it is characters coded as Russian who are actually engaged in the criminal espionage), there are still echoes of ideological difference. The iconography of Nazism is only evident in some of the stock footage sequences (the straight arm salute), and the Swastika is absent from the film, although the German police are represented within discourses of the authoritarian regulation of society to make Nazi tyranny and German nationalism absent centres informing the film's ideology. The most overt displays of patriotism are, however, on the side of the Americans who cheer and shout as their compatriots win gold medal after gold medal, both in the actual events shown in stock footage (Jesse Owens) and in the fiction of the narrative (Bruce Masters and Lee Chan). This patriotic fervour applauds the United States as an inclusive democratic nation where white Americans not only cheer on fellow whites (Masters), but also African-Americans (Owens) and Asian-Americans (Lee). In representing the United States as a land of equality, opportunity and achievement, irrespective of ethnicity, the film does not need to emphasise Nazi racial ideologies because it is the unspoken sub-text against which the diversity of the United States is to be read.

Charlie Chan at the Olympics also shows Chan as less composed than in previous films and more perturbed by events that go on around him, most evidently in the kidnap of Lee. This suggests an important element within the series as it develops into the Toler years in its representation of the world as a troubling and strange place. Criminality is a necessary component of the detective format, but the series moves from the more comforting motives associated with the whodunnit (personal profit or jealousy) to representations that are more troubling, such as narcotics in *Charlie Chan in Shanghai*, graft in *Charlie Chan on Broadway*, gangster criminality in *Charlie Chan at the Wax Museum* and Rhadini's systematised bureaucracy of blackmail in *Charlie Chan at Treasure Island*, even if conventional whodunnit crime is still present. Anxieties about modern forms of crime are supplemented by wider concerns about global political instability. While the series had always implied that the modern world is a hostile place, as suggested by the fact that the vast majority of the films have an attempt on Charlie Chan's life (more than any other series detective, including Mr Moto), in the form of bullets, knives, darts, crossbow bolts or lumps of rock sent in his direction, the films at the end of the Oland period and during the Toler era address such concerns more overtly. The dominant modes in the Toler years are the spine-chiller and the espionage film and both seem to derive from an apprehension of the strangeness of the world and the incomprehensibility of both material and political reality. Charlie Chan is sent around global trouble spots, as well as facing those in the United States, to hint therefore that it is not just American modernity that lacks logic and order but that the world situation at the end of the 1930s is also chaotic or lacking in meaning.

The shift in setting and narrative attention is not only the product of topical concerns, however, and must also be understood by reference to the mode of production of the B-series, particularly in the change from Warner Oland to Sidney Toler after the death of the former actor in 1938. The first two Toler films, *Charlie Chan in Honolulu* (1938) and *Charlie Chan in Reno* (1939), replicate the format of the Oland films by using the closed world format (which also recurs in *Charlie Chan's Murder Cruise* [1940], *Murder Over New York* [1940] and *Charlie Chan at the Wax Museum* [1940]) and there are other continuities in this period, including the representation of Charlie Chan as a caring father to surrogate children (Marcel in *Charlie Chan in City in Darkness* [1939] and to Paula and Dick in *Charlie Chan's Murder Cruise*) and the use of a son as an assistant with the introduction of Jimmy Chan. The series also revisits themes from earlier films, such as the unmasking of supernatural fraud in *Charlie Chan at Treasure Island* (1939) which re-works ideas from *Charlie Chan's Secret*, or offers remakes in *Charlie Chan's Murder Cruise* (a remake of the lost film *Charlie Chan Carries On*), *Murder Over New York* (an espionage version of another lost film, *Charlie Chan's Chance*) and in the reworking of *The Black Camel* in *Charlie Chan in Rio* (1941), which replaces the blackmail sub-plot with Jimmy Chan's false detection and romantic diversion. Significant differences develop in order to vary the format, however, most obviously in the heightening of comedy to provide entertainment in plots that were increasingly repetitious. In addition, the films in the Toler period created several tropes of their own, such as the criminal boss eliminating a henchman who is the only person to know their identity (*Charlie Chan at Treasure Island, Murder Cruise, Charlie Chan in Panama* [1940], *Murder Over New York*), the use of masks (*Treasure Island, Murder Cruise, Dead Men Tell* [1941]) or new faces (*Wax Museum, Murder Over New York*), and the variation of the 'old dark house' format using ingenious settings (*Wax Museum, Dead Men Tell, Castle in the Desert*).

The amplification of cinematic vaudeville in the form of Jimmy Chan's slapstick antics is particularly important in changing the emphasis of the series from whodunnit to comedy thriller. When Jimmy Chan is reduced to his underwear (*Reno*), gibbers in terror (*Honolulu, Panama, Wax Museum*), or tumbles down stairs or into the water as a running joke (*Castle in the Desert, Dead Men Tell*), the focus shifts away from Charlie Chan's investigation to Jimmy's parallel comedy detection to make the cinematic vaudeville that it provides as important as Chan's investigation narrative. This situation becomes even more pronounced in the comedy provided by the racial stereotyping of Mantan Moreland as Chan's cowardly African-American chauffeur, Birmingham Brown, when the series went to Monogram.[6] Toler's version of Charlie Chan also changes because the films downplay ratiocination in favour of tricks, deceptions and traps as a means to capture criminals, such as a fake fire in *Charlie Chan in Reno*, the time-bomb deception in *Charlie Chan in Panama* and the trick to reveal the true identity of Narvo the master criminal in *Murder Over New York*. The shift of the series' paradigm is most obvious in *Charlie Chan at Treasure Island*, not only in the setting of a trap for Rhadini the murderer, but also in the fact that, despite taking possession of a manuscript called 'The Secret of the Pygmy Arrow', which provides an account of the murderer's methods, Charlie Chan still cannot deduce later on that another murder is committed using a pygmy arrow. The move away from classical whodunnit ratiocination operates in parallel with the shifting generic composition of the films which offer a multiplicity of styles within the thriller format, albeit with an emphasis on espionage and horror elements, even if the latter are deployed within the comedy spine-chiller style, as signified by the large number of black cats that wander through the films.

The series' espionage films pre-date the Nazi spy ring cycle that Hollywood produced after the attack on Pearl Harbor and develop to provide stylistic variation, in this case by drawing on topical concerns, in the same way that the travelogue dimension had Charlie Chan visiting various places around the globe to create new settings for the similar mystery plots. The later Monogram films similarly responded to contemporary issues at the end of World War II in order to offer textual variety, focusing on 'atom spies' and related scientific espionage in *Charlie Chan in the Secret Service* (1944), *The Shanghai Cobra* (1945), *The Red Dragon* (1945) and *The Scarlet Clue* (1945) while also spinning out formats that had become established within the series, such as the spine-chiller in *Meeting at Midnight*, aka *Charlie Chan in Black Magic* (1944) and the closed world in *The Jade Mask* (1945) and *Dangerous Money* (1946). The first of the Toler espionage films, *Charlie Chan in City in Darkness* (Herbert I. Leeds, 1939) makes more overt reference to international affairs than *Charlie Chan at the Olympics* because it is set in Paris as France prepares for impending war with Germany, after the occupation of the Sudetenland, and ends with a coded warning by the detective about Hitler's intentions at the Munich Conference ('Beware of spider who invite fly into parlour'). Very little of the plot, however, relates to the international and political situation or, indeed, with the rounding up of the spy ring delivering French munitions to the Nazis because much of the narrative material is mystification provided by two unrelated sub-plots involving burglary and blackmail. Despite early hints of espionage activity, the existence of the spy ring is only revealed in the last reel and its members are abruptly terminated when the airplane carrying them crashes on take-off, after which there is a brief denouement in which Chan reveals that the murderer is the butler Antoine, whose killing of Petroff the arms-dealer is justified as a patriotic act. The film marginalises the whodunnit investigation even further when Charlie Chan disappears from the narrative for long periods and even when he is onscreen it is the cinematic vaudeville provided by Harold Huber's incompetent investigator, Marcel, which dominates the action.

In the context of the dominant whodunnit mode of the series it seems as if the film cannot conceive of an investigation that doesn't conform to this type, although it is the very normality of this mode of investigation that is important, not only for the espionage films, but also the spine-chillers and gangster-related thrillers. Charlie Chan becomes more than just a detective in such films because in neutralising threats to normality (the spine-chillers), national security (espionage films) or American ideology (gangster criminality), he also becomes a protector of reality and the everyday life of American society. As importantly, by using the same mode of detection in these films as he does for conventional whodunnit crimes, he provides reassurance that any threat (gangster, supernatural, political) can be contained by the same means. *Charlie Chan in Panama* (Norman Foster, 1940) and *Murder Over New York* (Harry Lachman, 1940) provide a similar style of resolution to subterfuge and sabotage even if their use of a secret mastermind behind the espionage activities suggests they are more clearly spy thrillers. *Charlie Chan in Panama* concerns a Nazi threat to the American fleet's passage through the Panama Canal and provides a multitude of mystifications that signify espionage, such as one character ordering tobacco from another as if he were speaking in code, suspicions over the allegiances of a Czech refugee, and an experiment with bubonic plague (which leads to fears of biological terror). It also, as a sign of its espionage credentials, gathers together an Austrian, an Englishman, a Czechoslovakian refugee, an Arab, a Panamanian and assorted Americans, among whom is a German secret agent, but this arrangement only replicates the closed circle of the whodunnit and allows Chan to use standard methods of detection. The same closed circle is on show in *Murder Over New York*, which deals with the sabotage of a prototype airplane, although there is also a MacGuffin motif in the pursuit of a briefcase containing the fingerprints that will identify the secret mastermind of a spy ring, but Charlie Chan uses whodunnit methods, by means of a ruse, to once again unmask the murderer and bring order to a chaotic world. Controlling the world through such everyday and ordinary tactics suggests that nothing special is required to combat enemies and their devious subterfuges.[7] This normalises the threats, makes them comprehensible, and suggests that the United States can just be itself within its own ideological conception of its values (moral, decent, inclusive and ordinary) to face dangers from within as well as from around the world. That Charlie Chan is the most upright and conventional detective in the most conventional form of whodunnit also contributes to this effect even as it also makes Charlie Chan's ethnicity normative and reassuring because of the very conformity of persona and form.

"Gee, it's bewildering": The world of Mr Moto

Charlie Chan is not the only Asian detective at work in Hollywood in the 1930s and 1940s and he is complemented by Mr Wong, whose investigations follow the narrative patterns of the 'Charlie Chan' series, and the 'Mr Moto' series, which is more varied in its generic references and more wide-ranging in its textualisation of world affairs. The 'Mr Wong' films, created by Monogram to take advantage of the fame achieved by Boris Karloff in the Universal horror films while they had him under contract (Everson, 1972: 82), present James Lee Wong as an amateur detective version of Charlie Chan.[8] Karloff's performance of Wong emphasises the detective's urbane manner, signified by his European dress and speech, in opposition to Chan's homeliness, but he is problematically assimilated because he is usually only called on to assist in investigations that require knowledge of Chinese culture, artefacts or people and this reduces his identity to an ethnic type. The series also plays on suspicions of Asian criminality so that, although the murders are always committed by Westerners, the series still deploys signifiers that contribute to such associations in references to Chinese tongs in *Doomed to Die* (1940) and smuggling from the East in *The Fatal Hour* (1940). The films maintain a conventional whodunnit format, established in the first film, *Mr Wong, Detective* (1938), which calls upon Mr Wong to investigate a series of locked room murders during which he establishes a relationship with a police officer, Sam Street, who provides false detection for Wong to counter, although the film quite skilfully shows Street to have been right in his initial accusations against a disgruntled scientist, Roemer, who Wong finally proves to be the murderer having initially exonerated him. *Mr Wong, Detective* also introduces a recurrent motif in the ingenious methods used and alibis created by the murderers, in this case the vibrations caused by the sound of a police siren which shatter a poison gas capsule. Further ingenious murders, such as a shooting during a game of charades in *The Mystery of Mr Wong* (1939), and alibis, such as the complex rigging up of a radio and telephone in *The Fatal Hour*, occur throughout the series, but the most persistent tropes in the series are those shared with the 'Charlie Chan' series, such as the gathering of suspects and sudden revelations in the denouement to unmask the murderer.

The 'Mr Moto' series provides a more nuanced set of significations not only because it is more varied in style, but also because Mr Moto is more closely associated with modernity. He is also a source of ideological anxiety because he signifies concerns about threats to American power in the Pacific generated by Japan's embrace of technological modernity and this worry helped to end the series just before the start of World War II when a Japanese hero was becoming a problem (Everson, 1972: 82; Hardy, 1997: 233). Mr Moto is therefore a more complex figure than Mr Wong, not least because his association with modernity is accompanied by physical and intellectual abilities coded as 'Asian', which contribute to his representation as a latent threat even when he is a servant of American or European imperialist interests. Peter Lorre's performance as Mr Moto contributes to this complexity in his 'intriguing combination of Japanese and *mittel*-European mannerisms' (Miller, 1973: 48) because as a Hungarian émigré from Nazi Germany playing a Japanese agent he draws attention to the placelessness of the textual world of the series and its representations of the dislocations of global politics to suggest that personal allegiances are variable and temporary. Only one film in the series has resonances with the 'Charlie Chan' and 'Mr Wong' films, *Mr Moto's Gamble* (James Tinling, 1938), and this was because the film's narrative was refashioned out of *Charlie Chan at the Ringside* after Warner Oland fell ill. Mr Moto is a more distant detective in this film as a result, on the margin of events, and displaced from a central role by the comedy provided by Lee Chan, who was retained in the film, and a fellow trainee detective, Knockout Wellington. Both of these characters are introduced in a criminology class being taught by Mr Moto and thereafter provide a false detection entirely unrelated to Mr Moto's investigation of the murder of a boxer. They nevertheless fill up a good deal of the running time with gags about Wellington's kleptomania and his lack of knowledge about his larcenous tendency, as well as providing slapstick when Lee punches Wellington, at his own request, to try to help him remember where he found the murder weapon, although this information arrives too late to help the inquiry. Otherwise, the film betrays its origins at several points, such as when Moto allows Lee to go to jail to keep him off the case, in the gathering of suspects at the training camp for an initial questioning midway through the film and in Moto's occasional aphorisms, but most obviously in his sedentary detection from the margins and out of the blue revelation in the denouement.

It is the sedentary quality of the detection in *Mr Moto's Gamble* that is most clearly out of place in the series, because the films are more often adventure and espionage movies than they are detective mysteries. This is signified by the range of their settings, with the series beginning in San Francisco before moving to Shanghai in *Think Fast, Mr Moto*, after which locations include China again in *Thank You, Mr Moto*, Southeast Asia in *Mr Moto Takes a Chance*, Devil's Island and England in *Mysterious Mr Moto*, the Suez Canal in *Mr Moto's Last Warning*, and Puerto Rico in

Mr Moto in Danger Island. In these travels around the globe, Mr Moto is more clearly a trouble-shooter than Charlie Chan, protecting Western interests, so that although he is 'other', he channels his abilities into the protection of nations other than his own, even if this is not always, as Gates argues, the United States (Gates, 2006: 79) because, as Denzin points out (Denzin, 1995: 101), he more generally helps to avert 'disaster for the white world'. In *Think Fast, Mr Moto* his protection of global capitalism does have an emphasis on the defence of American interests, but Mr Moto defends Chinese tradition against Russian and German rapacity in *Thank You, Mr Moto,* French imperialism in *Mr Moto Takes a Chance,* and British national security against enemies coded as German in *Mysterious Mr Moto* and *Mr Moto's Last Warning,* while he also serves European powers friendly to Britain in the former film in saving from assassination a Czech industrialist portrayed as an English gentleman. Throughout, he has an ambiguous role, however, and although he is normalised after the first entry in the series by his appointment to the fictional 'International Police, he is nevertheless a man of mystery himself, free to rove and uncertain in his allegiances except insofar as they serve the global political and legal status quo.

The concealment of his motivations is a significant part of his persona and although this contributes to Orientalist discourses of Asian inscrutability, it also serves a similar ideological function to the criminal ambiguity of detectives such as The Saint and the Falcon in placing him outside social bonds (even if he is co-opted into serving Western powers), while also creating a narrative space for actions that are less obviously moral and legal than those undertaken by Charlie Chan and Mr Wong. Although justification for Mr Moto's actions is always provided, very often this legitimation depends upon context, such as the stabbing of a Mongol trader several times in *Thank You, Mr Moto,* the hurling of a smuggler into the ocean in *Think Fast, Mr Moto,* or his apparent lack of concern for the film-makers, Marty and Chick, in *Mr Moto Takes a Chance* (when, to suggest he cares nothing for their safety, he lets them know that he uncovered the cause of the death of the Rajah's wife before they were taken off to be executed for the killing), all of which serve his interests by protecting his identity or his immediate safety. Although in the latter example, he has already rescued Marty and Chick from execution by the time he tells them of his discovery, they are unaware of his altruism because he was in disguise when he saved them. His revelation helps therefore to promote a public persona that conceals a deeper sense of morality and duty, but Moto's duty is not necessarily bound to morality or legality because it is directed only to the successful completion of an assignment. Moto consciously adopts an air of ambiguity as to his criminal and moral disposition in order to conceal his identity as a detective, turning sleuth into secret agent by drawing on espionage motifs, and this creates the impression that there are no rules governing Moto except those he deems pertinent to a specific circumstance or those which accord with his personal sense of honour and justice.

Moto's ambiguity also creates greater narrative freedom so that he is not restricted by modes of action appropriate to the detective of the classical whodunnit. The whodunnit format is on show in the first film of the series, *Think Fast, Mr Moto* (Norman Foster, 1937),[9] which starts out with Moto as a detective in the mould of Sherlock Holmes taking on the disguise of an 'oriental' street trader in San Francisco before boarding a ship to Shanghai to follow a lead in a diamond smuggling case. The film also provides a body in a hamper in the curio shop that Moto enters in order to start his investigation, provides appropriate mystification along the way, and ends with the stock unmasking of a secret criminal mastermind inside the respectable Western community of Shanghai. The differences in style are generated by the detective persona of Moto, who is a more active detective than Charlie Chan, a feature immediately shown when he throws a police officer and becomes involved in a brawl after the proprietor of the curio shop shoots at him. Although he becomes a polite and gentle figure once he has returned home and divested himself of his disguise, he retains an active persona in his investigation, going out into the world from San Francisco to Shanghai to follow a trail before then roving about the latter city chasing the tiger symbol which is the sign of the smuggling ring. The film also places Moto in a world that seems pervasively disordered, signified by the chaotic street scene in which he is first encountered and then by the riotous party of American revellers he meets aboard ship. These scenes enact the textual disruption that Moto is required to fix but they also have an ideological dimension because the friendly riot of the Americans is contrasted with the seeming calm of Shanghai where, however, the real disruptions within the world economic order are located and which spin back to cause disorder in the United States.

Mr Moto's world more clearly articulates the ideological enforcement of the global political order than the espionage films of the 'Charlie Chan' series, although this is muted in the next film in the series. *Thank You, Mr Moto* (1937) is set entirely in China, but makes no reference to the tensions between Japan and China that form the background to Marquand's novel of the same title. Instead, the film removes many aspects of the novel, including a peasant uprising and reference to Japanese intervention in China, to provide a standard adventure thriller about the acquisition of a set of scrolls which reveal the location of the tomb of Genghis Khan.[10] The film does, however, advance Mr Moto's mystery and air of danger, not only in his brutal killing of the Mongol trader, but also in other killings he performs, one of which (Koerger) is effectively assassination. The narrative shows him much less bound by moral considerations than other series detectives by representing him as more ruthless, albeit in the name of justice, and places him in situations where he is also under threat. Clearly such moments are driven by the needs of the B-format to provide entertaining action sequences, as are the regular fights in which Lorre's double displays Mr Moto's expertise in judo and no-holds-barred brawling, but they also dramatise the general danger of the world outside the United States. *Mr Moto Takes a Chance* (1938) more fully emphasises action for its own sake and its narrative of an uprising against imperial rule generates a standard B-Movie adventure, complemented by an iconography (jungle scenes, exotic entertainments, a ruined temple, tiger traps, blow-guns, and a captive chained to a pillar) and ideology driven by the format rather than wider concerns. *Mysterious Mr Moto* (Norman Foster, 1938) is a more Hitchcockian entertainment, in the espionage mode, but although it develops the representation of Moto as a secret agent, in his shifting disguises (including two that play on stereotypes when he plays at being a simple Japanese house boy and then an eccentric German art-lover), and codes the League of Assassins to signify Europe as a threat to British security, it nevertheless betrays its whodunnit conventionality by making the leader of the assassins a silly fool of an English aristocrat.

The mixing of codes exhibited by *Mysterious Mr Moto* provides the model, however, for the more integrated cross-generic adventures of the final three films of the series, particularly in the amplification of its Hitchcockian style in *Mr Moto's Last Warning* (1939), which combines espionage and music-hall comedy to reflect on topical matters, but also in the more complete integration of cinematic vaudeville in *Mr Moto in Danger Island* (1939) and the playful self-parody of *Mr Moto Takes a Vacation* (1939). *Mr Moto's Last Warning* more fully confirms Denzin's view that the Moto films 'make violence and danger their topic' (1997: 102) by presenting Mr Moto in peril in the displaced form of a double acting in his place who becomes the object of murder in scenes following the opening exposition. The film has already offered echoes of the Hitchcock suspense thriller by displaying its allegiances in the playing of a refrain from 'Rule Britannia' during the credits before establishing its scenario in the Suez Canal Zone by mapping out a plot concerning an attempt to rupture the Anglo-French alliance. This establishes the operation of German spies in Egypt without the film ever having to speak their name, although their activities form the focus for the narrative as they advance their plot to mine the canal and kill a British agent, Danforth, who has infiltrated the spy ring. Moto hovers on the edge of the action for much of the film, watching the agents in their hideout, from the curio shop across the street where he masquerades as Mr Kuroki, only entering the narrative to warn Danforth of the danger to him, to search the music-hall where the spies' leader, Fabian, performs as a ventriloquist to cover his activities, and to help the comic relief, a bumptious writer called Venables, evade a mugging outside his store by playing 'ping pong with a couple of bruisers'.

Moto's shift from observation to action in helping Venables, although it is peripheral to his investigation, identifies him to the spies, and after Danforth's murder he is subject to an assassination attempt (a time bomb) before being captured (alongside Venables) when he penetrates the recesses of the spies' hideout. Moto is only in danger when he becomes active and, indeed, he has to rely upon Fabian's girlfriend, Connie, to save him from death after he has foiled the spies' plan once she has realised that she has been inadvertently aiding Fabian's sabotage plans. Although the British are shown to need help because they are bumbling, foolish or incapable of fending off threats, Moto is nevertheless represented as superior only in his tenacity and ability to survive, wriggling out of dangerous situations rather than dominating them, and the ideological sign-off favours the British when Connie realises her patriotic duty and despatches Fabian. *Mr Moto's Last Warning* is, however, a B-entertainment and although it balances its investigation and action narratives with an integrated use of comedy through the means of Fabian's ventriloquism act, it still emphasises its light-hearted aspects through the intrusions of Venables' buffoonery. A similar balance of generic elements, this time adding Twister McGurk, a dumb lug of a wrestler, to provide comic vaudeville in the role of Moto's assistant, is on show in *Mr Moto in Danger Island*. Although the film favours action, there is a more complete detection narrative through the investigation of diamond smuggling in Puerto Rico, complemented by McGurk's false detection in the comedy mode to counterpoint Moto's hermeneutic activity, so that the film shifts from thriller mode to bring it closer in style to the other detective series. It is also a more diverse film because its signifying patterns mesh together cross-generic codes, so that its use of espionage motifs (the smugglers' hideout in a swamp reputed to be haunted) also draws on Gothic inspired mystery codes deployed by the comedy whodunnit. In addition to its variable generic codes and styles (comedy, thriller, whodunnit, action, suspense, mystery, subterfuge), it also integrates McGurk's cinematic vaudeville, even in his self-inflicted pratfalls, and generates multiple twists and turns through effective mystification (pointing in several places at once) to provide a variety of entertainment.

A running joke throughout *Mr Moto in Danger Island* is McGurk's inability to learn a new wrestling hold from Moto, which usually leaves him on the floor muttering 'Gee, it's bewildering'. While the routine is primarily for comic effect, McGurk's comment also describes the confusions of the onscreen world of Mr Moto, around which he trails, confounded like a surrogate member of the audience, to highlight in opposition Moto's superior understanding of events. A similar situation is on show in *Mr Moto's Vacation* which playfully parodies the whodunnit format by providing an excess of mystification and self-conscious comedy, the latter most obvious in the double-act provided by two old professors, which also helps to obscure the identity of the super-criminal, Metaxa, for whom Moto is searching. Because of the self-parodic humour provided by Lionel Atwill's performance as one of the professors, which draws on associations with the actor's previous roles to point the finger in his direction, the comedy created by the pair helps not only to conceal that Manderson, his associate, is Metaxa, but also to mesh with the mystification provided by a cops-and-robbers subplot involving a gang of hoods and the false detection supplied by a bogus insurance investigator, all of whom are, like Metaxa, after the mythical crown of the Queen of Sheba. Textual style therefore contributes to the misdirections that Mr Moto must negotiate, along with the interferences of the comic relief he has to contend with (George R. Huntley Jr as a detective from Scotland Yard), although here Moto uses ratiocination, rather than his menace and physical abilities, to solve the case by deducing from a set of footprints that the limping Manderson is actually the able-bodied Metaxa. Just as Mr Moto is transformed from a dangerous man of mystery to a comforting whodunnit detective, however, the series was cancelled and whether it was because Lorre wanted to move on to more prestigious features (Everson, 1972: 82) or because of increasing tensions between the United States and Japan, the series concludes with the taming of Mr Moto.

6
The Rise of the Hard-boiled Detective

Although the hard-boiled style has been regarded as a dominant mode of the detective film in Hollywood in the 1940s, as Steve Neale describes (2000: 72), the number of hard-boiled films in this period that actually have a detective, in the conventional form of the private eye, is much less than most people suppose.[1] The intersections of private eye format with the wider phenomenon of *film noir*, the iconic status of the hard-boiled detective, and the canonicity of films such as *The Big Sleep* and *The Maltese Falcon* within the 1940s Hollywood crime film have made the hard-boiled detective film seem more widespread than it is. If Frank Krutnik's list of films from *In a Lonely Street* is taken as indicative of the output of '"Hard-boiled" Hollywood' (1991: 183–7), however, there are more films within his categories of 'suspense thriller' and 'criminal-adventure thriller' than the 'investigative thriller' of which the private-eye film is a sub-type. Of those within the investigative thriller type, some are focused on pseudo-detectives, such as the insurance agent Riordan in *The Killers* or Krutnik's 'investigative veteran' (100) in *Cornered* (1945), *The Blue Dahlia* (1946) and *Dead Reckoning* (1947), to which can be added *Somewhere in the Night* (1946) and, in a lighter vein, *The Big Steal* (1949), while the gangster or gambler as detective from *The Glass Key* (1942) and *Johnny O'Clock* (1947) could also be added to this category. Also included are *The Dark Corner* (1946) and *Out of the Past* (aka *Build My Gallows High* [1947]), both of which contain private detectives, although Krutnik considers these films to be hybrids of the investigative and suspense thriller because of their 'displacements of the investigative narrative through suspense' (130). There are also investigative films involving police detectives, but, except in the police procedural, these tend to have their detection narratives interrupted by or deflected on to other tropes. *Crossfire* (1947), for example, doubles its narrative of detection by having an investigative veteran in addition to a police detective (and explores *noir*-related discourses such as lack of trust, betrayal and hatred), while *I Wake Up Screaming* (1941), *Laura* (1944) and *Where The Sidewalk Ends* (1950) form a group of films which transfer their investigation from crime to an exploration of the compromised or obsessed police officers conducting a detection.

Setting aside for the moment those investigative thrillers which contain police detectives or pseudo-detectives in order to offer a strict definition of the hard-boiled detective film as one that includes a professional private eye, it would seem that Hollywood's contribution to this area during the 1940s is composed of *The Big Sleep*; *The Maltese Falcon*; *Murder, My Sweet*; *The Brasher Doubloon*; *The Lady in the Lake*; *The Dark Corner*; *Out of the Past* and the films in the Michael Shayne 'B' crime series. The Shayne films even seem to comprise most of Hollywood's output of hard-boiled detective films during the 'high period' of the form in 1940s, amounting to twelve films between 1940 and 1947, even if they align more with the detective series mode than the hard-boiled style. The diverse nature of both *film noir* (Walker, 1992: 8) and Krutnik's investigative thriller, however, make such categories slightly arbitrary and there are many more films in the 1940s that incorporate detection or mystery in a hard-boiled style, often in unconventional forms or in unusual places. These include *Johnny Angel* (1945) in which George Raft portrays a sea captain investigating a mystery aboard his father's ship, *Deadline at Dawn* (1946), in which events surrounding a mystery all take place during one night, and *Shadow of a Doubt* (1943) in which a young girl, Charlie, is drawn to and then repelled by the uncle who shares her name when she gradually learns the truth about him. To these could be added many other mysteries, although it is arguably still the crime series that produces Hollywood's most significant output in the detective film during the 1940s. The 'Sherlock Holmes' series continued until 1946, 'The Falcon' went on until 1947 (although there were a further three entries at Film Classics with a different version of the Falcon), 'Charlie Chan' carried on at Monogram until 1949, the same year in which the 'Boston Blackie', 'Lone Wolf' and 'Crime Doctor' series all ended, and in the meanwhile the unusual investigative film series, 'The Whistler', starring Richard Dix in different roles (with one appearance by Michael Duane), arrived in 1944 and finished in 1948. The Whistler series of films at Columbia, in using the same actor to play different characters in different situations (for example, a widower who hires a hitman to kill himself in *The Whistler* [1944], a drifter who takes on another man's identity to find that he is a target for murder in his new guise in *Mark of the Whistler* [1944], or more conventionally a private detective in *Mysterious Intruder* [1946]), is typical of the ingenuity of the Hollywood studios of the period with regard to the deployment of mystery narratives, which could take place anywhere and involve anyone.

This emphasises wider shared concerns of *film noir* and hard-boiled texts with the pervasiveness of crime and the pervasive need for its investigation. In *film noir*'s criminalised society, for example, a mystery can involve the female detective activity of the girlfriend of a man wrongly accused of murder in *The Stranger on the Third Floor* (1940), the investigation of the Nazi past of a college professor by one of his ex-soldiers in *The Stranger* (1946), or the ingenuity of a man announcing to the police that he has been murdered in the first scene of *D.O.A.* (1949) followed by an investigation in flashback narration. Many of these films concern issues of wrongful arrest or conviction, along with a general sense that everyone is either implicated or threatened by crime, and suggest a key aspect of both hard-boiled and *noir* forms: the cupidity and viciousness of everyday life in the United States. The consonance of the two kinds of film in representing the permeation of American society by corruption and all manner of sins (deceit, avarice and hatred) or transgressive and criminal behaviour (murder, blackmail, larceny, petty theft or perverse desire) offers a different vision to that of the detective crime series, which still tended, even as the hard-boiled or *noir* styles became more widespread in the mid-1940s, to isolate criminality in deviant individuals. This more comforting vision perhaps goes some way towards explaining the persistence of the crime series, even if they had to confront the variety and pervasiveness of crime that, in hard-boiled and *noir* forms, seemed to question the probity of most American citizens. 'The Whistler' series directly contends with this new textual sensibility, while Sherlock Holmes encounters versions of the *femme fatale* in the form of the Spider Woman or female vamp and the Falcon enters a world derived from *film noir* in *The Falcon's Alibi*.

Hard-boiled detectives in a hard-boiled world

The mapping of a society or culture that is pervaded by criminality and corruption in hard-boiled and *noir* films leads to a variety of investigative or detection narratives across the United States in both cities and small towns. Persistent instances of individual violence, hatred, perversity or crime and a multitude of little corruptions (of which the Mexican small businessman trying to defraud the Pacific All Risk insurance company in *Double Indemnity* [1944] is a minor example to act as a backdrop for the murder and fraud planned by Walter Neff and Phyllis Dietrichson) suggest that American society requires investigation at all levels and by everyone, including those who come from the underworld such as Ed Beaumont in *The Glass Key*. This also perhaps explains why the hard-boiled style of the detective film is considered to be so widespread in the 1940s. Not only are there so many figures mimicking the detection style of the private eye in becoming pseudo-detectives, but the crime, suspense and mystery thrillers of the 1940s also code certain kinds of criminality, associated either with the underworld or with a more pervasive everyday viciousness, as 'hard-boiled'. The term also becomes synonymous with embitterment and can therefore be used to describe the cynical self-interest of most of the criminals and upright folk that Roy Earle encounters in *High Sierra* (1941), Agnes Moorehead's Madge in *Dark Passage* (1947), not because she commits murder, but because of her petty and vicious hatred for Bogart's Vincent, or the mistrustful house detective of *The Blue Dahlia* who ends up carrying the can for murder. In Krutnik's use of 'hard-boiled' to signify 'toughness' (1991: 42–3), or Scaggs' further addition of 'shrewdness' (2005: 55), everyone who is 'tough', hard-bitten, cynical, weathered or merely resilient partakes of the concept of being 'hard-boiled', whether it is Nancy Hobson, whose hard-boiled love for the eponymous Johnny O'Clock ultimately saves him from death, Edward G. Robinson's irascible and gnarled insurance claims adjuster Keyes in *Double Indemnity* or, just outside the 1940s, Ida Lupino as a widow surviving the psychological terror inflicted by Robert Ryan's handyman in *Beware, My Lovely* (1952).

'Hard-boiled' describes a society in which living is not easy because people are affected by everyday troubles that make them subject to the 'paranoia and despair' that Ralph Willett attributes to the *noir* city (Willett, 1996: 89). This description applies more widely to American society in 1940s crime texts because the troubles, anxieties and failed schemes to triumph, or simply survive, make everyone 'hard-boiled'. The alternative to being 'hard-boiled' is to be one of society's losers, such as the 'old men with faces like lost battles' and women 'with faces like stale beer' who mix with tough 'fly cops with granite faces and unwavering eyes' in the Bunker Hill area of Los Angeles in Chandler's *The High Window* (1979: 53). The hard-boiled film often represents both a society of failures and hard-boiled survivors, although the two states are not mutually exclusive because characters such as Agnes in *The Big Sleep* or Vincent in *Dark Passage* can be losers who only endure and persist because of their hard-boiled cynicism. Such characters are supplemented in criminal texts associated with investigative or suspense forms by the 'cheap chiseller', as Anzelmo (Fritz Kortner) in *Somewhere in the Night* refers to himself, who suggests a society pervaded by widespread petty criminality (Messent, 1997: 7) as apparent proof of Mandel's view that 'the American crime story presented crime as far more completely integrated into society as a whole than the British did' (1984: 46). Many critics have also seen the United States represented in hard-boiled fiction and film as a corrupt or shallow place 'populated by various fakers, frauds, and charlatans' (Scaggs, 2005: 72), a view that is often allied to a perception that hard-boiled fiction is more authentic or realist in form. This opinion of the hard-boiled style derives from Raymond Chandler's well-known pronouncement in 'The Simple Art of Murder' (1995: 989) that Hammett's fiction is more authentic than the British whodunnit because it gives 'murder back to the kind of people that commit it for reasons, not just to provide a corpse; and with the means at hand, not with hand-wrought duelling pistols, curare, and tropical fish'.[2]

Hard-boiled fiction and film in *noir* forms is also regarded as a style that more fully offers a critique of American society than the whodunnit's confirmation of existing social and ideological structures. A particular focus for the hard-boiled form's critique of American society is the failure of the detective to return it to order through the solution of a crime. Instead, the hard-boiled detective form represents 'a society of flux', which Clarens offers as a view of crime films generally (1980: 13), in which, as Schatz notes in relation to hard-boiled *noir* detections, 'the solution to the detective's case, when there is one, fails to resolve the deeper issues and conflicts at hand or to bring the appropriate culprits to justice' (Schatz, 1997: 237). Neither of these accounts highlights the critique of American society, but the lack of conviction that order can be restored forms the basis for other views that do, such as Leitch's argument (2002: 195) that even when a crime is solved 'the original social evils – the inequalities aggravated by unbridled capitalism, the dependence of developers on crooked deals, the government's abuse of power – are only contained, never resolved'. These views very often rely on analysis of the literary hard-boiled text or the perceived intersection of hard-boiled film with a radicalised version of *film noir*. In literary forms, there is no reason to believe that criticisms of American society derive from a left perspective as Jameson notes in his judgment of Raymond Chandler as a writer who 'gives vent to everything racist, sexist, homophobic, and otherwise socially resentful and reactionary in the American collective unconscious' (Jameson, 1993: 37), even if Knight sees left wing views running throughout Hammett's career (Knight. 2004: 115) and Pepper argues that Hammett's *Red*

Harvest 'exhibits Marxist sympathies' (Pepper, 2010: 334). Similarly, with regard to *film noir*, it can be argued that its detectives, where they appear, are less concerned with challenging the capitalist system of monetary exchange and with rectifying the abuses performed by corrupt institutions than with controlling the former (by, for example, punishing opportunistic women or working class criminals who seek to use capitalism's economic freedoms to circumvent political and social hierarchies) and sneering at the latter.

Nevertheless, there is certainly a squalor and emptiness represented in hard-boiled film and fiction that is highlighted by one of the key tropes of the form, the 'mean streets' that Chandler identifies as the setting for its narratives. Chandler's description suggests a general sense of the United States as a fallen society even if the specific reference is to the landscapes of crime that the detective must enter, but because the detection as often occurs in mansions and private homes as in bars and criminal hideouts in Chandler's novels, there is little distinction between official bourgeois society and the underworld, as Naremore discusses in relation to Chandler's *Farewell, My Lovely* (Naremore, 1998: 234). Of particular importance within the hard-boiled form, however, is the detective's entry into the world of crime that the streets of the city symbolise, even if as a professional detective paid for his labour, he is always already inside the world of crime because he needs it to make a living. One of the differences between the classical and clue-puzzle forms of the whodunnit and the hard-boiled style is that the detective in the former type of fiction is objective and detached from the events of the crime and society, whereas the detective in the latter kind of text is detached from neither. The hard-boiled detective is often plunged into the crime world as an active or causative agent triggering subsequent events, which Todorov notes is a key aspect of the suspense form as the detective is 'integrated into the universe of the other characters' (Todorov, 1977: 51). The detective's presence and involvement in the act of detection is often enough to cause criminals to try to neutralise him either by administering a beating as a warning (*The Big Sleep*), threatening or attempting murder (*Kiss Me Deadly*), or by putting him in the frame for a crime (*The Dark Corner* and *Out of the Past*). In these cases, the detective is a passive figure, acting less as a subject driving forward events than as an object to which criminals and suspects respond.[3] The detective can be more active in determining events once in the world of crime, by setting traps (Marlowe arranging for Mrs Grayle to visit him when he expects Moose Malloy to be around in *Farewell, My Lovely*), tampering with the evidence (Marlowe's cleaning up of Geiger's house to cover for Carmen in the film of *The Big Sleep*), taking or withholding important clues (a stolen ring in *The Gay Falcon*), engaging in acts of deception in relation to evidence or witness testimony (Michael Shayne's repeated lies in *Michael Shayne, Private Detective*), or becoming involved with the criminals (Soitos, 1996: 53) either as an agent provocateur (the gangster-detective Ed Beaumont in *The Glass Key*) or as a facsimile stooge seemingly ignorant of the identity of the criminals and their crimes (Spade's involvement with Gutman and Brigid in *The Maltese Falcon*).

The condition of passivity is regularly visited upon the detective in the hard-boiled form (although it was for the crime series detective very often in the form of captivity, when the generic coding of the film tended towards the thriller) and the private detective is both a figure of 'self-sufficient phallic potency' (Krutnik, 1991: 95), seemingly invulnerable to everything that is thrown at him, and a suffering figure, whose masculinity and endurance are tested by the vicissitudes he experiences in his investigation, such as 'the occasional beating that is the ritualised proof of a private eye's power to survive in a tough world' (Porter, 2003: 109). Unlike the transcendental subjectivity associated with the classical detective, the private eye is submerged within a narrative of threats which arise from his urban location, within which he is a contradictory figure. The paradox of the private detective is expressed most clearly in the detective's licence which gives him the power to be a mobile agent pursuing the investigation through city streets and into any building, but which does not endow him with the authority or protected status of the police. His licence to act is therefore limited, meaning that he must often trick his way into spaces from which he is barred. More significantly he is placed precariously between police and criminals, with the former able to invoke their authority to call the detective to book, sometimes arbitrarily simply as a sign of their power, while the latter, with the fear of conviction to motivate them, feel no remorse in visiting pain upon someone without similar authority who might yet bring them to justice. However, unlike the police, the private detective's licence means he isn't governed by a rule-book, other than his own code of honour, and this gives him more freedom in some ways, to circumvent the law for example, but unlike the criminals he does have a code of honour and this restrains his actions to breaches of the law that can be justified in the service of justice.[4]

The paradox of the hard-boiled detective is most clearly expressed through the investigation which is not only a way toward truth, but also an entanglement that inflicts upon the hero recurring ordeals, dead-ends or tight corners, from which he must find a way out in order to arrive at the solution. The investigation-as-entanglement is an examination of the fortitude of the detective (most obviously in *The Dark Corner*), but also his integrity (in, for example, *Murder, My Sweet* or *The Maltese Falcon*), so that he can remain, like Chandler's Marlowe, 'virtually the only man of integrity in a landscape teeming with gamblers, blackmailers, pornographers, and their equally degenerate victims' (Leitch, 2002: 196–7). There are therefore two narratives within the private detective form, one in which the private eye is an active mobile investigator engaged in the detection of crime, while in the other he is the passive subject of investigation tested by threats to his masculinity and individual autonomy. The former kind of detective is referred to by Michael Walker as the 'seeker hero' and the latter kind as the 'victim hero' (1992a: 10–2). The first position comes closest to the transcendental subjectivity of the classical detective in depicting the private eye as a fantasy of individuality by making him a non-alienated form of labour able to traverse society and to enter the world of capital without however being captured by its seductions. The private eye is able to operate outside of social and political forces, creating a position of integrity or authenticity there, while also being able to affect events as if he were a fully fledged and free individual. The second position is most often associated with the suffering or bewildered investigator of *film noir*, who will be discussed in the Conclusion, although it is sometimes difficult to separate the two conditions in hard-boiled film because the threats that form the narrative for the 'victim hero' are only encountered as a result of the detective's activity as a 'seeker hero' within the investigation.[5]

These threats involve sexual and economic temptation to divert him from his condition of activity as an investigator, violence to the body of the detective (beatings and attempts on his life), captivity or attempts by the police to curtail the detective's freedom (by implicating him in a crime that might imprison him) or various attempts to curtail his economic activity as a detective by warning him off a case. For Krutnik, such tests determine whether the detective in the form of the *noir* hero is 'tough' or otherwise, with a particular emphasis being placed upon the negotiation of the heterosexual encounter with an actively sexual woman. This is a confrontation, or 'struggle' for Krutnik (1991: 99), in which sexual attraction does not merely create a romance narrative within the investigation narrative for the *noir* hero as a parallel to the move to resolution in the latter, because desire arouses fractured and complex impulses in constructions of masculinity as a result of tensions in gender relationships which endanger the hero unless he successfully constrains the feminine threat. Such impulses are, for example, whether to control, possess, redeem, destroy, or submit to the female agent, although the complexity of these urges lies not only in the fact that they often operate in combination, but also in the fact that the hero might delude himself, by misrecognising his motives and desires, into believing that he is the centre of activity either because ideologies of masculinity tell him that he is or because his social position or employment (as a detective, for example) lead him to presume he is a 'seeker hero' rather than 'victim hero'. This also means that threats to masculine agency and autonomy are not only external, in the form of the female threat and in the competition with other masculine agents, but also internal because the hero is subject to rival and fracturing impulses between desire and perceived duty to masculine ideology.

Canonical private eyes: Sam Spade and Philip Marlowe

Film noir versions of the detective film suggest 'victim heroes' stumbling about blindly or powerlessly within a world that they cannot control, subject to the corruptions and seductions of a fallen American society, particularly in the form of desire and money, both as an obstacle to masculine empowerment, but also as a false sign of its achievement. What might be considered to be the hard-boiled film proper negotiates these concerns, but does so by finally resolving the detective into an active hero by allowing him to control or reject the desiring narrative provided by the female protagonists he encounters while also showing him to be mainly immune to the lures of capital. This is largely because most of the canonical hard-boiled films of the 1940s are based on Chandler's novels where Philip Marlowe's constant reiteration that he takes only 'twenty-five dollars a day and expenses' measures the detective's integrity by his resistance to economic temptation. *The Maltese Falcon* (John Huston, 1941) seems to falter in this regard by showing Sam Spade as somewhat covetous of wealth, although it too draws back to represent Spade as above the dirty chase after money in which Gutman, Cairo and Brigid are all engaged. Although the film has often been defined by its representation of the detective's relationship with Brigid O'Shaughnessy's *femme fatale*, with Krutnik arguing that it offers a paradigm of 'the rigid constraint of the feminine' (1991: 101), the film is as much about how capital circulates. The focus for attention is confused, however, by the fact that there are several competing strands within the film and by the lack of clarity over what constitutes the narrative of detection. For the police (Lieutenant Dundy and Tom Polhaus) it is the murders of Miles Archer and Floyd Thursby, who both die in the manner of a classic whodunnit with little or no screen-time to set events in motion, but Spade spends very little time investigating these cases throughout the film. It is the mystery of Brigid, beginning with her prior visit to Spade's offices to supply herself with a patsy so she can be rid of Thursby, that forms Spade's main investigation as he tries to discover her loyalties (if she has any), which also involves Spade with Brigid in her role as sexual agent. The mystery of Brigid is displaced when Cairo and then Gutman appear, whereupon the schemes to acquire the falcon of the title take precedence. These draw in Spade, who is apparently entangled in the affairs of the adventurers and criminals, and Brigid, in her role as economic agent, although her sexual and economic roles are so confused because her pursuit of money depends upon sexual desire that to be one is also to be the other.

The plot maps out convolutions typical of *noir* narrations, in which mystifications and confusion derive from narrative complexity rather than retardations to the more linear narratives of the films of the crime series, particularly in the displacement away from the active pursuit of the investigation. Much of this complexity is drawn from Hammett's novel, to which the film is generally faithful not only in its narrative, but in its retention of much of Hammett's dialogue. The film's complexity also derives from the concern with money and its circulation, with the different strands enacting the confusions that muddle the focus of Spade's detection once he begins to take money from different people as retainers for his services. His attention is dispersed across different areas as a consequence, and even if the falcon narrative ultimately prevails it is still unclear who Spade is working for because the circulation of money has confused his loyalties as it has confused those of Gutman, Cairo, Brigid and Wilmer.[6] Each of them is shown betraying at least one of the others during the film (as Brigid betrays Thursby), most obviously when they gather to wait for the delivery of the falcon, and the back-story reveals that they have been double-crossing each other from Istanbul to Hong Kong to San Francisco, all for the wealth that the falcon symbolises. That the falcon turns out to be a worthless copy can be taken as a comment on the emptiness of both their enterprise and, more widely, the economic structures of capitalism in which money is constantly on the move, while also revealing the dispossession or powerlessness of those without capital. This is demonstrated twice in the film when Spade effectively coerces retainers out of Brigid and Cairo, with his seeming knowledge that this is the only money they have left, leaving them helpless (so that Brigid has to rely on Spade and Cairo has to turn to Gutman), even while it strengthens his position.

Spade's domination of characters he encounters indicates, despite his dispersed attentions, failure to pursue the investigation of his partner's death, and the confusions of the narrative, that he is as in control of events as the crime series detectives. Because a crucial scene from the novel is missing in the film, in which, to ensure her dependency, Spade fakes a break-in of Brigid's hotel room (which is instead attributed to one of the other criminals to enhance the mystery), he is also less ambiguous in his motives. In the novel, it is unclear for a long time whether Spade will be corrupted by the attractions of money (even if he clearly resists and controls Brigid's attempts to seduce him), so that even when he explains to Brigid why he is turning her over to the police there are reasons to suspect he is only doing it to protect himself. In the film, he lies less frequently and shows signs of remorse as he tells Brigid he is sending her over, while there is also more of a focus on his loyalty to his dead partner in the speech justifying his actions. Despite his interest in money, Spade's integrity is never in doubt, even if he is played by Humphrey Bogart at a point when he was only just emerging from gangster roles, and it is this that allows him to perceive Brigid's deceptions rather than any shared duplicity. Throughout, he exercises the detective's penetrating gaze, seeing through Brigid's masquerades because he seems to understand her from the opening scene (Maxfield, 1996: 17). Here, the composition of shots in the standard shot-reverse shot structure always includes Brigid when he is in shot but always shows Brigid on her own in reverse to frame her as if she were on the witness stand in court. His awareness of her deceptions is most clearly shown when she adopts the guise of a homely woman in a sensible dressing gown which only leads him to a show of superiority by revealing his knowledge that she is feigning ('You're good, chiefly your eyes, I think, and that throb you get in your voice when you say things like "Be generous, Mr Spade"') and then doing it again ('Now you are dangerous') when Brigid affects honesty.

The same exercise of control is demonstrated repeatedly with other characters, albeit in different ways. Krutnik notes Spade's manipulation of others when, after apparently displaying weakness in losing his temper with Gutman, he smiles on leaving the room to reveal his outburst was an act (Krutnik, 1991: 93–4) and Spade laughs or smiles on many other occasions as a sign of his mastery. He laughs when Cairo uses a gun that Spade has just returned to him to insist on searching Spade's office, when he throws Wilmer off his tail by outwitting him and even after he has taken a punch from Dundy to indicate that the latter offers no threat to his masculine self-identity. He also uses physical strength to assert his self-sufficiency, dispossessing both Wilmer and Cairo of guns, although it is the confrontational attitude he offers to figures of authority that is most significant, not only because it shows him triumphing in the contests of masculinity, but also because it represents his hard-boiled invulnerability. On several occasions when the police or the district attorney physically touch him or interfere in his affairs, he rebuffs them by a sudden controlled outburst. He fends off Polhaus' insistent questions about his business at the scene of Archer's murder with a simple 'Don't crowd me', browbeats Dundy when he is accused of killing Thursby with a terse 'Get your paws off me' (before showing his confidence and authority by sharing a drink with him), and adopts a confrontational response to the district attorney's questions to successfully repel him. Although the urban odysseys that Spade takes in Hammett's novel are reduced in the film to make the narrative more compact, thereby reducing the sense of his mobility and control of the city, Spade is nevertheless shown to be able to negotiate the corruption, greed, and temptations that come his way with ease. His integrity also remains intact as he forfeits the money offered as a bribe by Gutman and importantly he preserves a contained sense of himself and his place in the world when in the conclusion he answers Polhaus' question about the falcon by replying that it is 'the stuff that dreams are made of' to signify that the pursuit of money is a meaningless goal for his version of masculinity.[7]

The opening of RKO's *Murder, My Sweet* (Edward Dmytryk, 1944) offers a detective in a more precarious position by showing Philip Marlowe (Dick Powell) sitting at a desk in a police station with his eyes bandaged, being interrogated by a circle of police officers. Although his wisecracks fend off accusations of murder, the sense that Marlowe is surrounded or contained emerges more fully as the film enters its flashback narration when the camera moves from Marlowe's face to look down through a window on to a bright neon city which, after a montage of shots, leads back to Marlowe as he is picked out through his office window talking on the telephone. The neon lights intermittently illuminate Marlowe and then reveal the reflection of Moose Malloy in the window, making him oversized and ghostly as he appears and disappears when the lights flash on and off before revealing him standing behind the detective. Although Moose is a less menacing figure than he is in Chandler's source novel *Farewell, My Lovely,* offering Marlowe a paid job rather than forcing him along in the search for Velma, he nevertheless draws Marlowe down into a neon city that the detective finds difficult to comprehend and control. Marlowe is an observer to whom things happen, rather than a controlling subjectivity, standing as an onlooker to Moose's destruction of Florian's bar, and even though he is seemingly more composed with Jessie Florian and then a nervous and fidgety Marriott, with whom he adopts an aggressive attitude before belittling him, this is an illusion, because Marriott's entry into the narrative more fully transforms Marlowe into a passive object of events, even if he is only sapped rather than murdered at the arranged pay-off with a heist mob. Marriott's brief entry into the narrative also causes a hostile interrogation by the police, who are antagonistic thereafter, and Marlowe is then passively sucked further into events by Anne Grayle's appearance which, after a meeting with Velma/Helen Grayle, results in his forced visit to Amthor's (where he is throttled by Moose and pistol-whipped by Amthor) and his captivity in a drugged state, during which the narrational strategies of a dream sequence map his destabilisation as an active subject. Although he emerges from this experience in chipper mood and with a smile on his face, he only briefly becomes an active agent in escaping his captivity by administering a sapping to his guard at Sonderborg's, and soon needs Moose's help to fully escape and then Anne's to recuperate.

Marlowe's lack of knowledge compounds his destabilisation as an active agent in *Murder, My Sweet*. Even in the opening scene before the flashback narration, when all the events have occurred, he is presented in such a condition when he announces with bemusement that he understands that he is supposed to have committed 'a couple of murders'. Although he knows that he hasn't, as he also knows that he isn't the finger-man for a jewel heist gang despite rhetorically accepting the hinted accusation from the police after Marriott's murder, Marlowe nevertheless repeatedly draws attention to his own lack of understanding of the investigation, particularly with regard to relationships between various suspects and the reasons why people want him involved in the case and then want to be rid of him. His announcements that he doesn't know things that he does in fact know, such as whether he had met Marriott or not before the latter visited him, continue to emphasise his uncertainty. His confusion is mapped through his seemingly directionless movement from one conversation to another, immersed in a world of empty talk from which he learns little until Helen Grayle reveals her identity and crimes in the denouement (Bordwell, 1985: 68). Marlowe is literally 'clueless' because there are no telling objects to reveal information (unlike the cigarettes that lead to Amthor in Chandler's novel) and he moves around randomly without being in control because he has nothing substantial to direct his path through the meaningless society into which he has been dropped. Velma/Helen is the more active mover of events, creating Marlowe's discomfiture by setting him up for the shakedown by Amthor while also being the murderer of Marriott and the thief of her own jade necklace whereas in Chandler's novel, although she is involved in the narrative, she is more significant as an absent centre (as the object of Malloy's search for Velma and the target of blackmail). The transformation of Anne from the daughter of a cop in Chandler's novel to the daughter of Mr Grayle in *Murder, My Sweet* further emphasises Velma's importance by showing her as having more obviously disrupted the world of the wealthy to become its corrupt centre as Helen Grayle. On Marlowe's first visit to the Grayle mansion, for example, she is placed at the centre of a tableau (with a focus on her legs to emphasise her sexual presence) with Anne outside the circle created by Velma, Marlowe and Grayle, after which Grayle and Anne leave Velma alone with Marlowe to signify that she is now the power controlling legitimate wealth.

Velma is represented as the person who makes society meaningless because her usurpation of official structures of power and capital not only overturns masculine hierarchy but also, in proving that 'Marlowe's sexual bravado is a lie' (Buchsbaum, 1992: 97), reveals that male potency is empty. The story of crime that the film tells, therefore, is the ideological story of feminine disruptions to the masculine ordering of society as a place of certainty and stability, signified through Velma's re-naming as Helen Grayle, which is represented as a form of criminal imposture. This story only becomes evident through the story of investigation once Moose has reappeared and the confusions to masculine meaning, certainty and rationality are exposed as Velma seeks to defend her destabilising influence. Grayle is shown to be an impotent patriarch who is a stranger in his own home and money is seen to be scattered outside legitimate channels to criminals such as Marriott and Amthor (whose crookedness signifies the 'crime' of such dispersal of capital), without structure and purpose, the negation of economic order being emphasised when several characters hire Marlowe not to do his job as a detective. Marlowe's incomprehension is not only expressed by his failure to understand the mystery but also by his failure to understand the confused society in which he operates, even if the former is caused by the latter. Marlowe is shown therefore not as a triumphant male agent in *Murder, My Sweet* because by the end of the film (when he is blind and helpless) he has become someone who has merely survived everything that has been thrown at him. Although he is as capable in word as Spade, he is less able in actions, and his 'agency' is primarily expressed through a playful childishness that has him playing hopscotch in the Grayle mansion and striking a match on the rear end of a statue. More significantly, although Marlowe's integrity is taken for granted in Chandler's novels, in *Murder, My Sweet* Marlowe must more obviously prove that the accusations of being 'grubby' or 'dirty' have no validity by giving up claims to the jade necklace in the conclusion. In so doing, however, he confirms Velma's view of him that, despite having the 'name of a duke', he is 'just a nice mug'.

The suffering detective is also evident in the lesser adaptations of Chandler's novels, *The Lady in the Lake* (Robert Montgomery, 1946) and *The Brasher Doubloon* (John Brahm, 1947), although Marlowe has a greater understanding of events and romantic narratives to sexually empower him in both films. *The Lady in the Lake* is most notable for its use of the subjective camera to suggest that the audience sees events through the detective's eyes, '"the real thing'" according to Telotte (1989: 103), although a voice-over narration provided by Montgomery, who takes the role of Marlowe as well as directing, still guides the spectator to particular clues. There is also a frame in which Marlowe talks to the audience, a device that is repeated on occasions to provide narrative exegesis. Despite its technical experiment, the narrative is conventionally in the thriller mode and involves a missing person and a case of imposture, revealing another female killer, Mildred Haveland, and a corrupt police officer, De Garmot, as the main villains during a showdown in a hotel room. Marlowe suffers mainly at the hands of De Garmot, who administers a beating, hauls him in for interrogation and forces his car off the road before attempting to frame him for drunk-driving, although he is also smashed across the face with some brass knuckles wielded by a lover of a missing woman. *The Lady in the Lake* makes little of De Garmot's dishonesty as part of any wider concerns with institutional corruption, because it offers a good cop to balance his bad cop, although *The Brasher Doubloon*, based on *The High Window*, offers a fuller criticism of the idle rich. The film is a quickie, similar in style to the films of the crime series, with Marlowe more like a whodunnit detective directing the narrative towards a gathering of suspects in the denouement, even if there are also aspects of the Gothic style in the film's shooting (Phillips, 2000: 85). Although *Murder, My Sweet* has a similar arrangement in bringing together key characters in its conclusion, it offers a more melodramatic finale in which all the murderers in the film meet their ends. *The Brasher Doubloon* has a more conventional conclusion which reveals the truth about murder and blackmail while also providing a confession to resolve the story of the investigation and its preceding story of crime, or *récit,* which Jameson refers to as 'the classic tale-telling of events that are over and done with before the story begins' (Jameson, 1993: 36). The film, however, presents Marlowe as a more active hard-boiled agent, his apparent control of events signified by his taking possession of the valuable Brasher Doubloon, even if this act also leads to threats to both his integrity and physical safety because once he has the coin he is subject to a gunpoint questioning, a kidnapping and a beating. The taking of possession of capital (the doubloon) seems therefore to embody Marlowe, albeit as a vulnerable suffering body initially before it finally embodies him sexually in his relations with Merle, the apparent cause of crime and mystery for much of the narrative, with whom he proves his masculine agency by curing her of her phobia of being touched by men.

Bogart's Marlowe as a 'right guy'

Perhaps the most significant film in the canon of hard-boiled detective movies is Warners' adaptation of Chandler's *The Big Sleep* (Howard Hawks, 1946), a big-budget feature that was afforded re-shoots to make more of the relationship between Humphrey Bogart as Marlowe and Lauren Bacall as Vivian Rutledge, the daughter of the impotent patriarch, General Sternwood, who calls on Marlowe to settle a case of blackmail involving his youngest daughter Carmen (Martha Vickers). *The Big Sleep* is famously convoluted (Hagopian, 2004: 33), labyrinthine and incomprehensible (Phillips, 2000: 67) or 'impossible to follow' (Hardy, 1997: 49), and involves several instances of blackmail, a pornography racket, gambling, deception and fraud, and several murders (one of which, Owen Taylor's, remains famously unexplained), as well as a complex *récit* uncovered by Marlowe. The complexity derives from the way in which the investigation spirals out from the initial blackmail case, which itself draws in pornography, drug use and murder, to continue even when the first case has been resolved. The pattern is repeated from Chandler's novel which goes beyond its original bounds to reveal not only further crimes in the search for Regan, but also an archaeology of pre-narrative crime to map a society that is destabilised already and which remains so at the end. The film offers a symbolic destruction of gangsterism in the killing of Eddie Mars, after the sleight of hand that makes him the chief purveyor of crime, rather than Carmen, but the brutality of his death, hoist by his own petard, suggests that the heterosexual union between Marlowe and Vivian and the sound of police sirens that follow Mars' killing are not signs of the restoration of civic and sexual order, but proof that legitimate society can only persist by 'othering' itself to become like him. The investigation itself becomes an entanglement in this configuration of American society as a confused realm of machination and corruption, rather than a path towards truth, and Marlowe's success is simply to emerge from the 'investigative maze' (Walker, 1992b: 191) to prove, unlike Harry Jones, Sean Regan and Owen Taylor, that he is able to survive this society.

Chandler's novels very often represent Los Angeles as a fallen society, offering a nostalgic vision of the city as one that was once governed by an honourable brotherhood of men who are now ineffectual (General Sternwood), marginalised (Bernie Ohls and Marlowe) or dead (Sean Regan). In its place, a representation that the film draws out, is a divided city founded upon antagonism and competition (symbolised by the betrayals of Geiger's gang once he is dead), in which domestic conflicts are stressed because the dissolution of family hierarchy (the wildness of General Sternwood's daughters) enacts a wider sense of a ruptured and chaotic city which is even more significant when it is the families of the wealthy (as symbolic rulers of society) that have crumbled. The city of *The Big Sleep* is an 'unruled' society (a post-Camelot world in Chandler's novels), a place of distrust and deceit in which gender relations, social relations, and masculine trust have disintegrated to fracture hierarchies and create a fragmented city of isolated individuals. The city becomes a microcosm of the flows of capitalism, and the film uses the avarice of petty criminals, 'grafters' and gangsters as a metaphor for the uncontrolled movements of money. Blackmail is particularly significant as a sign of the breakdown of legitimate economic and social control of capital because it allows anyone access to money without labour and without concern for their criminal inclination, irrespective of their social status, while also suggesting not only that money has no morality but also that it creates a society without morality or hierarchy. In addition, in a familiar hard-boiled trope, *The Big Sleep* puts on display the 'unspeakable' as far as it can within the confines of the Production Code, often by implication (homosexuality, pornography and drugs), in order, as Hagopian argues, to show 'the illicit come out of the shadows to overtake and upend the licit' (2004: 38).[8] Although the sites of the illicit or the illegal are hidden in places that are off the beaten track (Geiger's house, Eddie Mars' club, Mona Mars' hideout) or concealed behind shop-fronts and hotel lobbies (the operation run by Geiger and then Agnes), they also extend into the heart of society by reaching into the Sternwood home through Vivian and Carmen (Marling, 1995: 201–2) while the use of pastoral leafy settings for Mars' club and Geiger's home suggests that they have become normal and everyday.

This does not mean that *The Big Sleep* necessarily offers a thorough critique of capitalism because, as Krutnik argues in relation to the 'dark enticements' of the *film noir* city (1997: 88), there are freedoms in this society for Marlowe to experience, such as his urban odyssey of flirtations with sexually open women (including his wooing of the glamorous upper class Vivian) and bars and clubs to visit.[9] There is nevertheless a more far-reaching sense that everything is sordid or tarnished in *The Big Sleep* than is found in *The Maltese Falcon*, whose narrative of a fabulous artefact has resonances with some of the Sherlock Holmes' stories despite its concerns with betrayal and double-dealing. Although *The Big Sleep* has similar continuities with the classical detective form in 'the romantic pursuit of truth and justice' by a chivalric detective protecting 'damsels in distress' (Mandel, 1984: 35), the other would-be knights riding to the rescue are a petty-thief (Harry Jones), who dies to protect a hard-boiled woman who cares nothing for him (although he proves he is a 'right guy' and earns the approving monicker of 'Jonesy' from Marlowe in the process), and a chauffeur (Owen Taylor), who dies for nothing in his defence of Carmen's non-existent honour. The film suggests that this is a society mainly without honour and where it does exist it is compromised by criminal association (Jones) or misdirected towards undeserving causes (Taylor). In these cases, the honour on show is destroyed because it has been manipulated by the new breed of active or sexual women interested only in money or pleasure who have displaced masculine tradition, resolve and duty. The film uses women as a sign of the crimes of this new society, with its interests in vice, self-indulgence and desire, offering an implicitly reactionary nostalgia for a lost male-dominated past. The dying body of General Sternwood (who has no 'blood in his veins') is contrasted to the bodies of his daughters to symbolise the shift, his withered flesh opposed to the endless carnal pleasures of Carmen and, to some extent, Vivian. However, it is questionable whether they find satisfaction or whether they are endlessly yearning for further pleasures because their desires cannot be fulfilled (and indeed Vivian is only ultimately shown as finding fulfilment in her domestication by Marlowe).

Marlowe's role in the film is to be a 'right guy', the term Jones uses to describe Marlowe and himself, thereby showing he is a worthy replacement for General Sternwood's surrogate son, Sean Regan, in his union with Vivian. He achieves these things by exhibiting the values of the old masculine order, in displaying integrity as a sign of tradition (his refusal to be bought off by Vivian), composure as a sign of his Stoic resolve when he is either threatened (by Eddie Mars at Geiger's) or suffering (his captivity at Art Huck's garage), and loyalty (to Vivian, in wanting to extricate her from her difficulties, or to Regan in wanting to discover his murderer) as a sign of his sense of duty in order to prove that he is not 'Doghouse Reilly', the name he uses with Carmen, which carries hints of shabbiness, sleaziness and failure. The narrative only ever uses this name as a self-conscious joke to indicate what Marlowe is not, however, and his path through the complications of the narrative is far more purposeful and knowledgeable than Powell's Marlowe in *Murder, My Sweet* because he knows, for example, how to identify characters by inspecting the driver's tags in their cars and understands not only the set-up between Vivian and Mars when she is hijacked, but also the reason for this incident. He clearly recognises the motivations and desires of those he encounters, and while this might suggest he is more fully of the society he traverses, he is always represented as honest. When Eddie Mars tells Marlowe he might make the detective's business his business, his reply that 'you wouldn't like it, the pay's too small' indicates that he cannot be bought by the society of loose money. Marlowe's wisecracks are also used to prove that he is superior (intellectually and morally) to the schemers and gangsters who dominate society, the most notable in this regard being his comment when Brody pulls a gun on him: 'My, my, such a lot of guns around town, [and] so few brains'. This quip signifies Marlowe's view that he is dealing with 'losers', people who are busy to no purpose on the edge of power and money, but his wisecracks also indicate that he is only an observer who is just as marginal, his superiority created only by the knowledge and integrity that allow him to recognise his powerless position.

The paradox that Marlowe has a superior position only by understanding his own social and economic insignificance is more fully played out in Chandler's novel, which leaves him with only the compensation of his intellectual superiority and honesty, but Hawks' film provides Marlowe with a romantic union with Vivian to draw him into the world of capital that signifies power. Marlowe triumphs by transforming Vivian from the 'exacting, smart and ruthless' woman described by General Sternwood into his own construction of her as 'Wonderful', even while he allows her to retain the 'cool, laconic, sexually assured and independent' qualities of her 'good-bad girl' persona

(Spicer, 2002: 92). He does this partly by showing faith in Vivian's honesty and integrity, but also by being contrary and insubordinate, deliberately asking for a drink and then changing his mind, for example, when she summons him in after his meeting with General Sternwood, but most obviously in the 'sugar won't work' scene after Vivian tries to pay him off and Marlowe refuses to submit. He then inverts their relationship by threatening the hard-boiled veneer she puts on display (signified by her fetishised lamé jacket and fur stole) when, in asking what hold Eddie Mars has over her, he tells her that she is not the independent, assured agent she thinks she is (the fiction of which is both sustained and revealed in the following scene when Mars arranges for her to win money at his casino before sending a man to take it back), but controlled and directed for corrupt purposes. He subsequently restores her to a simulation of independence by ending Mars' influence, although the film presents this as an acceptable simulation because even though Vivian has been brought under masculine control, she is allowed to retain vestiges of her assured self when she toughs things out with Marlowe in the final scene. Power, however, ultimately resides with Marlowe's mobile masculine self-sufficiency as 'a culturally iconized fantasy male deriv[ing] from his role as the perpetually liminal self who can move freely among the diverse social worlds thrown up by the city' (Krutnik, 1997: 90), and his assimilation into official society in the union with Vivian does not presage a loss of freedom. Instead, his centred individuality is confirmed, although the location of its validation in the off-centre world of Geiger's house also still suggests that Marlowe is off-centre, even if he now seems to be free of connotations of the threatened decentred alienated lone male that his previous occupation of solitary spaces (office and bachelor apartment) and the invasion of his home by Carmen signified.

Michael Shayne and the 'Hard-boiled' detective series

Although Michael Shayne is a private detective with hard-boiled origins (in the fiction of Brett Halliday), the films in the Shayne series more closely resemble those of the other crime series of the 1930s and 1940s. Designed to replace the 'Mr Moto' series, the films used narrative material from a variety of other detective novels with only one of the seven films in the Twentieth Century Fox series (*Michael Shayne, Private Detective*) and one of the five films made at the independent Producers Releasing Corporation (PRC) (*Blonde for a Day*) having a basis in Halliday's works.[10] This means that, like Sherlock Holmes, the Falcon and other series detectives, Shayne (played by Lloyd Nolan for Fox and then Hugh Beaumont for PRC) was scattered across different settings and cities (moving away from the Miami base of the novels) to face different types of crime in a variety of sub-genres of the crime film, such as comedy thriller in the first entry in the series, *Michael Shayne, Private Detective*, the suspense thriller in *Sleepers West* and the who-dunnit in *Dressed to Kill*. The character of Michael Shayne is one of the few hard-boiled signs within the series until the late PRC films placed him alongside members of the criminal underworld in *Blonde for a Day, Three on a Ticket* and *Too Many Winners*, because the films draw on the same kinds of B-Movie cinematic vaudeville used by the other crime series, thereby muting the tough style. Familiar tropes such as bungling or dimwitted police officers (Painter in *Michael Shayne, Private Detective* or Pierson in *Dressed to Kill*), humorous situations, and occasional interludes involving music (*Just Off Broadway*), dance (*Dressed to Kill*) and magic (*The Man Who Wouldn't Die*), as well as the pastiche of crime forms, provide distractions that unsettle the hard-boiled discourses. These also channel into Shayne's representation so that his persona is built more around comedy, with the result that his wise-cracking becomes less a matter of proving he is 'tough' than a way of providing burlesque humour, without need of a sidekick, to lighten the mood of the films. His breeziness and flippancy also reflect on his competence as a detective and on occasions he is more like the clumsy police officers who either inconvenience other series detectives or who chase investigations down blind alleys.

These devices are also, however, a way of coding Shayne as less perfect than the impossible detectives of the crime series or the masculine fantasies of the hard-boiled films in order to attach signs of authenticity to his representation. He is a rather downbeat ordinary detective who lacks the perfect integrity of Philip Marlowe because he often impersonates people, lies, tampers with evidence or uses unscrupulous tactics in order to earn money. Although these reality effects suggest an authentic portrayal of a detective, they are somewhat disrupted by the textual contrivances of the cinematic vaudeville customary within the B-Movie. The problematic authenticity of Shayne is established in *Michael Shayne, Private Detective* (Eugene Forde, 1941), which revolves around the contrivance of Shayne playing a practical joke to fake the murder of a gambler, Harry Grange, who is then subsequently found murdered apparently with a bullet from Shayne's gun. Unlike the hard-boiled detectives, who are entangled by narrative complexities which derive from and enact the destabilised society they inhabit, Shayne is entangled by a fictional device familiar from the B-Movie crime series from which he must extricate himself, even if he does it to protect Phyllis Brighton, the daughter of a wealthy man who has hired him to keep her away from Grange. Throughout the film he is the prime suspect for the police after being treated as a fall-guy by another gambler, Gordon, who implicates him in the murder of Grange to protect his own daughter. Shayne moves from one complication to another, hatching schemes, conniving and telling lies to try to find the real killer, but never reaching the condition of active agent because not only are his plans constantly frustrated, but they also mire him further in trouble (as when he swaps the barrel of his pistol for that of the actual murder weapon). He becomes the object of investigation, never able to become an effective agent of detection even when he tampers with evidence to implicate Gordon's daughter in order to turn the tables on Gordon so that he will not only hire him but also provide him with protection. His less than legitimate tactics still leave him bemused, however, and even enlisting Phyllis' crime-obsessed Aunt Olivia to provide whodunnit expertise (as well as a burlesque parody of whodunnit codes) only leads to a denouement, not to Shayne's command of it. He is saved by another fictional device when the real murderer confesses before the film concludes on a comic note when Shayne hugs his new partner, Aunt Olivia, to backtrack on the film's attempts to offer an authentic representation of a private detective.

The second film in the series, *Sleepers West* (Eugene Forde, 1941), is more melodrama than mystery even though it offers a suspense narrative in which Shayne escorts a surprise witness, Helen Carlson, by train to give evidence in a trial that will both exonerate a man wrongly accused of murder (a reformed crook called Callahan) and reveal political corruption. Shayne has little to do within the narrative except to remain watchful, retain his integrity by proving that he is helping Callahan for honourable reasons, and to resist the temptations of a corrupt private detective, Izzard, who has been hired to neutralise Helen before she gets to trial. Izzard represents the kind of detective Shayne must avoid becoming (despite his unscrupulous tactics in the previous film), but so too do other detectives because also present are the railroad inspector, Trautwein, who has been sent on a wild-goose chase (although he inadvertently helps Shayne at a key moment), and a pseudo-detective in the form of Kay, a newspaper reporter and ex-girlfriend of Shayne's. Shayne must counter their interferences in order to distinguish himself from their incompetence and, in Kay's case, from her conniving for her own ends. Shayne has little opportunity to demonstrate his competence until the final reel, however, and much of the narrative is filled with other matters, such as the mystification involving Izzard's attempts to find Helen. This sub-plot nevertheless draws out the film's melodramatic mode when Izzard embroils Linscott, an aide of the politician whose son committed the murder for which Callahan is on trial. Linscott, who is aboard the train with Kay, who is now his fiancée, is given the opportunity to make the right choice, in refusing to help Izzard, but fails and loses Kay as a consequence. Although the film uses Linscott to emphasise Shayne's integrity, because he puts money and career before honesty and love, there is little political comment in his failure because politics is collapsed into melodrama by presenting his choice as a moral and romantic decision. He is also used as a narrative device to counterbalance the right choices that are made by Helen and the man she meets on the train, Everett Jason, who is leaving behind his wife and a life of security in order to find himself. The narrative of Jason and Helen forms much of the film's focus as it displays their brief romance, allows them the opportunity to tell their life-stories, and puts them in a situation where they choose to go on to help justice (Helen) or turn back to responsibility (Jason). It is only when there is a sudden burst of action after the train collides with an oil tanker that has broken down on the line that Shayne is drawn in from the sidelines, having been marginalised by the omniscient narration that foregrounds other characters, but he is more a moral guardian than a detective when he reminds Helen and Jason of their duty by setting an example in following his own sense of duty to Callahan.

Shayne has moments that signal his investigative abilities in *Sleepers West*, such as spotting one of Kay's ruses when she tries to find Helen and then successfully frustrating her search. This makes him more quietly competent and wiser than he had been in the previous film and these talents are developed in *Dressed to Kill* (Eugene Forde, 1941) where he drives the narrative action. In particular, his control is signified by a return to a restricted narration, which follows him as he controls and moves forward the action, even as it showed him floundering in *Michael Shayne, Private Detective*. The film, however, begins to diffuse hard-boiled and suspense codes into the whodunnit form (effectively of the 'butler did it' variety in making its murderer an odd-job man with a secret history and a grudge against the victims) and Shayne is initially presented as a classical detective in using methods of ratiocination after he is sidetracked from his impending marriage by a scream. At the scene of the murder of a theatrical producer and an actress, he quickly locates clues (such as a playbill which provides suspects), deciphers the number of people who attended a dinner from the place settings, finds the murder weapons, and identifies the scorch-mark from a gunshot on a serving hatch that has been disguised as a cigarette burn to ultimately work out the means by which two people were killed at the same time. His re-enactment of the murder also codes him as a reasoning detective, although he still maintains a hard-boiled control of events by mapping a purposeful path through the narrative, following evidence from the murder-scene to various suspects and accurately interpreting testimony and mystification along the way so that, even though he is hampered in the trap he sets for the murderer, he still manages to disarm and overpower the killer. Shayne is a hybrid of the classical and the hard-boiled detective in *Dressed to Kill,* although he never aspires to the disinterested status of the former and describes himself as having 'turned in his Boy Scout badge' at one point. As a professional detective he has a concern for money that leads him to adopt some unscrupulous tactics, such as effectively blackmailing a suspect, Julian Davis, into hiring him or tricking Inspector Pierson out of crucial information so that he can forward his investigation and earn the money promised to him when he finds Davis innocent. He does demonstrate signs of integrity in protecting his client and this ambivalence means that he becomes as much Philip Marlowe as 'Doghouse Reilly'.

The attenuation of the hard-boiled style is furthered in *Blue, White and Perfect* (Herbert I. Leeds, 1942), a standard Nazi-hunting flag-waver of the kind popular after Pearl Harbor involving Germans smuggling industrial diamonds to the Third Reich. Shayne retains aspects of his conniving persona, conning his fiancée out of $1000 so that he can follow his investigation aboard ship to Honolulu, but the film is dominated by the usual tropes of the wartime pseudo-espionage film. These include Shayne's use of disguises; the obligatory character of Latin American origins as a helper of the United States (here as an FBI agent) to please South American allies; a spy-ring operating behind a respectable business; a revelation scene in which the chief Nazi is revealed to be a minor, seemingly innocuous, but ever-present character; an American woman unaware she is helping the Nazis but who reforms when she finds out (to be immediately rubbed out); and a validation of tough American masculinity when Shayne bests three larger German spies by throwing one of them to knock the other two down. There is some mystification and confusion regarding the FBI agent to extend the plot, along with a mystery about how the diamonds are being smuggled, but wartime production trends and B-Movie mystery conventions divert Shayne away from all but the most tenuous hard-boiled associations into available or topical situations. *The Man Who Wouldn't Die* (Herbert I. Leeds, 1942) has very little reference to war, but draws on the comedy ghost story, re-popularised by the Bob Hope films, *The Cat and the Canary* (1939) and *The Ghost Breakers* (1940), to present an old dark house mystery whose whodunnit aspects are confined to the denouement (a brief wrap-up telling a story of blackmail and double-crossing) because its narrative primarily comprises a grab-bag of Gothic and action-based thriller tropes. Its style is set in the opening scene when Gothic lighting effects are deployed as a camera pans across the front of a mansion to show a body being loaded into a station-wagon before intermittently using shadowed effects and uplighting on faces to create further suspense while also articulating related tropes (howling wind, rattling windows, thunder and lightning) as well as offering scattered horror codes such as a laboratory in the cellar and adapting codes of the monstrous threat in the form of a seemingly unstoppable swami able to simulate death through 'shallow breathing'.

The last two films in the Nolan incarnation of the series return to a more conventional murder-mystery format. *Just Off Broadway* (Herbert I. Leeds, 1942) draws on the burlesque humour deriving from the Shayne's clumsiness in *The Man Who Wouldn't Die* (where he electrocutes himself and exits the film in the conclusion by sliding down a banister into the sound of smashing china), but uses Phil Silvers' portrayal of a photographer who follows Shayne around to provide the comic vaudeville. The narrative is very much of the conventional whodunnit style despite (or because) of the contrived ingenuity that makes the killer the attorney defending a socialite (Lillian Hubbard) accused of murdering her fiancé who has been trying to frame others (a night-club owner and singer) so that he can to clear Lillian and achieve romantic union with her. The film is also ingenious in offering a hybrid courtroom drama and detective film, beginning with Shayne as a member of the jury before he sneaks out of the hotel where the jury are sequestered so that he can pursue his own investigation. The film ends back in the courtroom where Shayne takes on the role that all detectives effectively perform in the whodunnit denouement by acting as a prosecutor who reveals the truth and delivers justice. The last film at Fox, *Time to Kill* (Herbert I. Leeds, 1942), is a generally faithful adaptation of Chandler's *The High Window*, but even so, there are few traces of the hard-boiled style remaining here despite Shayne being allowed to wise-crack in the manner of Marlowe, because the film still uses such quips as burlesque one-liners ('I've got good news for the old lioness; pry her loose from her raw meat and put her on the phone'). This may be because Chandler's novel is more conventionally of the whodunnit style in plotting a linear path towards the denouement and it provides an apt end to Nolan's tenure as Shayne, before the PRC cheapies, by suggesting hard-boiled suspense but delivering crime series comedy murder mystery.

Conclusion: *Noir* Detectives, Rogue Cops, Undercover Men and Police Procedurals

The crime series persisted into the late 1940s, but the detective crime genre in this period, and into the 1950s, became increasingly fractured, as if the comforting formal style of the mystery series could no longer contain the complexity of post-war American society. A range of thrillers and investigate narratives emerged in detective and police dramas, including hard-boiled *noir*, investigative thrillers in the *noir* mode, the police procedural, undercover narratives, and rogue cop films, even though, as noted in the previous chapters, many crime series persisted until the end of the 1940s. The closure of the B production units and the development of unit and independent production aided the demise of the series because more flexible forms of production created more autonomy and experimentation in Hollywood film-making (Maltby, 1983: 75) and the series no longer aligned with the less centralised planning structure of the studios. Although some units and independent companies focused on particular styles, such as the Val Lewton unit at RKO which continued to produce cheaply made horror films, others such as the Mark Hellinger unit at Universal, while focusing on crime, deployed a diversity of styles (Schatz, 1997: 386–7). Spicer (2002: 34) also discusses how independent producers, such as Enterprise Productions, which operated in the late 1940s, had the opportunity to develop a particular style as a result of aesthetic and political choices, in this case *noir* crime movies such as *Body and Soul* and *Force of Evil*, a freedom that would not have been possible a few years earlier. There are therefore matters of production that help to account for the rise of new forms of crime film in addition to whatever cultural factors might have contributed to their emergence, whether it is the post-war disillusionment and misogynistic fear of female empowerment that Leitch describes as the usual reasons ascribed to the rise of *film noir* (2002: 127), or a crisis of

American modernity arising from tensions surrounding the increased systematisation of society at the expense of individual liberty in parallel with a counteracting perception that social institutions had failed and cast individuals out into a disconnected society. However deeply felt these tensions might have been in American society, there are nevertheless concerns in the texts from the varied crime formats with either a disjointed modern experience (Luhr and Lehman, 2006: 175) in which individuals are cut loose from social bonds and the apparatuses of the State (*noir* heroes and rogue cops) or with a routinised world in which bureaucratic legal systems efface identity (police procedural and undercover cops).

Film noir and the investigative thriller

Film noir is the area in which texts most closely related to the detective film can be found, producing styles that include hard-boiled *noir* and the investigative thriller, predominantly involving pseudo-detectives, as well as some undercover cop narratives and a subset of films focalised through the figure Krutnik (1991) refers to as the 'investigative veteran'. The overall category of the investigative thriller includes films such as *The Glass Key, The Killers, Deadline at Dawn* and *Johnny Angel*, with the sub-category of the 'investigative veteran' film contributing films such as the amnesiac veteran film *Somewhere in the Night, Cornered* (involving a veteran abroad), *The Blue Dahlia* and *Dead Reckoning. The Killers* (Robert Siodmak, 1946) is one of the paradigmatic forms of the former investigative style in focalising events through an insurance investigator, Riordan (Edmond O'Brien), as he pieces together the fragments of the life of The Swede (Burt Lancaster), a boxer and petty hood, after the opening sequence has presented the latter's unexplained murder in a small town. The film has a fractured centre of narration because much of it is told in flashbacks which are presented in non-linear fashion as O'Brien uncovers evidence through the stories of various characters even if O'Brien's investigation maps a linear trajectory towards the truth of the betrayal of The Swede by Kitty (Ava Gardner), the woman to whom he submitted because of his obsessive desire for her. In offering parallel narrational strategies, the film enacts the fractured masculinity of The Swede in complex and fragmentary flashback narrations in order to explain his mysterious passivity in allowing his assassins to kill him. This approach reveals a flawed masculinity by showing that The Swede's passivity has already been articulated through his surrender to his desires for Kitty, but also allows O'Brien to be centred by his more structured narrative investigation through which he reasserts masculine authority and takes revenge on Kitty for her creation of what the film considers to be The Swede's aberrant masculinity.

The Glass Key (Stuart Heisler, 1942), adapted from a novel by Dashiell Hammett, offers an investigation emanating from the criminal underworld and has resonances with the hard-boiled style by portraying a gangster as a detective in the form of Ed Beaumont (Alan Ladd) who is the right-hand man of gang boss Paul Madvig (Brian Donlevy). The case concerns the murder of a local politician's son during a period of tension between Madvig and a rival boss who wants to take over the city and is set against the backdrop of an election in which the father of the murder victim is running on an anti-mob platform. The narrative traces connections between the criminal underworld and high society in the manner of the hard-boiled text and offers Beaumont as a suffering detective taken into captivity to receive a number of beatings from Jeff, a thug from the rival gang, who feminises him in the process by calling him 'Sweetheart' or 'Cuddles' during the beatings, although there is a homo-erotic subtext which is revealed when Jeff seeks to intimidate Beaumont after the latter's escape by getting so close to him that it appears as if he is cuddling up against him. The narrative involving the gang is all mystification, however, because Beaumont reveals that it is the politician who killed his own son after using the ruse of having a warrant sworn out for the arrest of the murder victim's sister, Janet (Veronica Lake), in order to force a confession out of her father. Alan Ladd returned to investigative mode as Johnny Morrison in *The Blue Dahlia* (George Marshall, 1946), a 'maladjusted veteran' film (Spicer, 2002: 86) scripted by Raymond Chandler. The film concerns the murder of Johnny's wife, Helen, with evidence seeming to incriminate him until he is exonerated with the help of Joyce (Veronica Lake) and a police detective who coaxes a confession out of a blackmailing hotel detective, even though Chandler's original script had his Navy buddy, Buzz (William Bendix), killing Helen, because of bouts of mental instability caused by a head injury suffered in the war, until the Navy Department persuaded Paramount to change the ending (Clark, 1982: 62).

One of the most interesting of the investigative veteran films is *Dead Reckoning* (John Cromwell, 1947), which sets its hero, Rip Murdock (Humphrey Bogart), on an investigation to find an army buddy. Rip begins in a state of ignorance except for the real name of his army buddy, Johnny, which means that he has to piece together a world and a criminal reality from scratch. The investigation becomes more a matter of understanding the mystery of the *femme fatale*, Coral Chandler (Lizabeth Scott), the woman with whom Johnny is obsessed, who forms the central problem in Rip's quest for truth (Krutnik, 1991: 170), partly because she is in a condition of knowledge to Rip's condition of ignorance, but also because she incarnates Rip's inability to understand women as a result of a misogynistic view of female duplicity arising from his masculine attachment to order and meaning. In beginning his investigation he displays 'masculine competence' (Krutnik, 1991: 168) by finding his way in strange landscapes (the urban landscape of Gulf City and the world of crime) using old newspapers and the phone book to discover Johnny's history before he enlisted in the army (his apparent murder of Coral's husband, Stuart Chandler) and to map a path around the city to start his detection when a visit to the morgue reveals Johnny is dead and the finding of the Sanctuary Club uncovers some leads. The film is mainly narrated in flashback as Rip recounts his story to a priest, but by the end of the flashback narration the result of his 'masculine competence' is that he knows nothing about Johnny, Coral, and the other characters he has encountered because the pre-narrative *récit* which explains the totality of the situation is still a complete mystery. He only comes to knowledge when he confronts the night club owner, Martinelli, who reveals that he is Coral's real husband and that he killed Chandler, but this is only legitimated as truth when Coral proves Rip's misogynistic suspicion by trying to kill him, even if she only manages to shoot Martinelli by mistake. Coral is ultimately punished by death when Rip reasserts masculine authority, but the film still articulates anxieties about a vulnerable masculinity trapped by an ineffable femininity to which the only responses seem to be either obsessive submission or destruction of the cause of emasculation.

Hard-boiled *noir* detectives

This is an area of particular concern in the hard-boiled *noir* style, which bears further analysis because of its similarities with and inversions of the classic hard-boiled style. *Out of the Past* (Jacques Tourneur, 1947) dramatises a similar pattern to that on display in *Dead Reckoning* in the representation of the choices made by its detective-hero, Jeff Markham (Robert Mitchum), who ultimately decides to control the film's *femme fatale*, Kathie Moffett (Jane Greer), by destroying her in order to atone for his earlier submission to her. His subordination to Kathie is shown in a flashback sequence set in Acapulco where he has followed her after being hired by the gangster Whit Sterling (Kirk Douglas) to bring her back along with $40,000 she has taken. In Acapulco, Jeff gives in to his desire for Kathie, negating the autonomy of the detective, by allowing himself to be drawn to the meeting places she chooses, knowing he is a 'chump' but holding out the hope that she will follow him (and thereby submit to his control) when he asks her to leave with him in order to escape Whit. When Whit arrives in Acapulco, Jeff seeks to convince himself he is still active as a masculine subject by briefly resuming the mask of the detective persona but the self-sufficiency it seemingly bolsters is revealed to be fragile when Jeff responds with anger to Whit's seeming accusations that he is a failure for not having found Kathie. Although this is part of an act to conceal his relationship with Kathie (and her imminent arrival at the bar where he, Whit and Joe Stephanos, Whit's henchman, are waiting), Jeff's anger is nevertheless still an attempt to re-empower himself for the failure that he perceives, but to which Whit, sitting calmly beside him under a mask of composed masculinity, is oblivious. Jeff's display of uncontrolled emotion also emphasises that, in submitting to Kathie, he has abandoned the composed self-sufficiency associated with the detective agent, as signified by his telling Whit that he is giving up his search, although it is only when Whit tells him that 'I fire people, but nobody quits me' that he properly understands that he has no control over his actions. This places Jeff in a submissive position, ideologically feminine, not least because there are suggestions within the film that Whit sees Kathie as an object that signifies his power (particularly economic) whereas his true desires are for Jeff (indicated by the fact he later hates Jeff as Jeff hates Kathie, suggesting that he is also a betrayed lover). This complicates the masculine relationships, not least because Jeff has created a sense of his own insufficiency by projecting into Whit's position as a competing and economically powerful masculinity and looked back at himself through Whit's eyes to find himself wanting.

The money that Kathie takes from Whit is significant in this regard, because it signifies Kathie's aspirations to masculine economic independence and because it signifies Kathie as a metonymy for money and the success that money brings; it is not the loss of Kathie (as 'one dame in a million') that concerns Whit, but the sign of success and money she represents. The 'million' in Whit's description of Kathie in Acapulco seems also to be displaced on to money in the context of both Jeff's previous concerns about wasting Whit's money pursuing Kathie and the slightly disparaging reference to Kathie as a 'dame'. Within this network, once he has submitted to his desire rather than maintained his masculine duty as a detective, Jeff is powerless before either Whit or Kathie, because when he begins to disparage her, after she betrays him, he is also disparaging and negating himself, both in terms of his lost masculine sufficiency and the desires that led to this loss. The sense of desiring as a synonym for insufficiency, as a lack in both self-fulfilment and ideological completion (which can also be extended to economic deficiency because this bears upon both social and sexual articulations of power) is significant in the construction of Jeff who, once he has failed to redeem Kathie after their flight to San Francisco, retreats to a small town called Bridgeport to hide from Whit under a new name (Jeff Bailey), which is where the film starts. Here, he has a business (as a garage owner) and a more normative domestic heterosexual relationship with a new girlfriend, Ann, through which he seeks to establish both economic and sexual independence in order to reconstitute a version of masculine sufficiency in tune with the 'archaic American dream' of Bridgeport (Grist, 1992: 205). He finds, however, that he is called back into his old life as a detective, where he has already failed, when he is spotted by Stephanos and he is set up to fail again in Whit's plan to make him a fall-guy for murder. Jeff uses the narrative of the detective provided for him, however, to 'prove his worth as a "tough" private eye' (Krutnik, 1991: 105), keeping his new name of Bailey to signify his distance from his previous failed detective persona, turning his detection into a contest with Kathie, to prove he is free of his desire for her, and with Whit, to re-emasculate himself by becoming what he sees in Whit in order to reverse their situations.

Jeff's path to redemptive masculine autonomy involves an encounter with another dangerous female, the duplicitous Meta Carson, who sets Jeff to steal some tax files from Whit's attorney which might incriminate him, although this time he remains free from seduction, and a further meeting with Kathie, who he deceives so that he can act out his plans to take possession of the tax files. Jeff is coded as an active detective agent through his use of unlawful methods, involving several acts of breaking and entering and an assertion of masculine power to force the files out of the night club manager who is holding them, and although these suggest disempowerment because he has to resort to criminal acts, they also correspond with the shrewdness and physical power associated with the private eye, while Jeff's stealth and mobility as he moves quickly and silently around San Francisco suggest his ability when acting autonomously. Jeff, however, is defeated by chance when the body of the attorney, for whose murder he has been framed, is discovered sooner than expected and he has to confront Whit in his mansion. However, after using the tax files as a bargaining chip to free himself from the frame, Kathie negates all Jeff has done to reassert his self-sufficiency by killing Whit while he is reconciling with Ann, thereby thwarting both his deal with Whit (leaving him in the frame) and his plans for heterosexual domesticity. The film therefore creates more than a competition with women, even if Kathie takes the upper hand, but also between men, a contest in which Jeff fails because it is Kathie who deals with Whit as she deals with Jeff's partner, Fisher, when he arrives in San Francisco where the couple have holed up after returning from Acapulco, having stuck to the task of being a detective, albeit a corrupt one who is only after the money that Kathie stole from Whit. Jeff can only therefore find compensation by destroying Kathie, but he does so by proxy, by deception and in a self-destructive manner, in leading her into a police trap that results in both their deaths. Jeff thus gives up his masculinity in the ending even as he seems to assert it in the destruction of the active female agent, making him a failed detective for a second time in 'his inability to become something other than he once was' (Palmer, 2004: 60) and in his failure to redeem himself after failing to redeem Kathie, who has no interest in matters other than more material concerns such as power and money and who shows more masculine resolve throughout the film as she clocks up three murders and only pays for one.

The vulnerable detective of *film noir* can also be seen in *The Dark Corner* (Henry Hathaway, 1946) although in this case it is the power of money and the services it can buy that destabilise the private eye, who has only his own subjectivity to hold at bay the threats he encounters. Although Bradford Galt (Mark Stevens), the detective of the film, is not subjected to the temptations of money, nevertheless the narrative suggests that if sexual desire is one obstacle to fulfilment as an autonomous agent for the detective, then money is the other obstacle. Hardy Cathcart (Clifton Webb), through his monetary power, seems to overcome the adultery that threatens his relationship with his wife, Mari, and re-establish his control over her as his aestheticised object (created because of her resemblance to a portrait he worshipped before he met her), by using hired muscle, 'White Suit' (William Bendix), to both kill her lover, Tony Jardine, and to frame Galt. This keeps him at a distance from the crime, protected by his money, especially once he has killed 'White Suit'. However, Mari refuses to take on the role he has created for her and kills Cathcart instead, thereby rescuing Galt, although her revenge seems more a product of sulky petulance at her own dependency than the result of any willed agency. Mari's childish self-regard makes her a degraded version of Cathcart's ideal, although this seems less a comment on Cathcart's misguided fetishisation of her than a way of framing her failures as a distorted reflection of Galt, who is as weak, dependent and petulantly despairing of his condition. Galt's compromised position is hinted at early in the film when he receives a visit from a police lieutenant, Reeves, who seems to be persecuting him for his convict past, and his impotency is further revealed when he tells Kathleen (Lucille Ball), his assistant, that he was set up for manslaughter by Jardine, his ex-partner, who now works with Cathcart. Before this, he receives a visit from 'White Suit' during which he seems to assert his hard-boiled masculinity, but although 'White Suit' submits to Galt's tough-guy act, it is a facsimile of fear designed to falsely bolster Galt's sense of his own toughness. When 'White Suit' allows Galt to threaten and slap him around to coerce a false client's name out of him (Jardine) it snares Galt in the plan concocted by Cathcart that ultimately makes him powerless. His failure to achieve masculine potency is signified, however, by the drunk he throws as soon as he learns Jardine's name and by his distracted state in the night club afterwards.

He tries to retrieve his self-sufficiency by taking Kathleen in his arms and kissing her and then by posturing as tough and active (a seeker hero) when he masquerades a sneering hard-boiled front in his confrontation with Jardine, during which he seems to prove his 'toughness' by punching Jardine across a desk. However, in so doing, Galt actually becomes feminised and passive (a victim hero) because he misrecognises his sense of masculine agency without understanding that it is only a fabrication created by others to turn him into a fall-guy. 'White Suit' further reveals Galt's inadequacy on the telephone to Cathcart by reporting that it not only took Galt two days to spot him but that he also fell for the 'softie' routine, although it is the ease with which 'White Suit' overcomes Galt, murders Jardine with a poker and then fakes a convincing struggle by breaking furniture to create the frame-up that fully confirms Galt's futility as a detective-hero. Kathleen further confirms Galt's insufficiency when, after he crumples under the pressure, she proves herself more effective by cleaning up the murder scene in no time at all and then displays her sexual superiority by taking him into her apartment, signed by the milkman's surprised but unconcerned look when he realises Galt's presence there. Galt still refuses to avoid helplessness when he gives up after the Fred Foss lead goes nowhere, and even when the little girl provides him with information on where he can find 'White Suit', he still looks bewildered. Kathleen then proves to be the better detective when she realises that the girl's reference to 'cascara at the gallery' refers to the Cathcart Gallery. Galt only has a posed facsimile of hard-boiled masculinity, displayed in the language he uses, which seems tough, but which enacts his impotence ('I haven't got the answers, but the police will find them. They're laid out like road markers right up my alley') to make him a rhetorical masculine agent, rather than the genuine article. Fortunately, he has the help of a chirpy and hard-boiled Kathleen, who as well as being maternal is tougher than he is (because, as she says, he only 'thinks he's tough' whereas, as he says, she is 'the blow-torch type'). The result of their partnership is a perverse romance in which Galt is infantilised as a helpless, pusillanimous and needy child who fails even to achieve the masculine potency of Jardine even though the latter becomes the object of murder.

Rogue cops, undercover men and police procedurals

Perhaps the most influential strand of crime fiction that developed in the 1940s, because it ultimately displaces the styles associated with the amateur and private detectives that have been the object of study in this book, is the police investigation film, whether in the form of the rogue cop, undercover police officer or the police procedural. The first of these inflects its representations with *noir* motifs by focusing on obsessed or compromised police officers. *Laura* (Otto Preminger, 1944) offers an investigation of perverse desire by representing a police officer, Lieutenant McPherson (Dana Andrews), compromised by his seemingly necrophiliac love for a dead woman (until it is revealed that the eponymous Laura is still alive), but his love still seems to be of the same fetishistic order as the jealous possessiveness of Waldo Lydecker (Clifton Webb), not least because he demonstrates the same jealousy in his suspicion of Laura when she comes back from the dead. Laura (Gene Tierney) forms the focus for the obsessions of several characters, however, so that McPherson's infatuation seems normal within the skewed world of high society he enters. He still has to negotiate the bitchy acrimony that Lydecker, Carpenter (Laura's almost fiancé) and Ann Treadwell show towards each other in order to prove his 'self-sufficiency', even if he seems to display his impotence when, as Lydecker comments, he falls 'in love with a corpse', slave to a desire that is not only perverse but which he can never fulfil. Throughout, however, McPherson retains a deductive ability, albeit resonant of the whodunnit rather than the hard-boiled detective (Walker, 1992a: 10), proving his perception and knowledge at several points as well as in his deduction of the method used by Lydecker in his killing of the woman he mistook for Laura, although his ruse to incriminate his suspect (returning the shotgun used in the first murder to its hiding place inside a clock) almost miscarries when Lydecker retrieves it and goes after Laura again. He rescues himself by realising Laura's peril in time for her to rush into the safety of his arms, although this action is only a confirmation of his return to the hard-boiled agency he displayed on his first appearance in Lydecker's apartment as a casual, uncouth detective in a rumpled suit unimpressed by the perfect sheen of the sophisticated world of Lydecker and Laura. It is primarily through his control of Laura that he proves his masculinity when he browbeats the truth out of her in the interrogation room. In so doing, he returns himself to phallic potency by aligning legal authority with masculine power and cracks Laura's fetishistic power over himself and other men to make her willing to submit to his protection as she seeks to escape Lydecker for a second time.

I Wake Up Screaming and *Where the Sidewalk Ends* offer similarly compromised police officers and their narratives are less concerned with detection than with the revelation of the corruption or irrational passions that call into question the objectivity and impartiality of the institutions of law and justice. *I Wake Up Screaming* (H. Bruce Humberstone, 1941) offers an obsessed detective in Ed Cornell (Laird Cregar) who, although he knows that the killer of a model called Vicky Lynn is a desk clerk (Elisha Cook Jr in his role as perennial loser) still persecutes Frankie Christopher (Victor Mature), the promoter who created Vicky's career. The narrative focuses on Cornell's deranged hounding of Christopher, firstly when he is shown sitting in an armchair in Christopher's bedroom in the middle of the night and then when he proves he is more hard-boiled than Frankie by goading him into committing suicide to avoid conviction. He also demonstrates shrewdness in his cynical manipulation of Jill (Betty Grable) to create doubts in her mind over Frankie's innocence, although Jill turns out to be hard-boiled too because she refuses to be cowed and then displays agency and potency Frankie only ever affects in his front of toughness, perhaps turning out to be tougher even than Cornell whose sentimental fantasies are displayed in the conclusion when his shrine to Vicky is revealed. *Where the Sidewalk Ends* (Otto Preminger, 1950) tells the story of a tough detective, Mark Dixon (Dana Andrews), whose obsessive desire to punish criminals causes him to accidentally kill a suspect when he uses his usual violent methods on a veteran with a plate in his head. Dixon is as an ambiguous figure, the film seemingly questioning his methods when he receives a warning about his violence from Inspector Foley, his superior, but also treating him as a hero in the eyes of several characters, including a taxi driver, Jiggs Taylor, who is accused of the killing Dixon has committed, and his daughter, Morgan (Gene Tierney), whose admiration turns to love when Dixon does his utmost to exonerate her father. He is also, however, referred to as a 'gorilla' by another character while Scalise, the hood he is particularly keen to incriminate for another murder and to frame to clear Jiggs, describes him as 'a man full of hate' to problematise the more positive views. It is when Dixon takes a beating from three of Scalise's thugs in the manner of a private eye, giving a good account of himself against the odds to prove his masculine potency and fortitude, that focalisation leads to identification and thereafter his suffering and guilt are emphasised as he moves toward redemption. First of all, he admits that he has become a 'mobster' like his father in trying to cover up the killing in a letter he writes to Foley, then he sets himself up to be killed by Scalise to clear Jiggs and finally, once Scalise has been incriminated and he has become a hero, he insists that Foley reads his letter of confession instead of taking it back unread.

Dixon is a fore-runner of later rogue cops, but before then Hollywood balanced its representations of compromised or obsessed police officers with cops who are just dogged and methodical in their pursuit of crime or who are considerate and understanding liberals. Lieutenant Candella (Victor Mature) in *Cry of the City* (Robert Siodmak, 1948) is of the former type, but his rule-bound style is so ruthless that he becomes an unsympathetic depersonalised force in his pursuit of Richard Conte's gangster Martin Rome. He is so obsessive that his investigation takes the form of a vendetta similar to the one McQuigg in *The Racket* (John Cromwell, 1951) pursues against the gangster Nick Scanlon even if the latter is depicted as having a mission to serve society to legitimate his actions. Lieutenant Koch in *Johnny O'Clock* (Robert Rossen, 1947) offers a corrective for the compromised or troubled cops because, although he engages in a contest of tough guys with Dick Powell's Johnny he is considerate, dogged and watchful rather than obsessed or malicious so that, despite his apparent grudge against Johnny, he seems pleased finally to exonerate him of the murder of a crooked cop and his girlfriend. On the liberal side are Brian Donlevy's D'Angelo in *Kiss of Death* (Henry Hathaway, 1947), an Assistant District Attorney rather than a cop, and Captain Finlay (Robert Young) in *Crossfire* (Edward Dmytryk, 1947), who clears a troubled soldier of the murder of a Jewish veteran by finding the real killer, the anti-Semitic Montgomery (Robert Ryan). The film also has an investigative veteran in the form of Keeley (Robert Mitchum), although his role as detective is curtailed after his interference in Finlay's investigation causes Montgomery to kill again. Robert Ryan was often cast as a hard-nosed and brutal character and this is on display in his role as the tough cop, Wilson, in *On Dangerous Ground* (Nicholas Ray, 1951), although the sadistic disposition he shows during a manhunt is later tempered when he falls for a blind woman played by Ida Lupino.

Spicer considers *On Dangerous Ground* a rogue cop film (Spicer, 2002: 87), in which category he also includes many of the films discussed previously, although Leitch (2002: 143) considers it within a grouping of films about 'troubled-cop heroes', which also includes *Detective Story* (William Wyler, 1951). In this film, Kirk Douglas plays Detective McLeod as an intolerant cop with an unblemished record operating in a world in which the ugliness of crime is portrayed, who becomes unhinged by a personal crisis involving his wife's concealment of her past which causes him to use rough tactics against a sleazy abortionist with a connection to his wife. Like most troubled cops, McLeod finds redemption before he dies, although patrolman Johnny Kelly in the portentous *City That Never Sleeps* (John H. Auer, 1953) lives to find redemption, even if he helps to cause the death of his policeman father because he is tempted by money offered for his services by a crooked lawyer. *City That Never Sleeps* is an odd police drama because although it deploys the realistic style of the police procedural in its use of locations and offers *noir* betrayal and sexual infidelity among a circle of crooked, criminal or deceitful characters, it also has the city of Chicago joining Johnny on his night-beat, as a police sergeant called Joe Chicago, to watch over him until he makes the right choices to stay in the police force and to return to his wife. Other rogue cop films in the 1950s include *Private Hell 36* (Don Siegel, 1954), which focuses on the criminal activities of corrupt police officers, and *Rogue Cop* (Roy Rowland, 1954) and *The Big Heat* (Fritz Lang, 1953), which suggest that the police must 'other' themselves to become like criminals in order to assert the law. The latter film portrays Bannion (Glenn Ford) disgusted by crime, but effectively having to adopt its tactics in resigning from the police force so that he can pursue the gangsters in a syndicate who killed his wife. In the pursuit of his investigation, which is again more like a vendetta, he becomes a maverick racket-buster in the manner of the hard-boiled private eye, but he is so 'tough' that the imagery figures him, rather, as a gangster like Vince Stone (Lee Marvin) until he is humanised and redeemed by his contact with Debbie (Gloria Grahame), the doomed 'good-bad girl', who rescues him from crossing the boundary into criminal activity.

The other significant strains that developed within the police drama are the undercover cop narrative and the police procedural which overlap in some ways, as Luhr and Lehman (2006: 177) indicate by considering the undercover narrative of *T-Men* (Anthony Mann, 1947) within the procedural form. Other undercover cop films include *The Undercover Man* (Joseph H. Lewis, 1949), which concerns Treasury agents tracking down a syndicate boss in a story based on the entrapment of Al Capone, and *The Street with No Name* (William Keighley, 1948), while *White Heat* (Raoul Walsh, 1949) also marshals an undercover narrative, as well as including the technology of crime detection associated with the procedural, in parallel with a psychopathic gangster narrative dominated by James Cagney's Cody Jarrett. The film highlights one of the key motifs of undercover cop narratives in Cagney's bravura performance by emphasising his individuality, albeit presenting it as aberrant, in contrast to the facelessness of the undercover agent, Hank Fallon (Edmond O'Brien), in his impersonation of a criminal called Vic Pardo and the effacement of his own identity that the latter masquerade signifies in providing him with the personality that his cop-self, Fallon, lacks. This trope is repeated across the undercover cop film which represents the erasure of identity in the adoption of a criminal guise so that in *T-Men* the agents, Genaro (Alfred Ryder) and O'Brien (Dennis O'Keefe), gain new memories as well as clothes and documents when they are made anew as 'Galvani' and 'Harrigan'. This sense of the wiping of the self is signified in the use of montage effects when O'Brien enters the underworld, which are screened over him to create a spectral effect that suggests both that he is blurring into the criminal landscape and that he is a ghostly self. It is unclear whether the ghost self is his cop or criminal identity, although when he has to stand by and watch the execution of his partner, who in his criminal role has had to deny knowing his own wife to maintain his fictional undercover self, it is implied that it is his official identity that has disappeared in his powerlessness to step out of criminal character. *The Street with No Name* offers the same construction of identity, although Gene Cordell (Mark Stevens) finds that he is as faceless inside the gang as outside because he has to submit to the same system by which government law enforcement operates.

This latter film also draws on the procedural style initially in the fetishisation of routine, method and scientific detection that characterises procedural films, which include *Call Northside 777* (Henry Hathaway, 1948), *The Naked City* (Jules Dassin, 1948), and *He Walked By Night* (Alfred Werker, 1948). *The Naked City* has a semi-documentary style through which it suggests an authentic representation of crime and its investigation by focusing on the routine of detection. The film opens with a montage of shots of New York set against a narration by its producer, Mark Hellinger, who claims that the film will show 'the city as it is', as the shots pick out ordinary people who will not recur in the narrative before focusing on the crime that forms the investigation, the murder of a model, and then the murderer killing his accomplice by the river, before drawing in the two detectives, Dan Muldoon (Barry Fitzgerald) and Jimmy Halloran (Don Taylor), who will pursue the investigation. As Schatz notes (1997: 390), the film is 'authentic in its treatment of police procedures' and this is shown in the inspection of the crime scene in which clues, relevant or otherwise, are noted and methods such as the medical examination of the body, dusting for fingerprints, interviewing characters, photographing the scene and moving furniture for a thorough search are shown to indicate that this is not the cursory examination of a crime scene provided by the detective of the crime series. The film proceeds through other routine procedures, particularly focusing on the 'legwork' of searches and questioning, as well as showing forensic science on occasions, while also including pointless information and a false confession, although it highlights their irrelevance instead of using them as mystification. The film, however, does still offer dramatic moments to disrupt the mode of documentary realism, such as Muldoon's creation of a confrontation between two characters and the tension created by Garzah's attempt to evade the police as the film draws towards its conclusion. There are also occasions when the two detectives are humanised through the representation of home-life and their companionate relationship to prove that they have not been depersonalised by the system of bureaucracy signified by the 'step-by-step' routine of procedural detection. *He Walked by Night* offers similar signs of authenticity in its painstaking search of a crime scene and surrounding area, its use of forensics and the recurrent dragnets it includes, although unlike *The Naked City* it shows the criminal's activities outside of the investigation to disrupt the procedural format and more clearly has an ideological purpose in its representation of police procedure, which is described by a witness as 'amazing' at one point. In focusing attention on procedure, the film points to the way in which the police procedural, even if it doesn't kill off the detective (who appears consistently after the 1940s), does signal the death of the romantic individual detective of the crime series who has no place in the world in which the science of detection doesn't seem to need a detective.

Notes

1 Exploring Detective Films in the 1930s and 1940s: Genre, Society and Hollywood

1. For a discussion of Hollywood's predilection for action in narratives, see Elsaesser (1981) and the analysis of this essay in Maltby (1995: 352–4).
2. An important strand of recent criticism of literary detective fiction has emphasised the widening of the genre to incorporate female and non-white protagonists (Munt, 1994; Pepper, 2000; Bertens and D'Haen, 2001; Knight, 2004: 162–94) but, despite Hollywood's use of Asian detectives in the 1930s and 1940s, these accounts are more relevant to contemporary Hollywood crime films.
3. This was not only the case in B-Movies, however, as Warner's films, including headliners, in the early 1930s generally came in at only about an hour and one-quarter due to budgetary restraints and pace was a similar necessity. See Miller (1973: 4–5).
4. See Palmer (1991: 124) for an alternative view which argues that 'the criminal mystery dominates each text to the extent that all the events in the narrative contribute to the enigma and its solution by the hero'.
5. Field (2009: 27–8), for example, takes the second position in order to create a binary opposition between the cerebral British whodunnit and the visceral American suspense thriller.
6. The Republic serials were: *Dick Tracy* (1937), *Dick Tracy Returns* (1938), *Dick Tracy's G-Men* (1939) and *Dick Tracy vs Crime, Inc.* (1941) (Langman and Finn, 1995b: 80).
7. The use of the series' detectives in spy-hunter films after 1941, however, modifies this relationship by giving them at least an ideological affiliation with the discourses of freedom and democracy that Hollywood deploys in its propagandistic representation of the Allies in general and the United States in particular.
8. See Cross (1981: 7) for details with regard to the organisation of B units at specific studios.
9. See Taves (1993: 329) for details of the use of contract-players and other studio personnel in B film units.
10. Kerr (1986: 230) notes, in discussing *film noir*, that during the early 1940s as a result of escalating costs: 'Casts and crews on contract to B units were kept at a manageable minimum, so prohibiting plots with long cast lists, crowd scenes and complicated camera or lighting set-ups'.
11. I would like to thank Alasdair Spark for pointing out the similarity between the performances of detective and the magician in the act of revealing the truth.

2 'Such Lovely Friends': Class and Crime in 'The Thin Man' Series

1. Schatz (1997: 49) includes *The Thin Man* in the class of low budget films produced by MGM although Naremore (1998: 141) considers it as having an A budget in comparison to other studios' B productions.
2. Glitre argues that the screwball form was itself a product of two modes, the sophisticated comedy and the 'tough comedy', mixing 'the glamorous pleasure-filled lifestyle of the former with the wise-cracking sexual tension of the latter' (Glitre, 2006: 23). This means that *The Thin Man* draws its 'toughness' from within the comedy genre as much as it does from its source novel.
3. See Neve (1992: 28) for a discussion of populism's deployment of 'the opposition between elites and "the people"'.
4. An alternative view might, however, see Nick as a dabbler, taking on a profession similar to other screwball comedy heroes 'in a field middle America does not view as serious or "real" employment' (Gehring, 2002: 30).
5. See Bergman (1971: 141–5) for a discussion of the importance of innocence and simplicity in redeeming the United States in Capra's 1930s films.
6. The film offers a modified back-story for Nick who is now at work as a detective again, working as a consultant for the NYPD, rather than managing Nora's business affairs.

3 Between Law and Crime: The Chivalric 'Criminal' Detective

1. Boston Blackie and the Lone Wolf both first appeared in film in the silent era before being revived in the 1930s and 1940s. Boston Blackie appeared in a number of silent films beginning with *Boston Blackie's Little Pal* in 1918 while the Lone Wolf had been regularly portrayed by Bert Lytell after his first appearance in *The Lone Wolf* in 1917.
2. The granting of a temporary official licence to the criminal detective to allow him to engage in detection was an occasional device used by other series. Michael Lanyard, for example, is used by the police in *Secrets of the Lone Wolf* (1941) and Boston Blackie is given a police badge in *One Mysterious Night* (1944), although in both cases the pair come under later suspicion.
3. See Pepper (2010: 345) for a discussion of the Op's relations with political and economic power structures and the way that these undercut his sense of autonomy.
4. The character of Hymie Fanro, who pays deference to The Saint during *The Saint in New York*, was played by Paul Guilfoyle, who returned to the series as Pearly Gates in *The Saint Takes Over* and *The Saint in Palm Springs*, playing a more overtly subservient character in his role as The Saint's comedy sidekick.
5. Miller (1973: 225) and Hardy (1997: 123) report that the reasons for the change were either that Charteris withdrew the rights to 'The Saint' or recovered them.

6. The death of the first Falcon is a textual contrivance necessitated by George Sanders' desire to quit the 'Falcon' series, but it comes as a logical conclusion to the troubles that beset the Gay Lawrence incarnation.
7. Nick Charles is, however, a similar figure as Glitre comments in her discussion of the way in which *The Thin Man* plays a central role in 'the development of Powell's trickster persona' (Glitre, 2006: 81).

4 Englishness and America: Basil Rathbone's Sherlock Holmes

1. Ousby (1976: 153) notes, however, that Conan Doyle was responsible for something similar in converting complex issues into 'material for beguiling romance' as a part of a process of '*haute vulgarisation*'.
2. See Brooks (1994: 327) for a discussion of the interpretation of irrelevance in Conan Doyle's 'The Naval Treaty' as a paradigm of the classical detective's method.
3. In *The Adventures of Sherlock Holmes*, this insightful mind is less on display than in other films in the series, not only because Holmes cannot identify an albatross in the drawing sent to Ann Brandon's brother, but also because he doesn't seem able to identify the murder weapon as a bolas nor connect it with the South American Gaucho band at Lady Conyngham's party. Steinbrunner and Michaels comment that 'Moriarty's grand scheme is so complicated and unwieldy that it is embarrassing to see it almost work' (1978: 82) and this is in no small part due to the lack of intellect demonstrated by Holmes in the film.
4. All of the Universal entries, except for *Sherlock Holmes and the Voice of Terror*, were directed by Roy William Neill who was also involved in their production from *Spider Woman* onwards.
5. See Field (2009: 115–7) for a discussion of Holmes' end-words in *Sherlock Holmes and the Voice of Terror*, *Sherlock Holmes and the Secret Weapon*, and *Sherlock Holmes in Washington* and their enunciation of Holmes as the embodiment of several hundred years of humanist ideas. It should be noted that the end-words form the standard coda that concludes most films of the classical Hollywood period, in which comment is made reflecting back on events while also often suggesting a life after the film for the characters. Holmes' end-words are, arguably, therefore free of any ideological meaning in themselves because they only derive such meanings from the previous events on which they reflect.
6. See Field (2009: 165) for a counterview arguing that the science-supernatural opposition more fully informs the narrative.
7. One such example of this economy of shooting involves a shot through a church doorway when the priest arrives to find the body of Lady Penrose, which allows him to be shown dismounting a cart, walking up the path and then discovering the body while in the background Potts can be seen as he calls out a message and then rides off without any change of lighting, camera angle or focus.
8. See Leitch (2002: 138) for a discussion of the use of cigarettes as a sign of 'emotional intimacy' to imply homo-erotic discourses in *Double Indemnity*.

5 Ordering the World: The Uncompromising Logic of Charlie Chan and Mr Moto

1. *Charlie Chan Carries On* is not the only lost film in the series because *Charlie Chan's Chance* (1932), *Charlie Chan's Greatest Case* (1933) and *Charlie Chan's Courage* (1934) shared the same fate.
2. See Ousby (1976: 154) for a discussion of the importance of the use and reconstruction of the past in the 'Sherlock Holmes' stories.
3. The shooting script for *Charlie Chan's Greatest Case* indicates that the film had the same format, but that it flirted with a breach of the closed world in Chan's accusation of someone not of the circle only for this to be revealed as a ruse to catch the real killer within it.
4. *Charlie Chan's Greatest Case* seems also to have included a scene at home in which Chan has more modern American slang inflicted upon him.
5. Denzin (1995: 92) argues that because Charlie Chan, Mr Moto and Mr Wong were presented as sexually passive they became 'feminized Asian men', but this is problematic not only because they often enunciated masculine ideology, but also because the lack of sexual coding equally applies to detectives such as Sherlock Holmes and the Crime Doctor and, very often, to Boston Blackie, the Lone Wolf and even Michael Shayne because it is a general textual pre-requisite of the detective to be distant from romantic entanglement.
6. Such stereotyping of African-Americans as comic cowards was not new to the series and had already appeared in its most exaggerated form in *Charlie Chan in Egypt* in 'Stepin Fetchit's bizarre racist comedy as the racist stereotype to end them all' (Everson, 1972: 76).
7. The 'pragmatic method' that Denzin (1995: 97–8) attributes to Charlie Chan aligns with this strategy to produce an everyday pragmatism that reduces complex problems to puzzles that can be easily solved.
8. So similar were the two detectives that two of the 'Mr Wong' films were remade by Monogram as Charlie Chan vehicles, with *Mr Wong, Detective* becoming *Docks of New Orleans* and *Mr Wong in Chinatown* becoming *The Chinese Ring.*
9. Foster directed all but two of the 'Mr Moto' films, with James Tinling, a regular director of 'Charlie Chan' films, taking the helm for the Chan-derived *Mr Moto's Gamble* and Herbert I. Leeds providing direction for *Mr Moto in Danger Island.*
10. Also gone are Marquand's criticisms of the American economic ransack of Chinese treasures because the villains are transformed into a band of Russian and German gangsters and the Americans are turned into victims suffering the same troubles as the Chinese.

6 The Rise of the Hard-boiled Detective

1. Stephen Knight, for example, writing about the hard-boiled literary style, pronounces that it had a 'major impact' on Hollywood cinema: 'Film as a genre favoured the action and attitudinising of the private-eye form, while

the characters of the clue-puzzle, whether reticent or self-mocking, fitted awkwardly into the hyperbolic style of Hollywood film' (2004: 111).

2. See Gates (2006: 81), who concurs with the idea of the hard-boiled style as realist, and Malmgren (1999: 375–6) for a counter-position in which the authenticity of the style is questioned on the grounds that the hard-boiled world is fictionalised in order to justify the ideological need for a romanticised hero.
3. A paradigm of such passive causation occurs in Chandler's *Farewell, My Lovely* when all Marlowe has to do to set events in motion among those he is investigating is to visit Jessie Florian in order to find out something about Velma because his act of questioning prompts Mrs Florian to contact Lindsay Marriott who is then set up by Velma (now Mrs Grayle) to neutralise Marlowe.
4. This is one of the more problematic areas of the hard-boiled style in both film and fiction because such breaches of the law sometimes involve killing, such as Marlowe's shooting of Canino in *The Big Sleep* which, even though it is in self-defence, is also a murderous act of revenge for Canino's killing of Harry Jones.
5. Walker comments, for example, that Jeff Markham is transformed from 'seeker hero' to 'victim hero' (1992a: 12) in *Out of the Past*, the cause of which is his submission to the sexual threat derived from the investigation-as-entanglement.
6. See Fay and Nieland (2010: 33–4) for a discussion of the unclear motivations created by Spade's performance of inscrutability in his dealings with the criminals.
7. Harvey (1978: 43) sees Spade finding a 'lonely and frustrated freedom', like Michael O'Hara in *The Lady from Shanghai* (1948), rather than a sense of contained knowledge.
8. See Walker (1992b: 198–9) for a discussion for the way in which *The Big Sleep* represses Carmen's deviance as 'unspeakable'.
9. Christopher (1997: 46–7) also comments on the 'glamour' of the noir city, highlighting its origins in the corrupting power of money.
10. See Miller (1973: 140) for details of the fictional sources for the Fox movies.

Bibliography

Balio, Tino, ed. (1993) *Grand Design: Hollywood as a Modern Business Enterprise, 1930–1939*, Berkeley, CA: University of California Press.

Barer, Burl (1993) *The Saint: A Complete History in Print, Radio, Film and Television of Leslie Charteris' Robin Hood of Modern Crime, Simon Templar, 1928–1992*, Jefferson, NC: McFarland.

Bennett, Tony, Susan Boyd-Bowman, Colin Mercer, and Janet Woollacott, eds. (1981) *Popular Television and Film*, London: BFI.

Bergman, Andrew (1992) *We're in the Money: Depression America and its Films*, Chicago, IL: Elephant.

Bertens, Hans and Theo D'haen (2001) *Contemporary American Crime Fiction*, Basingstoke: Palgrave Macmillan.

Binyon, T.J. (1989) *Murder Will Out: The Detective in Fiction*, Oxford: Oxford University Press.

Black, Gregory D. (1994) *Hollywood Censored: Morality Codes, Catholics, and the Movies*, Cambridge: Cambridge University Press.

Bordwell, David (1985) *Narration in the Fiction Film*, London: Methuen.

David Bordwell, Janet Staiger and Kristin Thompson (1985), *The Classical Hollywood Cinema: Film Style and Mode of Production to 1960*, London: Routledge.

Brooks, Peter (1994) 'Reading for the Plot', in Hodgson (1994): 321–7.

Buchsbaum, Jonathan (1992) 'Tame Wolves and Phoney Claims: Paranoia and Film Noir', in Cameron (1992): 88–97.

Caillois, Roger (1983) 'The Detective Novel as Game', in Most and Stowe (1983): 1–12.

Cameron, Ian, ed. (1992) *The Movie Book of Film Noir*, London: Studio Vista.

Carr, Helen, ed. (1989) *From My Guy to Sci-Fi: Genre and Women's Writing in the Postmodern World*, London: Pandora.

Cawelti, John G. (1976) *Adventure, Mystery and Romance*, Chicago, IL: University of Chicago Press.

Cawelti, John G. (2004) *Mystery, Violence, and Popular Culture*, Madison, WI: University of Wisconsin Press.

Chandler, Raymond (1979 [1943]) *The High Window*, London: Pan.

Chandler, Raymond (1995 [1950]) 'The Simple Art of Murder', in *Later Novels and Other Writings*, New York: Library of America: 977–992.

Chesterton, G.K. (1983 [1902]), 'A Defence of Detective Stories', in Haycraft (1983): 3–6.

Christopher, Nicholas (1997) *Somewhere in the Night: Film Noir and the American City*, New York: Henry Holt.

Clarens, Carlos (1980) *Crime Movies: An Illustrated History*, London: Secker & Warburg.

Clark, Al (1982) *Raymond Chandler in Hollywood*, London and New York: Proteus.

Clarke, David B., ed. (1997) *The Cinematic City*, London and New York: Routledge.

Cook, Pam and Mieke Bernink eds. (1999) *The Cinema Book*, 2nd edn, London: BFI.
Copjec, Joan, ed. (1993) *Shades of Noir: A Reader*, London: Verso.
Copjec, Joan (1993) 'The Phenomenal Nonphenomenal: Private Space in *Film Noir*', in Copjec (1993): 167–197.
Coward, Rosalind and Linda Semple (1989) 'Tracking Down the Past: Women and Detective Fiction', in Carr (1989): 39–57.
Cross, Robin (1981) *The Big Book of B Movies, or How Low Was My Budget*, London: Frederick Muller.
Denzin, Norman K (1995) 'The Asian Eye: Charlie Chan and Mr Moto Go to the Movies', in *The Cinematic Society: The Voyeur's Gaze*, London: Sage, 88–113.
Doane, Mary Ann (1991) *Femmes Fatales: Feminism, Film Theory, Psychoanalysis*, New York and London: Routledge.
Dyer, Richard (2007) *Pastiche*, London and New York: Routledge.
Elsaesser, Thomas (1981) 'Narrative Cinema and Audience-oriented Aesthetics', in Bennett et al. (1981): 270–82.
Everson, William K. (1972) *The Detective in Film*, Secaucus: Citadel.
Fay, Jennifer and Justus Nieland (2010) *Film Noir: Hard-Boiled Modernity and Cultures of Globalization*. London and New York: Routledge.
Field, Amanda J. (2009) *England's Secret Weapon: The Wartime Films of Sherlock Holmes*, London: Middlesex University Press.
Finney, Gail, ed. (1994) *Look Who's Laughing: Gender and Comedy*, Langhorne, PA: Gordon and Breach.
Fowler, Alastair (1994) 'Sherlock Holmes and the Adventure of the Dancing Men and Women', in Hodgson (1994): 353–67.
Gates, Philippa (2006) *Detecting Men: Masculinity and the Hollywood Detective Film*, Albany, NY: State University of New York Press.
Gehring, Wes D. (2002) *Romantic vs Screwball Comedy: Charting the Difference*, Lanham, MD: Scarecrow.
Glitre, Kathrina (2006) *Hollywood Romantic Comedy: States of the Union 1934–65*, Manchester: Manchester University Press.
Grist, Leighton (1992) '*Out of the Past* a.k.a. *Build My Gallows High*', in Cameron (1992), 203–12.
Hagopian, Kevin (2004) '"How You Fixed for Red Points?": Anecdote and the World War II Home Front in *The Big Sleep*', in Silver and Ursini (2004): 33–52.
Haralovich, Mary Beth (1979) 'Sherlock Holmes: Genre and Industrial Practice', *Journal of the University Film Association*, 31: 2 (Spring 1979): 53–7.
Hardy, Phil (1997) *The BFI Companion to Crime*, London: BFI.
Harvey, James (1998) *Romantic Comedy in Hollywood, From Lubitsch to Sturges*, New York: Da Capo Press.
Harvey, Sylvia (1978) 'Woman's Place: The Absent Family in Film Noir', in Kaplan (1978): 22–34.
Haycraft, Howard, ed. (1983) *The Art of the Mystery Story*, New York: Carroll & Graf.
Hirsch, Foster (1981) *Film Noir: The Dark Side of the Screen*, New York: Da Capo.
Hodgson, John A., ed. (1994) *Sherlock Holmes: The Major Stories with Contemporary Critical Essays*, New York and Boston: St Martin's Press.
Horsley, Lee (2009) *The Noir Thriller*, Basingstoke: Palgrave Macmillan.

Huang, Yunte (2010) *Charlie Chan: The Untold Story of the Honorable Detective and his Rendezvous with American History*, New York: Norton.

Jameson, Fredric (1993) 'The Synoptic Chandler', in Copjec (1993): 33–56.

Kaplan, E Ann, ed. (1978) *Women in Film Noir*, London: BFI.

Kerr, Paul (1986) 'Out of what past? Notes on the B *film noir*', in Kerr, Paul, ed., *The Hollywood Film Industry: A Reader*, London: Routledge and Kegan Paul/BFI: 220–44.

Knight, Stephen (1980) *Form and Ideology in Crime Fiction*, Basingstoke: Macmillan.

Knight, Stephen (2003) 'The Golden Age', in Priestman (2003): 77–94.

Knight, Stephen (2004) *Crime Fiction, 1800–2000: Detection, Death, Diversity*, Basingstoke: Palgrave Macmillan.

Krutnik, Frank (1991) *In A Lonely Street: Film Noir, Genre, Masculinity*, London and New York: Routledge.

Krutnik, Frank (1997) 'Something More Than Night: Tales of the *Noir* City', in Clarke (1997): 83–109.

Kuhn, Annette (1999) 'Columbia Pictures' in Cook and Bernink (1999): 22–5.

Langman, Larry and Daniel Finn (1995a) *A Guide to American Crime Films of the Thirties*, Westport, CT and London: Greenwood.

Langman, Larry, and Daniel Finn (1995b) *A Guide to American Crime Films of the Forties and Fifties*, Westport, CT and London: Greenwood.

Leitch, Thomas (2002) *Crime Films*, Cambridge: Cambridge University Press.

Lehman, David (2000) *The Perfect Murder: A Study in Detection*, Ann Arbor, MI: University of Michigan Press.

Lemon, Lee T. and Marion J. Reis, eds. (1965) *Russian Formalist Criticism: Four Essays*, Lincoln, NE: University of Nebraska Press.

Luhr, William and Peter Lehman (2006) '*Experiment in Terror*: Dystopian Modernism, the Police Procedural, and the Space of Anxiety', in Pomerance (2006): 175–193.

McCann, Sean (2000) *Gumshoe America: Hard-Boiled Crime Fiction and the Rise and Fall of New Deal Liberalism*, Durham, NC and London: Duke University Press.

McClelland, Doug (1978) *The Golden Age of "B" Movies*, Nashville: Charter House

Malmgren, Carl D. (1999) 'The Crime of the Sign: Dashiell Hammett's Fiction', *Twentieth Century Literature*, 45: 3 (Autumn, 1999): 371–84.

Maltby, Richard (1983) *Harmless Entertainment: Hollywood and the Ideology of Consensus*, Metuchen, NJ: Scarecrow.

Maltby, Richard (1995) *Hollywood Cinema: An Introduction*, Oxford: Blackwell.

Mandel, Ernest (1984) *Delightful Murder: A Social History of the Crime Story*, Minneapolis, MN: University of Minnesota Press.

Marcus, Laura (2003) 'Detection and Literary Fiction', in Priestman (2003): 245–267.

Marling, William (1995) *The American Roman Noir: Hammett, Cain and Chandler*, Athens, GA and London: University of Georgia Press.

Maxfield, James F. (1996) *The Fatal Woman: Sources of Male Anxiety in American 'Film Noir', 1941–1991*, London: Associated University Press.

Messent, Peter (1997) 'Introduction: From Private Eye to Police Procedural – The Logic of Contemporary Crime Fiction,' in Messent, Peter, ed., *Criminal Proceedings: The Contemporary American Crime Novel*, London: Pluto: 1–21.

Miller, Don (1973) *B Movies*, New York: Ballantine.
Moretti, Franco (1988) *Signs Taken For Wonders*, rev. edn., London: Verso.
Most, Glenn W. and William W. Stowe, eds. (1983) *The Poetics of Murder: Detective Fiction and Literary Theory*, San Diego, CA: Harcourt Brace Jovanovich.
Munt, Sally R. (1994) *Murder by the Book?: Feminism and the Crime Novel*, London and New York, Routledge.
Naremore, James (1998) *More than Night: Film Noir in its Contexts*, Berkeley and Los Angeles, CA: University of California Press.
Neale, Steve (1990) 'Questions of genre', *Screen*, 31: 1 (Spring 1990): 45–66.
Neale, Steve (2000) *Genre and Hollywood*, London and New York: Routledge.
Neve, Brian (1992) *Film and Politics in America: A Social Tradition*. London and New York: Routledge.
Ousby, Ian (1976) *Bloodhounds of Heaven: The Detective in English Fiction from Godwin to Doyle*, Cambridge, MA: Harvard University Press.
Palmer, Jerry (1978) *Thrillers: Genesis and Structure of a Popular Genre*, London: Arnold.
Palmer, Jerry (1991) *Potboilers: Methods, Concepts and Case Studies in Popular Fiction*, London and New York: Routledge.
Palmer, R. Barton (2004) '"Lounge Time" Reconsidered: Spatial Discontinuity and Temporal Contingency in Out of the Past', in Silver and Ursini (2004): 53–65.
Parish, James Robert and Michael R Pitts (1990) *The Great Detective Pictures*, Metuchen, NJ: Scarecrow.
Pepper, Andrew (2000) *The Contemporary American Crime Novel: Race, Ethnicity, Gender, Class*, Edinburgh: Edinburgh University Press.
Pepper, Andrew (2010) '"Hegemony Protected by the Armour of Coercion": Dashiell Hammett's *Red Harvest* and the State', *Journal of American Studies*, 44: 2 (2010): 333–49.
Phillips, Gene D. (2000) *Creatures of Darkness: Raymond Chandler, Detective Fiction, and Film Noir*, Lexington, KY: University Press of Kentucky.
Pomerance, Murray, ed. (2006) *Cinema and Modernity*, New Brunswick, NJ: Rutgers University Press.
Porter, Dennis (1981) *The Pursuit of Crime, Art and Ideology in Detective Fiction*. New Haven, CT: Yale University Press.
Porter, Dennis (2003) 'The Private Eye', in Priestman (2003): 95–114.
Priestman, Martin, ed. (2003) *The Cambridge Companion to Crime Fiction*. Cambridge: Cambridge University Press.
Pyrhönen, Heta (1999) *Mayhem and Murder: Narrative and Moral Problems in the Detective Story*, Toronto: University of Toronto Press.
Rzepka, Charles J. (2005) *Detective Fiction*, Cambridge: Polity.
Scaggs, John (2005) *Crime Fiction*, London and New York: Routledge.
Schatz, Thomas (1981) *Hollywood Genres: Formulas, Film-making, and the Studio System*, New York: McGraw-Hill.
Schatz, Thomas (1996) *The Genius of the System: Hollywood Film-making in the Studio Era*, London: Faber and Faber.
Schatz, Thomas (1997) *Boom and Bust: American Cinema in the 1940s*, Berkeley: University of California Press.
Silver, Alain and James Ursini, eds. (1996) *Film Noir Reader*, New York: Limelight.

Silver, Alain and James Ursini, eds. (2004) *Film Noir Reader 4*, New York: Limelight.
Soitos, Stephen F. (1996) *The Blues Detective: A Study of African American Detective Fiction*. Amherst, MA: University of Massachusetts Press.
Soter, Tom (2002) *Investigating Couples: A Critical Analysis of 'The Thin Man', 'The Avengers' and 'The X-Files'*, London: McFarland.
Spicer, Andrew (2002) *Film Noir*, Harlow: Longman.
Steinbrunner, Chris, and Norman Michaels (1978) *The Films of Sherlock Holmes*, Secaucus, NJ: Citadel.
Symons, Julian (1972) *Bloody Murder, From the Detective Story to the Crime Novel: A History*, London: Faber.
Taves, Brian (1993) 'The B Film: Hollywood's Other Half', in Balio (1993): 313–50.
Telotte, J.P. (1989) *Voices in the Dark: The Narrative Patterns of 'Film Noir'*, Urbana and Chicago, IL: University of Illinois Press.
Thompson, Jon (1993) *Fiction, Crime, and Empire: Clues to Modernity and Postmodernity*, Urbana, IL: University of Illinois Press.
Thompson, Kristin (1988) '"No, Lestrade, in This Case Nothing Was Left to Chance": Motivation and Delay in *Terror By Night*', in *Breaking the Glass Armor: Neoformalist Film Analysis*, Princeton, NJ: Princeton UP: 49–86.
Todorov, Tzvetan (1977) 'The Typology of Detective Fiction', in *The Poetics of Prose*, Ithaca, NY: Cornell University Press: 42–52.
Tomashevsky, Boris (1965) 'Thematics', in Lemon and Reis (1965): 61–95.
Tuska, Jon (1984) *Dark Cinema: American Film Noir in Cultural Perspective*, Westport, CT and London: Greenwood.
Tuska, Jon (1988) *In Manors and Alleys: A Casebook on the American Detective Film*, New York and London: Greenwood.
Walker, Michael (1992a) 'Film Noir: An Introduction', in Cameron (1992): 8–38.
Walker, Michael (1992b) '*The Big Sleep*', in Cameron (1992): 191–202.
Willett, Ralph (1996) *The Naked City: Urban Crime Fiction in the USA*, Manchester: Manchester University Press.
Young, Kay (1994) 'Hollywood, 1934: "Inventing" romantic comedy', in Finney (1994): 257–94.

Index